FATAL
HARMONY

Kate Rhodes

Those who were seen dancing were considered insane by those who could not hear the music.'

FRIEDRICH WILHELM NIETZSCHE

Also By Kate Rhodes

The Alice Quentin series

Crossbones Yard
A Killing of Angels
The Winter Foundlings
River of Souls
Blood Symmetry

The Hell Bay series

Hell Bay
Ruin Beach
Burnt Island

Monday 21st March

Adrian Stone wakes early on the first day of spring. Somewhere in the distance music is playing, a solitary piano refrain that should be accompanied by weeping violins. It's imaginary, of course. None of the murderers and rapists on his wing share his musical skill. When he rubs sleep from his eyes, the sound falls silent, but his anticipation remains. He keeps his mind calm as he dresses. There is no mirror in his cell, only a piece of pearlised metal bolted to the wall; it returns the blurred image of a young man with blond hair and pale blue eyes.

'Time to start over,' he whispers.

The morning follows its usual pattern. Stone is escorted to the cafeteria, where more guards than patients populate the hall. He stares out at the grounds while eating his breakfast: daffodils are raising their yellow crowns to the sky, pigeons scrapping for food, half a mile of tinted window. He knows from experience that its transparency is deceiving. When he was younger and more reckless, he hurled himself at it, hoping to shatter the barrier between life and death, but receiving only a mess of bruises.

One of the guards greets him with a rapid nod. The officer is called Matthew Briar, a thin-faced young man with an intent stare. Stone finds his gauche manner irritating, but he's in no position to criticise. It's a relationship he's cultivated for years.

'Ready for your trip, Adrian?'

'Sorry, I didn't hear you.' Stone leans forward attentively, until their hands almost touch.

'It's your hospital visit today, isn't it?'

'That's right.'

Briar's voice lowers. 'Come on then, let's get you back to your cell.'

Stone follows the officer down the corridor at a steady pace, two more guards flanking him, another walking behind. The same men escort him to the ambulance. He has feigned deafness for weeks, forcing the chief medic to book an appointment with a specialist in Nottingham.

Years of good behaviour have won Stone an advantage. There are just three officers in the van when it leaves the compound: two guards in the front seats, then Matthew Briar locks him into the caged compartment, before sitting on the narrow bench by the doors. Behind the metal panel the driver and his colleague make conversation as villages tick past. It's only when the van enters open countryside that Stone nods at his guard. Music plays in his mind once more, reaching a crescendo, cymbals flaring, as Briar unlocks the metal cage. Stone gives a high-pitched scream and the van brakes suddenly. There's a stunned look on Briar's face as Stone throws his first punch, years of frustration giving him unnatural strength. Once the other guards wrench the doors open, light floods the confined space; the rage he has carried since childhood spills over as he kicks, bites and scratches his way to freedom. His thoughts spin out of control, mouth filling with the taste of blood.

Stone's mind finally clears as he scans the filthy ground. One of the guards is dead, the other two on the brink; his thoughts blank as he kicks first one skull then the other, hears the soft click of bones snapping. He leans down to press a small object into one of the men's mouths. When he straightens up again an old woman in a black car is slowing down; a rubbernecker, hungry for corpses. He raises his hand in a blood-stained wave.

'Leaving already, sweetheart?' The car roars away, engine trilling with panic.

Stone removes the keys from the ignition, noticing that the driver hit the panic button before exiting the vehicle. Sirens will squeal in his direction before long, yet he's smiling when he escapes the scene, a drum roll pounding in his skull as he sprints for the trees.

'What's the verdict?' Lola asked, gazing across at me.

I had taken a day off for her pre-wedding shopping trip. We stood in the changing room of an upmarket bridal boutique in Knightsbridge. She was dressed head to toe in ivory silk, auburn curls rippling down her back, tall and svelte as a mannequin, an assistant simpering approval in the background.

'Great,' I replied. 'Breath-taking, actually.'

'Be honest, Al, please. This is my last chance for alterations.'

'The dress is damn near perfect; I'll feel like a leprechaun beside you.'

'I've got wedding fever.' Her hands fumbled as she unzipped the dress. 'Get me to a pub, right now.'

'Good plan, but put some clothes on first.'

Under normal circumstances I enjoyed a good wedding, but not as maid of honour. Traipsing down the aisle dressed like a miniature Barbie, holding a bouquet of peace lilies wasn't my idea of fun, but Lola had been my closest friend since school. It would have been churlish to refuse.

The city was in slow motion as we crossed Sloane Street. Pedestrians were window shopping for designer handbags, cashmere and Italian shoes, enjoying the afternoon's first warm breath of spring. We ended up in a watering hole called the Gloucester, which had retained its traditional pub atmosphere, despite the area going upmarket. The ceiling was nicotine yellow even though smoking had been banned for a decade, tatty leather chairs grouped in clusters. I relaxed into one with a large glass of Chardonnay. It felt like the good old days, when Lola and I spent our weekends trawling from bar to bar, before her baby arrived. Pale sunshine filtered through the windows as Lola fretted over wedding details, from the food at her reception to the honeymoon weekend in Venice in two weeks' time.

'My parents are looking after Neve,' she said. 'But I'd rather take her with us.'

'You can't, Lo. Honeymoons are for romance and mindless sex. How is my god daughter anyway?'

'Wrapping Neal round her little finger, a total daddy's girl.'

'Is the Greek God ready for the big day?'

'The boy's unflappable.' She rolled her eyes. 'He's filming, so I've done all the work.'

Neal's acting career was going from strength to strength. He'd graduated from bit parts in soap operas to major roles in BBC costume dramas, his classic good looks making him an ideal leading man. When I looked at Lola again she was leaning forwards in her chair, cat-like green eyes scrutinising me.

'How's Burns these days?'

I shrugged. 'Pretty good. We meet between shifts, take the odd weekend away.'

'Is the sex still mind-blowing?'

'None of your business.'

'That sounds like a yes,' she replied, sniggering. 'How are you getting on with his kids?'

'Moray's coming round to the idea his dad's got a girlfriend, but Liam's in denial. He hardly ever meets my eye.'

'Is Liam the oldest?'

'Thirteen. It's a bad age for your family to fall apart.'

'At least his stepmother's not evil.'

'They might not agree.'

Lola looked amused. 'They're probably expecting you to get married.'

I couldn't summon a reply. My relationship with Burns survived because we took it one day at a time, the future rarely mentioned, which suited me fine. Given my track record, the whole enterprise might yet collapse like a house of cards. My attention wandered to the TV above the bar, to evade my friend's probing. A man's face filled the screen as the one o'clock news began, and suddenly the easy-going jazz that had been playing in the background fell silent. Adrian Stone looked unchanged since our last meeting six months before; he looked younger than his twenty-five years, giving the camera a winning smile. Words flashed across the screen, announcing that he had escaped, yet calmness flooded my system, not panic. My survival instinct had kicked in already; I would need a clear mind and rapid reactions to keep myself safe.

My phone had been on silent all morning, but now it vibrated wildly in my pocket. Six calls had arrived and a flurry of emails with angry red flags. The first was from my boss, Christine Jenkins, ordering me to report to the Forensic Psychology Unit immediately.

I stumbled to my feet, almost knocking over my wine glass. 'I have to go Lola, sorry.'

'Are you okay?'

'Fine, I'll call you tonight.'

I gave her a distracted kiss before hurrying outside. The rational part of me knew Stone could never track me down on a busy shopping street in the West End, unless he was clairvoyant, but the back of my neck still prickled with anxiety. The fifteen-minute cab ride to Dacre Street passed in a blur of expensive restaurants and shops. How could anyone escape from Rampton's secure psychiatric unit? The centre had rigid safety protocols, but for Stone, ordinary rules didn't apply. I looked out of the window as the cab drove east towards St James Park, passing elegant Georgian hotels. Stone must have spent years planning, it would have been impossible to escape without an accomplice, but right now the details were immaterial. His hatred for me was a matter of public record; he blamed me for denying him his liberty.

Squad cars were already parked outside the FPU when I arrived, the gravity of the situation hitting home. My role as Deputy Director had been announced on the internet. If Stone came looking for me, my workplace would be his first port of call. One of the young PCs on guard duty checked my ID card then waved me inside. My workplace carried its usual air of shabby gentility, photos of eminent psychoanalysts lining the walls as I jogged upstairs.

Christine Jenkins' expression was sombre. She was standing in her office, wearing a pale blue suit, which emphasised her slimness, no jewellery except small gold studs in her ears. I had known my boss several years but still found her enigmatic. Mike Donnelly was already seated at her meeting table. He was a long-time member of the FPU team and a world-renowned expert on juvenile psychopathology; a portly, avuncular figure with snow white hair and an unkempt beard. Donnelly had been my biggest ally since I started at the FPU and at that moment I felt like hugging him.

'Interesting times, Alice.' He looked up from an evidence file, eyebrows raised.

'Understatement of the year,' I replied.

Christine sat down at the head of the table. 'Burns is on his way. His team's leading the hunt for Stone.'

I almost spat out a curse but managed to suppress it. Working with Burns always caused tension, our private and professional lives competing, even though we lived apart. Christine must have clocked my reaction because she turned to me again.

'He's got the best conviction rate in the UK, Alice. We can't take chances.'

'Maybe we're overreacting,' I replied.

'Better safe than sorry.' Her expression hardened as she slid some photos across the desk. 'This is how Stone left his guards. Two of them are dead, one's in hospital, fighting for his life.'

The crime scene photographer had done a thorough job of capturing the fatalities from every angle, but the pictures took a while to compute. Two men's bodies lay piled on top of one another, as though they were locked in a lethal wrestling match. One face was a mass of torn flesh, the other bruised and swollen beyond recognition, blood pooling on the tarmac.

'Will the third man survive?'

'It's touch and go. They resuscitated him at the scene.'

Burns burst through the door as I closed the file. His dark hair was dishevelled, tie loose at his throat, his expression intense. He wore a charcoal grey suit, but his height and build made him look like a heavyweight boxer, masquerading as a detective. I felt my usual conflict of interests – in an ideal world our jobs would never connect, but I was in no position to argue. His body language signalled that he felt the same; he dropped into the seat beside me with a scowl on his face.

'Let's get started,' Christine said. 'Tell us how Stone escaped, Don.'

Burns stared back at her, eyes one shade lighter than black. 'It's Rampton's first break out in twenty years. He was being taken to a hospital appointment in a secure van. One of the officers, Matthew Briar, unlocked the cage just after ten this morning. Once he'd served his purpose, Stone attacked him, then killed the other two.'

'With a weapon?' Christine asked.

'Bare hands and the guard's keys. A woman saw him by the roadside; she thought it was a traffic accident until she spotted the bodies. He gave her a wave, with blood dripping down his arm. Stone had vanished by the time local police arrived. The van was heading for Nottingham. We think he's still roaming round Sherwood Forest, avoiding the sniffer dogs.'

'Robin Hood must be turning in his grave,' Donnelly muttered.

'What did he leave behind?' I asked.

Burns didn't meet my eye. 'A USB stick, in one of the men's mouths. We don't know what's on it yet; the IT guys are checking.'

'The message could be important,' I said, turning to Donnelly. 'What's your view, Mike?'

The Irishman's bonhomie was missing for once. 'I assessed Stone twice in his teens. He was one of the most plausible juvenile murderers on record. The boy almost convinced me that his killing impulse was situational not pathological, but his stories unravelled under the weight of proof. Narcissism is the one delusion he struggles to hide.'

'What about you, Alice? You've assessed him recently.' Christine said.

I tried to gather my thoughts. 'Stone was a musical prodigy, giving piano recitals since primary school. But something went badly wrong: he killed his mother, father and older sister when he turned sixteen, nine years ago. Then he went on the run. He's a skilled manipulator who can work any situation to his advantage. He killed two police officers who tried to apprehend him, and a middle-aged woman who'd let him stay in her home before he was recaptured. He kept under the radar by changing his appearance constantly. Stone gets his buzz from being in control; he must be thrilled to be back in the driving seat.'

Burns finally met my eye. 'Do you think he'll target you, Alice?'

'I'm not his favourite person. His defence team requested a review of his whole life tariff three months ago; I completed the assessment with a Home Office endorsed psychiatrist called Ian Carlisle. We spent a full day testing him. His specialist at Rampton thought he was well enough to go to a mainstream prison, with eventual release after twenty years, but we agreed he should never be freed.'

'Why not?' Christine asked.

'Stone can fool every psychological exam, even lie detectors. He did a good job of pretending to be contrite, but his control slipped when he described his musical gift. He thinks violence is the price he pays for his creativity.'

'That's convenient,' Burns muttered.

'He phoned me five times from the unit, until prison staff stopped him. I don't know whether he contacted Carlisle too. One of the letters he sent me is in my filing cabinet downstairs. It doesn't make pleasant reading.'

'Keep it as evidence, please. We'll need top level security for Carlisle too.' Christine scanned each of our faces, before opening her notepad. 'My first priority is keeping you out of danger, Alice. You'll be staying in the best safe house available.'

'I'll sort it today,' Burns replied.

I shook my head. 'His sister's the only member of his immediate family left alive; Melissa Stone needs immediate protection.'

I listened to their talk of security measures, transport, and team members trustworthy enough to watch my back. After a while their voices became a featureless drone as shock overtook me. Late afternoon sunshine flickered through the window, and I found myself distracted by noise from the street. Music must have been playing in a bar nearby. Somewhere in the distance a woman was singing a love song, the sound fading on the air, almost too faint to hear.

Dusk is falling by the time Stone finds his getaway car, parked on a cul-de-sac at the edge of the forest, fifty metres from the nearest house. He can hear the chatter of blackbirds, leaves shifting overhead as the breeze rises. These sounds have been denied him so long, he could spend hours absorbing each echo, but time is already against him.

Stone emerges from his hiding place among the bushes to find a key, taped to the chassis of a ten-year-old Hyundai. He takes a holdall from the boot and retreats again into the trees. His excitement rises as he riffles through the bag, like a child peering into a dressing up box. He tackles his hair first with a bottle of comb-through dye, then swipes the applicator across each eyebrow, using a mirror to apply it evenly. It would be foolish to allow a small mistake to ruin his one chance of freedom. His new clothes are different from the ones he wore last time he was free: skinny black jeans, a grey Superdry T shirt, baseball boots. The last adjustment is tinted contact lenses. He catches sight of himself in the car window; dark haired and studious-looking, eyes no longer blue, every trace of blood rinsed from his skin in a brook nearby.

He feels a rush of pleasure when he slips into the driver's seat. The glove compartment holds an envelope full of money, fake passport, driving license, a variety of ID cards, and a sat nav. But the item that pleases him most is the iPod, left on the passenger seat. When he scrolls through the playlist, he finds Rachmaninov, Debussy, and some of his jazz favourites too, Bill Evans and Oscar Peterson. He chooses Chopin for his journey, each arpeggio loaded with heartbreak. Stone sits in the driver's seat, allowing the melody to sing in his blood, blinking back tears as he begins to drive. Almost a decade has passed since he last sat behind a wheel, but he's confident again by the time he reaches the road block. A sour-faced WPC flags him down, her male colleague wearing a bored expression. She peers at him through the metal opening of his window.

'What's your name please, young man?'

'Seth Rivers. Has something happened?'

'Can I see some ID?' She scribbles his new name on her clipboard. 'There was an attack this morning. Didn't you hear?'

He offers a calm smile. 'I've driven from York, listening to music all the way.'

'You're making a long journey.'

'My girlfriend's in Grantham. It's her birthday.'

Her smile finally arrives. 'Best get moving then, hadn't you?'

The officer waves him through with her free hand. In his rear-view mirror Stone watches her repeat the process with the van behind, then turns up the volume on the car's stereo. London will be within reach in two hours. After so long in captivity, freedom feels like a form of ecstasy. He lets the music fill his mind, chanting its refrain in a calm tenor as darkness gathers on the road ahead.

By the time evening came, my life was no longer my own. I had until ten p.m. to pack a suitcase in my flat on Providence Square, then the two uniforms outside my door would take me to a secure location. I scanned my living room, with its hardwood floor, clear walls, and uncluttered shelves. The place had been my sanctuary for years, somewhere to lie low when work pressures grew overwhelming. Outside the window the square's floodlit gardens looked tranquil, filled with cherry trees ready to bloom. There was no guessing how long I would be away. I felt a quick pang of envy for the simplicity of Lola's life, planning her wedding with endless joie-de-vivre, but I had known from the start that forensic duties were risky. It was too late to complain. Working on high profile cases involving dangerous killers had given me an insight into human violence, yet it still felt like voyaging into the unknown. Advances had been made in neuroscience and psychological testing, but the psychopath's mind-set remained the final frontier.

I spent less than fifteen minutes packing outfits for work, running gear, my kindle and makeup bag. For good measure I threw in some heels and a little black dress, in case I needed to look smart during my time in exile. Once my suitcase was full I entered my Home Office password into my laptop, to access Adrian Stone's evidence file. It contained every police report on his first murderous attacks nine years before. The sheer number of documents was daunting. His crimes had generated thousands of interview transcripts, arrest reports and witness statements. I clicked on the scene of crime survey, detailing how Stone had massacred his parents and older sister in their lavish Richmond home. Only his thirteen-year-old sister

Melissa had survived by barricading herself in her room while her brother went on the rampage. The police photographer had included a picture of the three storey villa where he'd committed his crimes, surrounded by ornate gardens, bricks bleached to a dull rose by the passage of time. Stone had grown up with every creature comfort, yet none of it had satisfied him.

I flicked through more documents until Stone's childhood exploits filled my screen. His stubbornness and his musicality had both emerged early, according to reports from his Steiner school. The teachers couldn't keep him away from the piano; even as a six-year-old, Stone had been passionate about music. He would hit out, punching and kicking other children, if they tried to stop him playing. His behaviour had been interpreted as childish tantrums, but it was typical of the early violence shown by psychopathic killers. His parents had indulged his obsession. They provided him with a piano tutor until he'd passed every grade exam by age nine, and lessons became unnecessary. Stone blossomed into a musical prodigy, playing solo concerts and joining the London Youth Orchestra. He enrolled at the Royal College of music at thirteen, three years earlier than normal. I clicked on a picture of him performing as a child, his small figure dwarfed by the grand piano, drowning in a glare of floodlight.

'The loneliest boy in the world,' I whispered to myself.

Stone had refused to discuss his past when he was apprehended. I ran my eyes over the transcript from when his murder charge in Richmond: he had shown no remorse for killing two police officers and the elderly widow he had persuaded to shelter him, answering every question with 'no comment.' When his severe personality disorder was diagnosed, he was sent to Rampton's juvenile wing, instantly winning a place in the annals of crime history as one of the youngest male serial killers in Britain. Today's deaths brought his tally to eight murders. I stared at the screen again, hunting for patterns. Anyone who encroached on Stone's private world occupied dangerous territory, people he loved or loathed were equally vulnerable. On an objective level he fascinated me; an atypical psychopath, capable of controlling his violence for years. He had improved his musical skills during his time at Rampton, playing the piano regularly, and writing orchestral scores would might never be performed. Yet he also bore many of the standard traits of the psychotic manipulator: the ability to lie without detection, and an abundance of superficial charm.

By now I was on information overload. If Stone could evade a nationwide manhunt for four months as a teenager, how long could he hold out at twenty-five? It was possible that he might vanish from view permanently. The prospect sealed my tongue to the roof of my mouth. Until he was found, everyone he knew was vulnerable. Second-guessing where he would strike next would require more than ploughing through the backlog of evidence. I would need to understand his motives perfectly, and use psychological assessment techniques to gain information from his accomplice.

I was opening another report when the Skype symbol flashed on my screen. Burns's face appeared, and it struck me again that he was nothing like the men I usually dated. A haze of stubble darkening his jaw, all of his features exaggerated, from his hard-edged cheekbones to his broken Roman nose. It irritated me that I couldn't look away. In an ideal world we could ditch our jobs for a while, see how our relationship fared without any external pressure.

'Where are you?' I asked.

'Nottingham HQ. The search team have tracked footprints from the van into the forest, but we've got no confirmed sightings.'

'You've been to the scene?'

He rubbed his hand across his eyes. 'It's one hell of a mess. The survivor's nose was almost ripped from his face; he's in surgery now.'

'Was Matthew Briar definitely the helper?'

'No one else could have unlocked Stone's handcuffs; they were alone in the back of the van.'

'I need to see him.'

'He may not survive; the doctors say it's fifty-fifty.'

'Did the IT guys get anything off the USB stick?'

He nodded. 'The bugger's got a sense of humour. It's a piece of music; by Chopin, apparently.'

'Stone's had years to plan this, it must mean something.' I studied him again, noticing the tension in his face. 'Are you okay?'

'Fine, except a psycho knows where you work, and he's got a head start.'

'That's not my fault.'

'How come you're so calm?'

'Panicking won't help me.' My childhood had prepared me for violence; giving in to fear only made people unsafe. 'Let's talk tomorrow.'

His expression hardened. 'You'd prefer a nice quiet chat when all these messy emotions have died down, wouldn't you?'

'A car's waiting for me outside, but for the record, I'm not some bloodless machine. I'm as scared as the next person, but it won't get the better of me.'

'Nothing does,' he said quietly. 'You have to win every battle. We need to talk when I get back.'

'You know where I am.'

Burns's face vanished. When the screen blanked, it felt like a hot air balloon was deflating inside my ribs. I could forecast the discussion he wanted. Our relationship had survived nine months; my longest ever, and easily the happiest, but the strain of working together was tearing it apart. I slid my laptop into my briefcase then rose to my feet, all of my movements slower than before.

5

Stone abandons the car at Romford Tube station, then boards the first train west. After years of isolation, the press of bodies is overwhelming. He can feel the city's pulse racing, its staccato rhythm drumming on his senses. His calmness returns by the time he rides the escalator at South Kensington. Even the busker playing a badly-tuned concertina by the exit can't provoke his anger. It's only when he reaches street level that he congratulates himself on completing the first stage of his plan. London is heaving with humanity, no one will spot him unless he makes a mistake. He weaves north towards Hyde Park, joining the throng of evening strollers.

His first port of call is the Royal College of Music. He stands outside, studying its floodlit façade. This place was the scene of his greatest triumphs and disappointments. The building looks like a Gothic castle, five stories high, flanked by pointed towers. His anger bubbles to the surface again. Benjamin Britten studied here, Holst and Vaughan-Williams, yet the place failed to acknowledge him. He sinks his hands into his pockets and walks away, pausing beside the huge dome of the Albert Hall. An inscription circles the cupola: *Thine O Lord is the greatness and the power and the glory and the victory and the majesty.* Stone turns away with a half-smile, certain that the building's power lies in his hands now.

At half past ten the city's night-life is simmering. Bar doors hang open, releasing the reek of beer and pheromones, thousands of students circling each other.

Stone chooses a pub on Cromwell Road, ten minutes' walk from his old college; there's a battered piano in the corner, the room heaving with drinkers. He stands at the bar in silence, unwilling to rush as he orders a beer.

'Mind if I play the piano?'

The barman shrugs. 'Go ahead, mate. But be warned, it hasn't been tuned in a while.'

Stone smiles. 'Stop me, if I sound flat.'

He feels revived when his hands settle on the keys. A Cuban rumba first, high and carefree, then ragtime, until he secures the whole room's attention. Someone drops a fiver on the lid of the piano, asks for *Someone to Watch over Me*. He plays a slow version, full of longing, eyes closed. When he opens them again a young girl has edged nearer, watching his fingers caress each note, blushing when he catches her gaze. She's plainer than he would have liked, with a mass of brown curls, unpainted lips, a small crucifix around her neck.

'Amazing,' she whispers. 'I've never seen anyone play so well.'

'You're kidding, I kept dropping notes.'

'It sounded perfect.'

Stone lets his eyes linger on her face. 'Can I tell you a secret?'

She looks confused. 'Okay.'

'You're the prettiest girl here. What are you called?'

'Lily,' she says, blushing again.

'Beautiful name too. Can I play you something?'

'Whatever you like.'

'Then I'll buy you a drink. Don't go anywhere, will you?'

He plays the signature tune from *Porgy and Bess*, soft and lilting, full of dreamy southern heat. The girl leans against the wall, the power of his music rooting her to the spot. Her expression is rapt and hopeful when he finally closes the piano's lid and takes her hand.

6

Tuesday 22nd March

The sound of voices woke me early next morning. Daylight had an unforgiving effect on my temporary accommodations: the two-bedroom flat stood above a café on Borough High Street, outfitted with bottom of the range IKEA furniture, sickly yellow walls and drab carpet. The bathroom suite must have been in situ for years, cracks appearing in the dark blue tiles, an unpleasant smell of damp lingering on the air. But I could see why it had been picked as a safe house. Half a dozen locks and deadbolts adorned the front door, triple-glazed windows fitted with laser alarms, the entrance only accessible by a fire escape that must have been perilous in winter. A squad car was parked in the alley, waiting to catch anyone who approached. The best thing about the place was the smell of coffee rising through the floorboards, as early morning punters breakfasted in the café below. Their chatter was reassuring, proving that the rest of the world was going about its business undisturbed. I used my own soap in the shower; the scent of lemon verbena reminding me that home was a state of mind, not a specific location.

The buzzer bleeped loudly as I prised open a pack of Cornflakes that had been left in the kitchen. When Angie Wilcox's face appeared on the intercom I spent a full minute undoing security devices before the front door would open. She had filled out slightly in the past six months, but still looked elfin, cropped red hair framing a face dominated by freckles and a generous smile.

'Jesus, this place is grim,' she said. 'Are you okay?'

'I'll survive. I hear you passed your exam, Angie. Congratulations.'

'DI Wilcox sounds pretty good, doesn't it?' She sat at the table, flicking through her notebook, her face turning serious. 'We've got a busy day ahead.'

'Are we seeing Ian Carlisle first?'

She nodded her agreement. 'The boss called from Nottingham last night; he bit my head off twice for no reason.'

'He's feeling the heat, that's all.'

'I'm not surprised. The news channel's running the story twenty-four-seven.'

'That should flush Stone to the surface; someone will spot him, sooner or later.'

Angie's car had been upgraded since her promotion, a sleek grey Mondeo, dashboard glowing with screens and gizmos, her radio releasing a drone of static. I could tell she was trying to put me at ease as she navigated the morning traffic. She told me about her husband's delight over her promotion, and her plan to move to another division for more responsibility. I listened in silence as she rattled through personal details, grateful for the chance to forget that the Met had assessed my personal risk at the highest level. That decision was never made lightly, given the cost of round the clock security. By the time we had travelled through Finsbury Park and Islington, the streets looked more bohemian. Stoke Newington Church Street was packed with vintage clothes shops, delis, and trendy bistros.

Carlisle's house had a clear view across Clissold Park, where parents were pushing buggies towards the café, morning joggers lapping the circumference. I had known the psychiatrist professionally for years but never visited his home; the immaculate state of his Edwardian semi and the BMW on his drive let me know that his private consultancy was booming. He looked relaxed when he opened the front door, a tall fifty-year-old with a wry smile and athletic physique, grey hair cut short. A Hollywood actor with his looks would still have been playing romantic leads. He led us to an elegant but untidy living room, with books and magazines littering the furniture. An upright piano stood in the corner, guitar and violin cases leaning against the wall, hundreds of records filling his shelves.

'Forgive the mess,' he said. 'My wife collects vinyl and my daughters never puts anything away.'

'I thought she was at university.'

'Sacha graduated last summer. Our nest didn't stay empty for long.'

A few minutes of general chat gave me time to assess him. There was no sign of panic in Carlisle's behaviour, even though a squad car sat on the yellow lines outside.

'Does your family know you assessed Stone?' I asked.

His shoulders tensed. 'I've explained, but the chances of him coming after me are slim, aren't they?'

'We can't be sure,' I replied. 'He's got a track record of attacking people he sees as traitors.'

Angie looked up from her notes. 'Can I ask why you don't want to go into secure accommodation, Mr Carlisle?'

'This place is my practice as well as my home. I can't just pack up and leave. It's more secure than it looks; we've got a new burglar alarm and solid window and door locks.'

I studied him again. 'What do you think Stone will do next?'

'Adrian likes the idea of posterity; he'll want each stage to be memorable.'

'Because he sees it as a performance?'

'The whole world's his audience now. The longer he keeps killing, the more time he gets on stage.'

'We think he had at least one accomplice,' Angie said.

His eyebrows raised. 'That's interesting, given that he's had no contact with the outside world.'

'He turned one of his guards.'

'I'm not surprised. He can twist every conversation to his advantage; anyone vulnerable would be drawn to him.'

'Did Stone contact you after we quashed the Home Office review?' I asked.

Carlisle shook his head. 'He must have been expecting it. Adrian never showed full remorse, it was clear he couldn't be rehabilitated.'

'Are you a pianist, Dr Carlisle?' Angie asked, glancing at the instrument.

'Not a good one, but I keep taking lessons. It's a great antidote to stress.'

'Do you know Chopin's London nocturne?'

'My daughter learned it for a grade exam. I remember the first few bars.' Carlisle seated himself at the piano and slowly picked out a tune, the melody subdued and haunting. After he'd played for a couple of minutes, he faced us again.

'Melancholy isn't it?' he said, frowning. 'Is it relevant in some way?'

'Stone left a recording at the crime scene. Can you play it again?' The second time I recorded the phrases of music on my phone.

I thought about Carlisle's reactions on the drive to the police station for the senior team briefing, while Angie listened to messages on her radio. It seemed odd that he had rejected full security, despite having a family to protect. I didn't share his view that Stone would take his time. He had already killed two men and left another fighting for his life. His killing impulse had been revived; the typical pattern with psychopathic killers was for intervals between murders to shorten, the level of violence spiralling.

A small crowd of journalists was hanging around the police station on St Pancras Way when we arrived. Many were clutching coffee cups, as if they planned to stay alert for the next scoop. For once I appreciated having their interest; press coverage could keep the public safe. The station carried its usual smell of floor polish, coffee and adrenalin, the incident room heaving with detectives. The first person I bumped into was Pete Hancock, the station's chief scenes of crimes officer. He looked as forbidding as ever, even though an injury from our last case had kept him out of action for months. His black eyebrows were meshed in a permanent frown, beneath a crown of white hair, but I could tell he was suppressing a smile.

'Causing trouble again, Alice,' he commented.

'It wasn't me that set him free.'

'Some bugger did.'

'You look fit and well again, Pete.'

'Mustn't grumble.' His small eyes skimmed my face. 'We'll catch him, don't worry.'

The statement was Hancock's version of a pep talk, delivered in his lilting Tyneside accent, making me produce a grateful smile. When I looked up again Burns's deputy, DI Tania Goddard, was ushering staff into the meeting room. She looked tall and stylish, wearing a bottle green dress that emphasised her curves, black hair cut into in a glossy bob. Burns was at her side; he'd smartened up since the day before, the tallest man present, using the heft of his shoulders to steer his team into their seats. Yesterday's stubble had vanished, and he was dressed in a dark blue suit, his expression intense. The look on his face reminded me of his tendency to pursue each clue tirelessly, almost working himself into the ground. I stood at the back of the crowd as the meeting began, at least forty detectives packing the room, leaving standing room only. Many of the faces were unfamiliar, as some of the officers had travelled down from Nottingham for the meeting. Burns only had to raise his hand to call the room to silence.

'We all know why we're here. Adrian Stone absconded from a secure transport yesterday just after ten a.m., escaping into Sherwood Forest, where the sniffer dogs and search parties lost track of him. We think he washed in one of the streams to throw them off his scent. I want us to focus on protecting people at risk; we know Stone bears long grudges. Tania, can you give us the operational details?'

DI Goddard's turquoise gaze scanned the room. 'Stone attacks people close to him, supporters as well as enemies. You need to remember who you're dealing with. This guy may look like butter wouldn't melt in his mouth, but he enjoys killing and feels no remorse. The focus of our search is on the A1, M1 and stations in Nottinghamshire. It's possible that he hitched a ride or used public transport to travel south. We can't rule out the possibility that other staff members at Rampton helped Matthew Briar set up the escape. We think Stone's aiming for London, because his sister Melissa, and the mental health specialists who denied him his liberty are based here.' She paused to look in my direction. 'One of them is Alice Quentin from the Forensic Psychology Unit; she'll be working with us on the case. Alice can you talk us through the note Stone sent you?'

By the time I'd walked through the crowd, the letter Stone had sent me was projected on the facing wall. His backward-sloping handwriting would have given a graphologist a field day, each letter rigidly controlled, his outsized signature proving that his ego mattered more than his message. When I scanned the room, it was clear that Burns's team understood the challenge ahead. Even the old timers looked wide awake while they read Stone's message.

'Dr Quentin,

I heard about your decision today. I was disappointed but not surprised. I thought Dr Carlisle would be easier to convince, because he plays the piano. He understands musicianship and knows the demands of composing. My level of skill exacts a high personal cost; I've sacrificed my life to it. Music is a rigorous discipline, not that you would understand. There's no point in pleading with you to change your mind, but remember the words of George Bizet, next time you think of me.

'As a musician I tell you that if you were to suppress adultery, fanaticism, crime, evil, the supernatural, there would no longer be the means for writing one note.'

Great music comes from suffering, Dr Quentin. That will never change. Why blame me for a fact that will never change? If we ever meet again, face to face, alone, I will demonstrate what I mean.

Yours,
Adrian Stone'

The mood had changed when I studied my audience again. There was a buzz of anger in the room, triggered by the killer's threat.

'You can tell a lot about Stone's personality from his writing style. He's a true narcissist. His needs always come first, and he doesn't respect society's rules, which could stem from childhood trauma or be a feature of his personality disorder. Outwitting people makes him feel invincible; he'll change his look and identity often to stay underground. Stone turned one of his guards at Rampton, so don't underestimate how charming he can be, or how lethal. He left this piece of music at the murder scene, forced down the throat of one of his guards. The man choked to death on it.' I plugged my phone into the computer and Chopin's calm melody floated through the air. 'Beautiful, isn't it? This is the signature tune to Stone's campaign, but it's also his weak spot. Music should help us catch him, because it's the only thing he loves.'

The bed is empty when Stone wakes mid-morning. He stretches, letting himself enjoy the warm light flooding through the windows. His first action is to reach for his contact lenses, hiding the true colour of his eyes. When he looks up again the young girl from last night appears in the doorway. She's wrapped in a bathrobe, brown curls pulled into a ponytail, her expression awkward.

'I made you some coffee.'

He takes the mug from her hands. 'You're even better by daylight.'

'Flatterer.'

'Perfect skin,' he says, running a fingertip along her jaw. 'You look about seventeen.'

'I'm twenty,' she says, smiling. 'I don't know a single thing about you. Why are you in London, Seth?'

'To find work. I was playing on a cruise ship, but my contract ended.'

Lily drops her gaze. 'I don't make a habit of bringing men here. In fact, you're the first.'

'Then I'm the lucky one. Come back to bed, Lily.'

'I have to work,' she says, laughing.

'Call in sick.'

'I'm a trainee nurse. I'd get in trouble.'

He kisses her again. 'Dinner then, after your shift.'

Stone hides his impatience while she prepares to leave. Need and longing are written all over the girl's features; he will only have to pretend to care to gain everything she owns.

He leaves the flat by midday. His first action is to buy a pay-as-you-go phone, using cash from the envelope left in the car. Afterwards he walks to Hyde Park, enjoying the fresh air. He lingers in the flower gardens, admiring the tulips and bracts of scarlet dogwood, before heading for the café by the Serpentine. A copy of the *Times* lies on the table, his face emblazoned across the front page, but no one glances in his direction, except a waitress, offering a flirtatious smile. When Stone gazes out at the boating lake, he remembers the men he killed yesterday. The memory brings pleasure and pain. The power felt heady, but he regrets the speed and ugliness of their deaths. He plans to do better next time. Stone sips his coffee and watches pedestrians strolling across the grass, the names of people who have interrupted his destiny repeating in his mind, like a refrain. No need to rush, he decides. Each one will meet their fate at the right time.

I needed to interview Stone's accomplice, but he was too ill for visits. Second on my list was his sister, Melissa, who was refusing to leave her flat in Richmond. Her reluctance to see the police was understandable, but her brother's motives would only become clear once I had an insight into his past. She had been just thirteen when her family was destroyed; maybe her coping mechanisms wouldn't let her look back, but the meeting couldn't be delayed.

I expected Tania or Angie to accompany me to Richmond, but it was Burns who found me in the incident room at lunchtime.

'Ready to go?' he asked.

We headed for the car park in silence, the atmosphere between us thick enough to slice. I sensed that he could have driven all day without speaking, too locked in his thoughts to make a sound, yet he pulled up on a side street after less than a mile, his gaze fixed on the windscreen.

'Aren't you going to ask what's bothering me, Alice?'

'You'll say, when you're ready.'

'That's typical shrink's response.' His eyes were hot with anger.

'Go ahead then, Don, enlighten me.'

'Isn't it obvious?'

'Not at all.'

'I hate you being in this kind of danger.'

'What's the alternative? I can't just quit my job.'

'Maybe you should.'

'Don't be ridiculous. Your work's high risk too.' I touched the holster concealed inside his jacket. 'It's not me carrying a weapon.'

'Do you ever take advice?'

'All the time.'

'You're not safe,' he snapped. 'And this is getting us nowhere.'

I held his gaze. 'Why are you so angry?'

'It's all on your terms, no strings attached.'

'You don't usually complain.'

'Because you retreat if I mention the future. Every time I try to make plans you disappear for days.'

'That's not true.' His reactions suddenly made more sense; this was panic, not anger. I settled my hand on his arm. 'I promise not to take risks, Don. But let's not discuss the future with this hanging over us.'

'We'll have to, sooner or later.'

'I know.'

He gave a grudging nod, some of his tension draining away as the journey continued. He focused again on telling me about the case: Matthew Briar, the guard who had freed Stone was still in intensive care, no one at Rampton able to shed light on his actions. All the other staff who had come into contact with Stone were being interviewed, in case they too had succumbed to his manipulation. I looked out of the window as we drove through Kew, wishing for different circumstances. It would have done us both good to visit the botanical gardens, admire the exotic species thriving under glass, then take a long walk through the gardens. When I looked at Burns again his frown had vanished. I wished my own fears were that easy to exorcise. Since the news of Stone's escape, they kept surfacing at night, in gut-wrenching nightmares.

Richmond village green was full of life when we arrived. Retired couples sitting on benches, dog walkers and runners enjoying the spring air. I had always liked the area's bustling town centre, packed with designer shops and cafes, long avenues of genteel Victorian houses. Melissa Stone's apartment was on the edge of town in a plain modern block, wooden cladding peeling from the walls. It was clear that Burns was taking no chances with her safety, even though she was refusing to go into a safe house; an unmarked police car guarded the front of the building, another by the fire escape. I stared up at the small windows, wondering how she was coping. Top level surveillance had put us in the same boat; neither of us could go outside anywhere without a chaperone. Burns suggested that I should lead the questioning as we climbed the stairs, because she seemed more relaxed with women than men.

Melissa Stone responded to the knock on her door so rapidly, she must have been waiting in the hall. Her appearance took me by surprise. Her file stated that she was twenty-two, but she looked like a teenager; a willowy blonde, with porcelain skin, blue eyes glassy with fear. I felt a pang of sympathy. Her brother had wiped out every other member of her immediate family, and now his campaign had restarted. His violence must have blighted every day of her adulthood.

'Thanks for letting us visit,' I said quietly. 'I'm Alice Quentin and this is DCI Don Burns.'

'I know who you are. You'd better come in.'

Melissa was unsmiling as she led us to her small lounge. I studied her again as she perched on the settee; she was a classic English rose, but her beauty was going to waste. Dressed in leggings and a faded blue T shirt, her clothes seemed designed for anonymity, no makeup on a face that could have been show-stopping. Her living room was bland and impersonal too, few trinkets or photos on display.

'The guards keep checking on me every five minutes.' She turned to me, her gaze sharp as a laser. 'Is that why you're here, to assess my mental health?'

'I'm helping the police to find your brother, Melissa,' I replied. 'It would help a great deal if you can give us some background information.'

'You want me to discuss the past?'

'I need to unlock your brother's motives. None of us want him to kill again.'

When she rubbed her hand across her face her slim fingers looked brittle as icicles, waiting to snap. 'How would I know what's in his head? I haven't seen him since I was a kid.'

'This must be hard, but can you describe what your family was like, when you were growing up?'

Her voice was high and breathless. 'My parents were very hardworking. Dad was a finance manager and mum ran a travel company. My sister Jenny was eighteen when she died, the smartest girl in her year. She had a place to study science at Oxford.'

'Were you close to your siblings?'

She looked away. 'I was in their shadow, I suppose.'

'How do you mean?'

'Jenny and Adrian were the gifted ones. The only thing I liked at school was art. Dad found that hard to accept; he wanted all three of us to make a mark on the world.'

'Do you remember much about Adrian's behaviour?'

'He was the middle child, very self-contained. His emotions only came out when he played the piano.'

Burns leant forwards in his seat. 'How do you mean?'

'There's a film of him performing, when he was thirteen. It shows exactly how he was.'

'Could we see it?' I replied.

Melissa knew exactly where to look when she opened a drawer full of DVDs, which took me by surprise. If my brother had gone on a killing spree, I would have destroyed every relic. Once the film started it was impossible to look away. Adrian Stone was no more than a schoolboy, alone on a wide stage, yet the emotions on his face belonged to an adult: grief, combined with passion and anger. Notes flooded from his grand piano like an outburst of tears.

'What's he playing?' I asked.

'Rachmaninov's second concerto. My uncle says it's a huge technical challenge.'

'He makes it look easy,' Burns murmured.

I turned to Melissa again. 'Did something upset him, the day he attacked your family?'

'Nothing I can identify. I got home from school and went to my room to do homework, Adrian was practicing downstairs. I heard Jenny on her phone, laughing in the hall. Mum and dad got back around six, then the noises started.'

'Do you feel able to tell us what you heard?'

Her eyelids fluttered as she spoke again. 'Mum was screaming. I pulled open my door and Adrian was attacking her with a knife, out of control. Dad was running upstairs. I thought he'd stop him, but it was too late.'

'You hid in your room?'

'I can't talk about it anymore.' Her lips closed a thin white line, locking her words inside.

'That's not surprising, it must have been terrifying,' I said quietly.

'My aunt and uncle have been amazing. They adopted me. I only moved out last year.'

'We can give you extra support. Would you like a family liaison officer to stay here?'

'I don't want strangers in my home.'

'Do you have a boyfriend, Melissa?' I asked.

'How is that relevant?'

'This will be easier if someone's with you.'

'What kind of man would date someone with my history?'

'It wasn't your fault.' I studied her face. 'How about work? Do you have a job right now?'

Her face glowed for an instant. 'It's my first year of teaching at the Montessori school on Kew Avenue.'

'I'm afraid you can't go back until your brother's found.'

'He's taken everything, and now I'll lose my job as well.'

The interview ended abruptly. I could understand Melissa's behaviour from working with relatives of murder victims; her brother's escape had made her regress, rekindling her deepest fears. Yet behind all that damage, I sensed she was hiding something. Her feelings towards her brother seemed complex: he had killed her closest relatives, yet I had caught a glimmer of pride in his musical ability when we watched the film. She hesitated for a beat too long when asked about Stone's killing spree, her eye contact evasive. Melissa may only have been thirteen when her world fell apart, but she was holding onto family secrets that we needed to understand.

9

It's mid-afternoon when Stone returns to the Royal College of Music. He approaches the front entrance but a security guard is stationed in the foyer. When he peers through the doorway, it hasn't changed since he enrolled as a teenager. A marble statue of Prince Albert gazes across the open space, the floor an ornate mosaic, trodden smooth by generations of musicians over two centuries. He retreats before the guard catches sight of him. Luckily the back of the building is easier to access. The goods entrance is open, a gang of students are smoking outside the fire exit, one of them strumming a guitar. No one stops him when he slips inside the building, making his way up the wide staircase.

His heart lifts when he reaches the third floor. The corridor is flooded with light, portraits of eminent composers peering down from the walls. He spent his best days here, practising endlessly on the upright Bechstein he grew to love, memorising his repertoire, from Schubert to Prokofiev. But his happiness was wrenched away when his dream collapsed. He peers through an open doorway at a young girl, toiling over a Brahms requiem.

'Wrong tempo,' he mutters, 'stop racing.'

Behind every door pianists are learning their craft in solitude, disparate notes jangling from each room. None of them could equal him, even now, when he has only been able to practice for one hour each day. He absorbs the building's smell of floor polish, dust and history. He has spent years longing for the fierce competitiveness of this place, one musician pitted against another.

Stone slips from the building as quietly as he entered. He sits on the brick wall by the staff car park, until a familiar figure appears. The professor is instantly recognisable, thin and stoop-shouldered as he leans on his cane. Stone watches him approach. It seems incredible that he once put him on a pedestal. He waits until the old man is beside his car, fumbling for his keys.

'Remember me, Professor Keillor?' he asks in a pleasant voice.

Sunlight reflects from the old man's thick glasses. There's no sign of recognition at first, then a slow dawning terror. 'You shouldn't be here, Adrian.'

'That's no welcome for your best pupil.'

Keillor's briefcase falls to the ground as he backs away, but Stone seizes his wrist.

'Let's take a drive.'

He pushes the old man into the driving seat then slams the door, humming to himself as he slips into the passenger seat. Keillor struggles, then falls silent when he sees the knife in Stone's hand. His fingers tremble as he twists the key in the ignition.

10

I spent the last part of the afternoon in an office beside the incident room. Sounds leaked through the closed door: endless phones ringing, voices babbling, a printer grinding out documents. I focused on Stone's history, studying photos from the original crime scene, when two local coppers responded to Melissa Stone's terrified phone call on a hot June morning, nine years ago. Tania appeared at the door an hour later, dressed in a well-cut French navy suit. She looked more like a high-powered executive than a cop, her smile a few degrees warmer than normal. Over the years her attitude towards me had mellowed, from scepticism about all forensic psychologists to grudging acceptance. She glanced down at the photos spread across the table.

'It looks like the inside of an abattoir,' she murmured.

'Melissa seems remarkably sane for someone who's witnessed a massacre.'

The first image showed Stone's mother, curled in a foetal position at the bottom of a staircase, her sundress drenched with blood. Her husband was attacked on the landing, multiple stab wounds staining his shirt scarlet. It looked like Stone had killed his older sister Jenny for defending her parents. The girl's hands were slashed to ribbons; she must have tried to seize his knife, before her throat was cut.

'Culture mixed with savagery. It's an odd combination.'

Tania raised her head. 'How do you mean?'

'Not many classical pianists like cutting people to pieces.'

'You think he enjoyed killing them?'

'Of course, or we wouldn't be looking for him all over again.' I closed the folder. 'Is there any news from Nottingham?'

'Matthew Briar's recovering,' she said, frowning. 'I almost pity him. The papers will tear him apart.'

'Can I assess him tomorrow? I'll be in Nottingham, seeing Stone's psychiatrist.'

'I'll fix it.' She rose to her feet slowly. 'How long do you think Stone can hide?'

'Hard to say. We need some communication first, till then he's invisible.'

'Let's hope he makes contact soon.'

'How are you bearing up anyway?'

A quick smile lit her face. 'Good, thanks. Life moves in mysterious ways.'

'Sounds intriguing.'

'It may be nothing, but it's fun while it lasts.'

I grinned in reply, aware that she was talking about a new relationship. Tania could be prickly, but she was one of the hardest working detectives in the force; she deserved a decent run of luck. After she left, I carried on ploughing through files. The thing that interested me was the way Stone combined violence with calm. He'd been a model patient during most of his stretch at the personality disorder unit, rarely falling out with anyone, organising concerts and following a rigorous fitness regime. When I checked my watch again, it was seven-thirty. Afternoon had slipped into evening while I reassessed Stone's crimes. It had left me longing for a hot shower, to cleanse the images from my skin.

I recognised the middle-aged uniform who picked me up at six-thirty. His name was Reg Walker, and he had chaperoned me on the Foundlings case, several years before. The old timer seemed as curmudgeonly as ever, the skin around his mouth grooved with deep lines, as if disapproval was his default position. He followed me round Sainsbury's with a gloomy look on his face. When I got back to the flat in Borough I changed into leggings and a cashmere jumper, then put a readymade moussaka in the oven. Once I'd opened a bottle of Rioja and made a green salad, the meal was prepared, giving me time to watch Stone's escape act being reported on TV. The focus of the investigation was still in Nottinghamshire, even though I felt certain that he would have fled the area by now.

Stone was smart enough to find a location with guaranteed anonymity. He could be lying low in any major city, but sooner or later he would return to London, to complete unfinished business. I stood by the window gazing down at the dark alley where two uniforms sat in their squad car, sharing a takeaway. If I was Stone's first target, he would need ingenuity to pierce the layer of security surrounding me. My incoming calls, texts and emails were being monitored, police guards listening every time I breathed.

I flicked on my computer for a final check. No link had been established between Stone's escape and the recorded music left at the scene; Chopin had composed the nocturne in 1846, two years before his death. I listened to the slow, lilting melody one more time. My knowledge of classical music was limited, but even I could recognise beauty when I heard it. Why had Stone left that particular piece at a horrifying murder scene? He had spent years refining every detail of his escape. The music must hold a symbolic meaning that I couldn't yet grasp.

Burns arrived as the melody ended, his mood easy to read. I'd seen that distracted expression often over the years; there was something compelling about his dedication, even though it had ended his first marriage. Maybe his singlemindedness drew me because it was a trait we shared. He dropped a distracted kiss on top of my head in the hallway. I couldn't help smiling at his impatience when he tore off his tie, like it was strangling him.

'Any news?' I asked.

'Bugger all, except Melissa Stone's dismissed her security guards.'

'Is that legal?'

'We can't force her to stay safe, but my team'll keep watch anyway.' His Scottish accent was growing stronger with every word, a clear sign that he was annoyed.

'You can't be sure Stone wants his sister dead. His anger may have shifted from his family to another target by now. Have you checked his childhood home? It's possible he'll go back to Richmond to revisit the past. Whoever lives there could be in danger.'

'The property's been empty all year.' Burns hung up his jacket then toed off his shoes. 'Can we talk about something else, just for a while?'

I distracted him with food, drink and conversation. After some of the tension had eased from his face I studied him again. He was lounging on the settee, shoulders like a rugby fullback, dark eyes fixed out of focus.

'Say something in Gaelic, Don.'

The corners of his mouth quirked upwards. 'Chan eil mi 'tuigsinn thu.'

'What does that mean?'

'Take a guess.'

'Come to bed?'

'No, but it's a tempting thought.' His hands lingered on my waist. 'I have to leave, unfortunately.'

'This was just a meal break?'

'I'm on the dawn shift,' he said, with a half-smile. 'I thought you'd be glad to be rid of me, before the future raised its ugly head again.'

'Tease all you like, but you haven't said what you want either.'

'Less pressure and more holidays with you.' He kissed me, then disappeared out of the door.

It was only after he'd left that the worst details of the case re-entered my mind. I made myself do yoga relaxation exercises before going to bed at midnight, but sleep still took hours to arrive.

11

Wednesday 23rd March

At three a.m. Cromwell Road is quiet, little sign of humanity except black cabs plying their trade, a few homeless men huddled in doorways. Stone catches a night bus towards Mayfair, keeping his hood raised even though it's warm, weaving between street cameras.

The professor's car is parked behind deserted offices. He knows the old man is still alive as soon as he touches the bodywork, feeling it vibrate with his desperate movements. Stone removes his hooded top, then pulls on rubber gloves stolen from Lily's flat. This time there's no need to rush; the old man has had hours to contemplate his fate. He shines a torch into his victim's face when he opens the boot. The professor's eyes blink wildly in the unexpected light, jaws twitching as he bites his gag, the rope around his wrists soaked with blood.

'Anything to say, Professor?' Stone asks, loosening his gag. 'Any last words?'

'I'm sorry,' the old man mumbles. 'You deserved more respect.'

'You didn't listen, but now you will.' He takes an iPod from his pocket, jams the headphones over the old man's ears. 'Like what you hear?'

'Yes.' The professor's terrified face twitches as the soaring notes confuse his thoughts. 'It's extraordinary.'

'Liar. You never understood my music.'

The first thrusts of his knife are designed to inflict pain, the old man's body twitching in agony. Stone inflicts the final wound for pleasure alone. Once the act is complete, he lifts the bonnet of the car, to remove the battery. He takes care while draining the acid into a glass bottle, which he places in his bag. When he looks down, his white T shirt is spattered with blood. He yanks it over his head, dropping it into the boot with the rubber gloves, then replaces his hooded top. When he walks away, he feels lighter than before. He retraces his route back to Lily's flat, leaving her keys on the kitchen table. Stone leaves the bottle full of battery acid in his bag, then hides a small parcel wrapped in white plastic in her fridge, behind a cluster of jam jars. His final action is to take a shower then steal into the bedroom. Lily stirs drowsily when he climbs back into bed.

'Where did you go, Seth?' Her voice is a quiet mumble.

'The kitchen, for some water.'

'I thought you'd left me.'

'No, sweetheart. I never will.'

Soon her breathing steadies, and Stone falls into a dreamless sleep.

12

There was little evidence of Burns's visit by the time I woke. The apartment felt bare without him; the only possession he'd left behind was a grey woollen scarf hanging in the hallway, the musk of his aftershave lingering on the air. It was Angie who collected me at eight a.m. Despite informing me that she had hardly slept, she talked constantly as the car headed north.

'I need to know more about the music,' I said. 'It's his signature.'

'Maybe he's just showing us his expertise. It's quite obscure, isn't it?'

'It's one of Chopin's last nocturnes.'

'What is a nocturne anyway?' Angie asked.

'According to Wikipedia it's a musical composition inspired by the night.'

'So it's about darkness, fear, nightmares?'

'This one's more like a lullaby, dreamy and peaceful, which is pretty ironic.'

Angie kept up a stream of chat as we reached the A1, sharing details from the investigation. Melissa Stone still wasn't playing ball. She was staying at her aunt and uncles' home in Chiswick, unwilling to accept safety arrangements. I had the feeling that she was too terrified by her memories to confront them. The sense that she could be withholding information about Stone's original violence nagged at me, along with a concern that she might break down. So far there had been little fresh information, except calls from the general public, claiming to have spotted Stone on buses and trains, or boarding a plane from Aberdeen. Part of the problem was his bland good looks, allowing him to vanish into a crowd. He would have adopted a fresh disguise by now, making it even harder to track him down.

I looked out of the window as a road sign welcomed us to Sherwood Forest. We drove through an expanse of low heathland, scattered with copses of oak, birch and rowan. Stone would have needed maps to learn the terrain before making his escape. I stared at a pathway leading deep into the forest, wondering if he had used it for his getaway. The only person who could shed light on his actions was the guard who helped him escape, only to be rewarded by a savage attack that had almost claimed his life.

Matthew Briar was being treated in the high dependency unit at Nottingham City Hospital. The uniform stationed outside his door was armed with a taser, but Briar was in no state to escape. His facial injuries looked agonising. A blood-stained bandage held a splint to his nose, both eyes heavily bruised. One of the wounds on his forearm looked like a bite mark, ringed by purple scars. The extent of his injuries made me feel queasy; Stone had left his helper at death's door, yet sympathy seemed inappropriate. I needed to discover why Briar had released a violent inmate from a psychiatric unit, and whether he'd acted alone. The guard's psychology fascinated me; his vulnerabilities must be profound if a man with Stone's track record could win his loyalty.

Briar's face was so swollen his reactions were unreadable when we introduced ourselves. I studied my notes while Angie's questions met with silence. The former prison guard was thirty years old, living alone in a suburb of Nottingham, highly regarded by his seniors at Rampton until the escape. His previous job had been at Broadmoor, but he had moved north to become a wing manager three years ago.

'Say "no comment" if you won't answer, Mr Briar,' Angie said. 'The law requires it.'

Briar eyes were bloodshot slits, ringed by bruises. He appeared to be watching us, but hadn't spoken a word. I sat on the edge of his bed then touched his wrist.

'I'm sorry about your injuries, Matthew. You must be in so much pain, but your colleagues, Paul and Lenny are dead. Can you explain why you helped Adrian Stone escape?'

He gave a muffled 'no comment' angling his face away, making Angie tut under her breath. Luckily I had a longer fuse. My work as a psychologist had taught me to expect long silences while patients wrestled with their thoughts.

'He's charismatic, isn't he? Or were you afraid of him?' I shifted position so he was forced to look me in the eye. 'If you say where he's hiding it could reduce your sentence.'

'Right now you're looking at ten years,' Angie said.

Briar kept his eyes shut, clearly hoping we'd disappear. I decided to risk a different technique. 'I loved music as a child, but didn't have the gift. What instrument do you play, Matthew?'

There was a long pause. 'Saxophone, I was professional for a couple of years.'

'Is that how you met Stone?'

'I didn't know him before Rampton.'

'But you'd heard of him?

'Some of his music's online, the wildest free jazz ever.'

I gave a slow nod. 'He may be an amazing composer, but how much loyalty do you owe him now, Matthew? He left you for dead.'

Tears leaked down his battered face. 'We were going to change our identities, start a new life.'

'He brainwashed you. It's happened plenty of times before, psychopaths are very skilled. Try to forget his lies and tell us where he is, before someone else gets killed.'

'London, probably. He said it would be easier to hide in a crowd.'

'Did you arrange a getaway car?'

He dropped his gaze. 'No comment.'

'The arrangements were complex, you couldn't have done it all on your own.'

I saw a flicker of acknowledgement in his eyes. That shifty eye movement let me know that he wasn't the only one who wanted Stone free.

'Tell me who helped you, Matthew. Stone has a habit of turning on the people closest to him. He's in danger too.'

'Plenty of people wanted him out.' Briar's eyes were closing, pain and exhaustion levelling him. He understood the price he'd pay for being duped, but wouldn't reveal the name of his accomplice, no matter how much pressure we applied.

Angie turned to me when we got outside. 'Why would anyone fall for a twisted psycho like Stone?'

'The same reason people marry prisoners on death row. Fragile people are drawn to power, and Stone twisted him round his little finger. Briar was a frustrated musician, lonely and infatuated. He was the perfect mark.'

'I'm surprised they got enough time for long, intimate chats.'

'Briar was wing manager; he could engineer meetings whenever he liked. I hope they've got him on suicide watch.'

Angie nodded. 'He's being checked every fifteen minutes.'

'We need to push him to name his accomplice, until he cracks. He more or less admitted someone else was involved.'

'That could be bullshit, to make him look less guilty.'

'It would have been tough for him to pull off the whole escape on his own.'

'I'll see him again bright and early tomorrow.'

Angie still looked annoyed by Briar's reticence when we arrived at Rampton. I'd visited the place frequently over the years, to risk assess patients returning to prison, but its scale was always daunting. The hospital resembled a small town, wings built around well-maintained greens. Parts of the old red brick bedlam were still in use. Its long terraces would have been the last port of call for the incurably insane during Victorian times, but the personality disorders unit was a gleaming example of postmodernism. Its white roof glistened in the morning sun, heavy glass doors sliding back to admit us.

I sensed the subdued atmosphere immediately, a guard placed our phones and belongings in lockers, frisking us without any small talk. No doubt the news that two colleagues had been killed by a patient had decimated everyone's morale.

Dr Frances Pearce was waiting in her consulting room. She was an attractive brunette of around forty, with flawless olive skin, wearing a vivid blue dress. Her room showed her desire to make her patients feel comfortable, regardless of their crimes. A vase of tulips stood on her desk, water colours of rural landscapes in the seating area. She nodded as Angie explained our visit.

45

'I'm not sure I can help. We're all horrified, of course, but this was completely out of the blue.' Pearce's voice was edged with tension.

'When was your last meeting with Stone, Dr Pearce?' Angie asked.

'Call me Frances, please. I saw him last week. Adrian was in good spirits; he was planning a recital for our trustees.'

'How long have you been treating him, Frances?' I asked.

Her face was strained when she spoke again. 'I've been Adrian's psychiatrist since he arrived. I saw him weekly, for therapeutic reasons, and to assess his risk level.'

'You supported his plea to be released after serving a murder term, didn't you?'

'Adrian was a model patient for years. He worked in the gardens, played the piano and never harmed anyone. I questioned his original diagnosis of severe personality disorder. It seemed likely that a devastating psychotic episode had triggered his violence; every test indicated that he could be reintegrated into society eventually. I believed he'd learned to control his impulses.'

'Did he ever make you feel unsafe?'

'Not once. Patients are restrained during consultations, and a guard waits in the corridor, but his behaviour was never threatening. The opposite, actually. He could be good company.'

'You're joking.' Angie coughed out a laugh. 'The guy slaughtered most of his family in cold blood.'

'When he was ill,' the doctor said quietly. 'Our sessions proved he was recovering.'

'Did Stone show any regret?'

'His contrition struck me as genuine at the time.'

'How did he explain killing his relatives?'

'His motivations were complex.' Her dark eyes scanned my face. 'You're a psychologist, Dr Quentin. You know that violence is always multi-layered.'

Angie leant forwards in her seat. 'Can you guess where Stone may be hiding?'

'I'm afraid not. Adrian knew he would never be freed; he seemed focused on improving his life here.'

'Are you surprised he convinced Matthew Briar to set him free?'

The doctor's expression grew more sombre. 'Matthew organised concerts. He supervised Stone in the music room most days.'

'The perfect opportunity,' I said. 'Can I see Stone's case notes while I'm here, please?'

The doctor frowned. 'I'm afraid not.'

'Can I ask why?'

'The Board of Psychiatry has requisitioned them. They're questioning my professional judgement.'

Pearce's face was pinched with distress when I looked at her again. Stone's escape was causing a ripple effect on everyone inside his circle. In different ways he'd destroyed the lives of Matthew Briar and Frances Pearce. The prison guard would serve years in jail, and his psychiatrist faced losing her job. Wherever Stone was hiding, he would have been thrilled to be causing so much pain.

13

Stone takes Lily to the Troubadour café mid-morning. Last night's success has made him celebratory, and the place has an old-fashioned appeal. Its sofas are draped in dark green velvet, the coffee served from tarnished silverware; even the bebop jazz pulsing in the background pleases him.

'Happy?' He touches the girl's cheek with a fingertip.

'You know I am,' she replies, beaming. 'But I still don't see why you picked me. You could have had anyone, Seth. You only have to play the piano to make women fall for you.'

His gaze locks onto hers. 'I've been messed around before; I can't go through that again.'

'I'd never hurt you.'

'I sensed that straight away, sweetheart.' He sips his coffee. 'Today's a big day. I'm going flat-hunting.'

A look of panic crosses her face. 'I thought you'd be staying at mine, at least till you get a new job.'

'You'll want your own space. I'll cramp your style.'

'I love having you there.'

'Seriously?'

'Don't go, Seth. I'll get you a key cut today.'

'You're one in a million.'

She squeezes his hand then rises to her feet. 'I can't be late again, sister'll kill me.'

'Okay, angel. See you tonight.'

When she kisses him good bye, Stone notices that the girl is prettier than before, newfound happiness bringing a glow to her cheeks. She seems devoted already, pathetically willing to put herself at risk. Stone drains his cup, then studies the pedestrians hurrying down the street, bathed in watery sunshine. After years of confinement, he can do just as he pleases. The city is his to conquer.

14

Burns had been busy briefing the press when I updated him on that afternoon's visits. Stone's escape had been the top news story since he went on the run, even though there were few hard facts to report; Matthew Briar was still refusing to talk and the identity of the second accomplice remained a mystery. Members of the public had been phoning the help desk, terrified that a madman was on the loose, the archetypal image of the psychopath who loves inflicting pain on random strangers affecting the national mind-set.

I spent a frustrating half hour phoning the Board of Psychiatry, requesting Frances Pearce's case notes. The administrators reminded me that top level security permission would be required to access a criminal's treatment files. I pictured a room full of grey-suited drones consulting rule books, but decided to play ball, sending an email to Christine at the FPU requesting clearance.

At four o'clock a shout went up from the incident room. The sound was halfway between a scream and a victory cry. When I pushed open the door, the volume of conversation was deafening. I grabbed Tania's arm as she dashed past.

'What's happened?'

'A body's been found,' she replied.

'And it's relevant to the case?'

'The bloke was Stone's piano tutor.'

She hurried away before I could ask another question. I found out more on the way to the scene with Angie: Professor Keillor had overseen piano teaching at the Royal College for thirty years, following his successful career as a concert pianist. He had lost favour with Stone by blocking his admission to the college's professional music programme, arguing that he needed time to mature, before entering the stressful world of full-time performance.

Keillor had lived alone since his wife died two years before, much of his time devoted to arranging concerts and supporting students. Many of his protégés had secured positions in the world's finest orchestras, proving the professor's talent as a teacher.

Keillor's car was being held in a pound on the outskirts of Mayfair. It had been parked illegally then towed away. The police were notified when a patrolman saw blood dripping from the chassis. Two CSI vans were parked outside when we arrived, white-suited SOCOS buzzing around a new green Lexus. It took me a frustratingly long time to get through the inner cordon, the WPC from the Mayfair force making calls to check my identity, before lifting the crime scene tape. The forensics team were hard at work, plastic sheeting surrounding the car, objects being carted away in blue plastic boxes. Pete Hancock rose to his feet when I approached, thin as a ghost in his white suit, shaking his head in disbelief. He lowered his mask to speak to me.

'I thought musicians were sensitive souls,' he said.

'Not this one. Stone thinks violence is part of his creativity.'

Hancock let out a breath. 'In that case I'll stick to painting by numbers.'

'Me too. Can I take a look?'

'Go ahead, if you've got a strong stomach.'

One of the SOCOs was dusting the car bonnet by the time I peered into the boot. An old man lay on his side, his face twisted towards me, the smell overwhelming; urine and excrement, the bitter odour of fear. My anger towards Stone notched up another level. Whatever wrongs Keillor had committed, no one deserved such a brutal death. I forced myself to study the body again. His wrists had been chaffed by the rope that bound them, dark blood stains on his clothing. A vertical wound bisected his chest, half-covered by the torn remains of his shirt. The old man's face upset me most of all. His eyes were screwed shut, mouth stretched wide, as if he'd died screaming for help. A piece of paper had been folded into one of his hands.

'Can I have this?' I asked.

Hancock shook his head. 'The lab needs it till tomorrow.'

51

I noticed the SOCO's pallor when he stepped into the light. 'How long have you been here?'

'A few hours.'

'Take a break, Pete. I'll buy you a coffee.'

'You know I hate the stuff.'

'Juice, then.' I tapped his shoulder. 'Come on, let the pathologist do his work.'

He unzipped his Tyvek suit reluctantly, but didn't argue. It took us a couple of minutes to reach the nearest café, an Italian place close to Green Park. He ordered lemonade while I opted for espresso, a disapproving look on his face.

'Why do you drink that poison, Alice?'

I smiled. 'To upset you. Don't you have any vices?'

'Too much beer occasionally, long lie-ins at the weekend.'

'That's normal behaviour, no sin involved.'

He gave a sharp laugh. 'There is when you're plagued by Catholic guilt.'

Hancock's appearance had always been austere; white hair contrasting with black eyebrows that lowered over pebble-hard eyes. But today something was troubling him.

'This is just the start, isn't it?' he said. 'He's loving every minute.'

'How do you mean?'

'The details are so precise, right down to the figure of eight knots he used to tie the guy's hands. If we don't catch him, he'll keep going forever.'

'Sooner or later he'll make a mistake.'

Hancock's beady eyes fixed on me. 'How will you find him?'

'By thinking the way he does. Finding his helper would be a start.'

'No job's worth putting yourself in danger. Don't take any risks.'

'I won't.' I put down my cup. 'Where was the car parked, before it was towed to the pound?'

'Behind offices on Dover Street, that area's deserted at night.'

'Can you remember the number of the building?'

He looked puzzled. 'Forty-eight. Why?'

'Stone's giving us a music lesson. The location may be symbolic too.'

Hancock made his version of small talk on our way back to the crime scene. He told me that Newcastle's performance had almost made him sell his season ticket, and that his older son was planning a trip to Australia. In exchange I confessed that Burns's kids still felt like strangers; finding a way to speak to two monosyllabic teenagers who stayed in his flat on alternate weekends was taking a frustratingly long time. We snapped back to reality when we got back to the pound. A forty-minute break hadn't changed the facts: an old man had experienced an agonising death, and his killer was still at large. I stood on the threshold waiting for my taciturn escort to arrive, while the Met's photographer pointed his lens at the victim's wounds. A full set of images would be needed before the body could be removed for autopsy.

I made Reg drive down Dover Street on our way back to Borough. He complied, after whining about unnecessary detours. The road turned out to be an expensive Mayfair avenue, with a mixture of architectural styles. The original buildings were Regency, but bomb damage or neglect meant that many had been replaced. Number forty-eight was a modern office block, faced with sandstone, no distinguishing features. Its blankness bothered me so much that I flipped open my computer without removing my coat, the minute I reached the safe house. When I typed in the address, the information on my screen made me suck in a long breath.

'Bingo,' I muttered.

Chopin had stayed at number forty-eight Dover Street in 1846, two years before his death, composing several nocturnes during a concert tour. I carried on scanning information while placing a call to Burns. Ten minutes later he rang back, his voice breathless.

'Where are you?' I asked.

'Walking to University College Hospital. Fiona Lindstrop's agreed to do an emergency autopsy in half an hour.'

'I'll meet you there, but there's something you should know. The music Stone left at the Nottingham crime scene explains why Keillor's body was found in Mayfair.'

'How come?'

'Chopin composed the nocturne while lodging at forty-eight Dover Street. Keillor's car was parked outside the back door.'

There was a long pause before he replied. 'So the music gave us the location of the next crime?'

'There was a piece of paper in Keillor's hand; it could explain the next location.'

'How long do you think we've got before he strikes again?'

'Hours, not days. Serial killers accelerate; he's killed three victims already.'

Burns released a quick stream of expletives before hanging up.

15

Spring rain has soaked Stone's clothes, but he's too mesmerised to care. At dusk his former home in Richmond looks tall and imposing, surrounded by high walls, each brick burdened with memory. Stone smiles when he notices a 'for sale' sign over the entrance gate, wondering how many times the place has changed hands in recent years. The owners must have been afraid of the ghosts he created, but now he feels like a spectre in the gathering dark, returning to complete what he started.

He emerges from the shadows to open the gate. Luck is on his side again; some careless estate agent has left it unlocked. He glances up and down the street before disappearing inside. His mother's manicured lawn has gone to seed, with ragged weeds filling the borders, and the holly tree by the front door eclipses the path. He circles the building in silence, peering through windows. The gleaming parquet of his childhood still covers the living room floor. He would like to force a window and step inside for a trip down memory lane, but lingering could be dangerous.

Stone forces the door of the shed, wood splintering as he shoulders it down, then selects a spade. His movements are rapid when he retraces his steps. He stares through the window of his father's study; the room is empty now, a clean white box. But he imagines it in its original state, with his father's Chippendale desk dominating the room.

'This is a tribute for you, old man,' he mutters. 'No more than you deserve.'

Stone begins to dig in one of the flowerbeds, lifting the earth until sweat rises on the back of his neck. Once the hole is two feet deep, he takes the white plastic package from his pocket and places it at the bottom. His body floods with satisfaction as he covers it once more, tamping the ground flat with his foot. Gradually old scores are being settled, but his elation makes him careless. He strides through the gate without checking, then collides with a passer-by. A young boy in school uniform stands before him, eyes huge in the streetlight. It crosses Stone's mind to kill the child immediately, but a car's headlights distract him.

'Run, you idiot, before I change my mind,' Stone hisses.

The boy's gaze sharpens before he sprints into the dark, school bag bouncing on his shoulder. Stone's irritation fades as he vanishes down an alleyway. He pulls his iPod from his pocket then flicks through the menu, selecting *The Rites of Spring* for his journey back to town, the soaring notes of the opening movement reviving his mood.

16

Burns was waiting for me at University College Hospital by six p.m.
I found him in the basement corridor, checking his phone, his bulk
blocking out the light. It was only when he gave me a lopsided smile
that the usual jolt of attraction hit me, despite our surroundings. I
had visited the pathology department many times before, but the
place was always disturbing. Strip lights flickered above us,
releasing the same clinical light twenty-four-seven, the air tainted
by formaldehyde from the morgue next door.

'Ready for the dragon lady?' Burns asked.

'You can handle her.'

Fiona Lindstrop was hard at work when her assistant ushered us
into her theatre. The pathologist wore her usual look of fierce
determination, grey hair springing from her scalp in stiff curls. She
must have been near retirement age, with the reddened complexion
that comes from outdoor living, or a fondness for whisky. Professor
Keillor's body lay on a marble slab, covered to the chest by a white
sheet. The pathologist shone a small torch into the old man's eyes
then murmured a few words to the microphone suspended from the
ceiling, before acknowledging our arrival. When she finally looked
up her voice was just shy of ten decibels.

'There you are, Burns. Come to buy me dinner?'

'I'd love to, Fiona. But watching autopsies kills my appetite.'

'Pity, they always leave me starving.' Lindstrop turned to me.
'Good to see you again, Dr Quentin. I hope you remember the rules:
backs to the wall, no fainting. Talking will get you thrown out.'

Her advice turned out to be useful. Once the post-mortem began,
I needed the wall's solidity to stay upright. Despite my years at
medical school, pathology had never appealed to me. The wound at
the centre of Keillor's body was a foot long, deep enough to expose

his ribs. I heard Burns give a shallow moan when Lindstrop thrust her hand wrist-deep into his chest cavity. My eyes drifted to the other marks on the old man's thin frame; he had been stabbed repeatedly, most of the wounds to his chest and abdomen.

Lindstrop spent the next half hour performing a Y section, removing the major organs, before examining them minutely. Her face was stern when she finally drew the sheet back over Keillor's corpse, removing her surgical gloves, then scrubbing her hands with sterile soap that stained her skin yellow. She was frowning when she finally faced us again.

'The old fellow was held captive for hours. He tried to free his hands, but the ropes were too tight; his wrists are chafed to the bone. Several of the knife wounds are fifteen centimetres deep. It takes a sharp blade and physical strength to drive a knife that far through muscle and bone. There are sixteen wounds in total, all to the thorax. I suspect the blows were delivered in a frenzy.'

'Not a great way to go,' Burns replied.

'The killer fancies himself as a surgeon. Come over here, I'll show you.'

Burns groaned. 'I was afraid you'd say that.'

Lindstrop showed us a row of bowls on the metal table. Each contained one of the professor's organs, two dark purple kidneys lying side by side, lungs covered in pale pink foam. The smell of bile hit the back of my throat, raw and acidic.

'Is this a test of moral fibre?' Burns muttered.

'You can tell how he died, from the contents of this table,' the pathologist replied. 'Something's missing, isn't it?'

'The heart,' I said.

She gave a broad smile. 'Exactly, Alice. You're always an excellent pupil. The killer made a deep incision, breaking several lungs to remove it.'

Burns stared at her. 'The old man's heart was ripped from his chest?'

'He did a neat job. The aorta was cut cleanly in two.'

Burns still looked stunned when we got outside. We walked down the Euston Road in silence, his hand heavy on my shoulder. It felt good to breathe fresh air after two hours in Lindstrop's basement; the city's sights and sounds were a reminder that normality still existed. Buses hurtled through the dark, people marching to the Tube, going home to their families. We ended up in a dimly lit bar on Great Portland Street, with candles flickering and a bottle of Shiraz on the table between us. Burns knocked back his first glass without bothering to swallow. But when the waiter offered us bread and olives, he held up his hand to refuse.

'I've been in this job too long,' he said.

'Lindstrop affects me that way too.' I took a sip of wine. 'Stone's changed his MO since he was a teenager. He killed on impulse then, but this time he's leaving calling cards and taking mementoes.'

Burns stared at me. 'You'd call a human heart a souvenir?'

'Stone doesn't think like us. I still need to understand the link between the music he leaves and his violence. He's taunting us, but there has to be more to it.'

'I just want to know where he's hiding. There's an argument for gunning him down, isn't there? The tax payer will be paying for his bed and board for decades when we catch him again.'

'If you want to eradicate psychopaths from society, you'll be busy. Two percent of the population has a personality disorder.'

'Gene editing's the answer.' He gave a dry laugh. 'Right now I'd settle for Stone's head on a stick.'

'That's a balanced view, inspector.'

Burns was making light of it, but the tension on his face was easy to read. The responsibility for finding Stone rested on his shoulders. If the case dragged its heels, the press would attack him from all sides.

It was raining when we left the wine bar, a quick spring deluge that soaked me to the skin. Burns insisted on taking me back to the safe house in a taxi, rather than waiting for a patrol car. Sharing the back seat with him was an odd experience. We were safe, in the enclosed confines of the cab, but my safety felt paper thin. I knew for a fact that Stone was walking the streets that flickered past the window, preparing to strike again.

17

At ten thirty Stone and Lily are drinking wine in the bar where they first met. The place is packed with students, lingering over a final drink. He's pretending to enjoy the girl's chatter, but would rather be playing the piano in the corner, fingers itching to touch the keys. In an ideal world he could return once the place closes, practice to his heart's content. He concentrates on Lily's voice when he realises she's asked a question, naivety shining from her face.

'What did you do today, Seth?'

'I visited a few people, set up some job interviews.'

'That's brilliant.' Lily sips from her drink. 'You still haven't told me much about yourself. Have you got a family tucked away somewhere?'

'Just one sister, here, in London.'

Lily's face is solemn. 'I'd love to meet her. Is she like you?'

'She's younger. Maybe I'll introduce you one day.'

The conversation is straying onto dangerous territory. Part of him wonders how the girl would react if she knew he'd killed a man, less that twenty-four hours before. He short circuits her questions by lifting her hand to his cheek.

'I'm falling for you, Lily. I can't help myself.'

Her smile widens. 'You've only known me two days.'

'Who cares? I've waited years for you.'

She leans forward to kiss him. 'Thank God I walked into this place when you were playing.'

'Let me play for you again, then I'll take you home.'

It's a relief to escape the adoration in her eyes. When he sits at the piano, nothing matters except the sound vibrating from his fingertips. He plays Satie's third Gymnopedie. The piece is so overused it's become a cliché, but the harmony still moves him, minor chords echoing with sad purity. Its simplicity reminds him of his sister's gentleness as a child. He wonders if she's waiting for him already, too afraid to open her front door.

18

Thursday 24th March

My morning began with a quick scan of the headlines, as the patrol car edged north through thick traffic. The *Independent's* front page announced VIOLENT MURDER OF CLASSICAL LEGEND; the story gave a roll call of Professor Keillor's most gifted students, but no explicit claim that Stone could be the killer. Burns had worked hard to convince the press that the professor's death might have been a random attack, unwilling to spark more panic until Stone's whereabouts were known.

The patrol car dropped me outside the Royal College of Music at nine a.m. Reg and his sidekick remained in the vehicle, monitoring me from twenty metres, as if I might be snatched from the pavement. The building's imposing façade reminded me of a French chateau, door surrounds faced with marble, two sharp-roofed towers piercing the sky. Most of the windows were shuttered, confirming the college's reputation for secrecy. Despite producing some of the most successful performers in the world, its teaching methods were a closely guarded secret.

When Tania arrived ten minutes late the sight of her long legs unfolding from the back of a taxi made me wonder why Burns had chosen me. Their brief fling at training school years before was something I tried to forget. She looked more striking than ever, dressed in a cream mackintosh that accentuated her glowing skin. I made myself focus on the purpose of our visit. Stone's tutors might be able to explain why Professor Keillor had been the target of Stone's brutal attack.

'Busy morning?' I asked, as Tania approached at a brisk stride.

Thursday 24th March

'I've been checking CCTV. We've got some blurred shots of a man on Dover Street; the IT guys are cleaning them up to see if it's him.'

'Are we meeting the Principal first?'

She studied her notebook. 'Professor Susan Weinman. She decided against cancelling classes today.'

'How come?'

'Out of respect for Keillor. Apparently he hated giving his students a day off.' She turned to face me. 'She wasn't keen to see us. The place doesn't normally welcome visitors, unless there's a public concert.'

'To preserve their mystique, probably. I need to understand Stone's behaviour when he was a student. Can I lead the questions?'

'Feel free. I'll check details at the end.'

The place resonated with music as we climbed the stairs. Each floor seemed to be dedicated to a different family of instruments, the air pulsing with drum beats on the ground floor, melodious sounds greeting us as we climbed. The mournful song of cellos was followed by clarinets and flutes as we crossed the second landing; pianos were playing hectic scales as we reached the third floor.

The sign on Susan Weinman's door revealed a dozen letters after her name. The woman who greeted us was around forty-five, thin-faced with straight black hair tumbling over her shoulders, hazel eyes giving us an intent stare. Her dress sense made me envious: her emerald green dress skimmed her slim figure, heavy gold jewellery that looked hand-designed, but behind the effortless style her tension was easy to read.

'Forgive me if I don't make sense,' she said. 'The news about Gareth has knocked me sideways.'

'It's good of you to see us,' I replied. 'I know visitors are rarely allowed inside during teaching hours.'

Her laser-like gaze fixed on me. 'Our students have to be utterly focussed, without distractions. We're not guarding any secrets. It's a combination of talent, passion and hard graft that helps them get to the top.'

'That makes perfect sense. Can you tell us about Professor Keillor?'

Her face softened by a fraction. 'He was a great mentor to our younger tutors. Gareth was incredibly dedicated. At sixty-eight he was still fully committed, despite being in constant pain.'

'Was he ill?'

'Rheumatoid arthritis affected his mobility, but he never complained.'

'The professor lived alone?'

'His wife died a few years ago.' Weinman's grief showed in the nervous jitter of her fingers, twisting the ornate rings that burdened her hands.

'Did he have any problems while he was teaching Adrian Stone?'

Her amber gaze locked onto mine again. 'Are you suggesting that Adrian killed Gareth?'

'We're exploring every possibility. Did Stone take his courses?'

'They spent hundreds of hours together. Our students are assigned a practical tutor when they start here; on average they practice for thirty-five hours a week. It made sense that Gareth should work with Adrian, because he argued for the boy to be admitted. We rarely accept underage students, but Adrian auditioned for us at thirteen. His parents wanted him out of mainstream education.'

'Did they say why?'

'His teachers found his temper hard to handle. It was obvious he was gifted; conventional schooling frustrated him.'

I'd read about Stone's early tantrums in his file but now they made more sense, fitting the blueprint for most juvenile psychopaths. His violent impulses surfaced whenever his desires were thwarted.

'You broke your own rules to give him a place.'

'We agreed to a one term trial, to see if he'd cope. He graduated from our practical degree programme at sixteen.'

'That must have taken dedication.'

She frowned. 'Adrian was always first to arrive and last to leave. To be honest, I found him disturbing, even then.'

'Why?'

'Dedication is admirable, but he had no other interests. He spent little time making friends.'

'Was he close to Professor Keillor?'

'Most of his teaching was one to one, with Gareth and Stanley Yacoub. Neither reported any problems.'

'What about other students?'

'Adrian saw many of them as his competitors; he showed little interest in anything except practising.'

'His time here ended badly, didn't it?'

'Adrian wanted to enroll on our professional studies course, but we didn't think he was ready. The students work with orchestras, and receive intensive mentoring, with feedback on performances. It can be a tough transition, even for mature performers. His parents agreed to send him back to school for two years. It was Gareth who broke the news.'

'How did he react?'

'Calmly at first. I explained that we hoped he would return at eighteen, but he just stared at me with those unnaturally blue eyes.' Her tough veneer seemed to be slipping as she passed her hand across her face, like she was erasing the memory.

'What happened afterwards?'

'I've lived with that for years.' Her hands fell still in her lap. 'He attacked his family that evening. I've often wondered if we could have saved their lives, by handling things differently.'

'The events may not have been linked.'

Weinman shook her head. 'He travelled home to Richmond on the Tube. Less than two hours later, he did those terrible things.'

I listened in silence while Tania quizzed the principal about security arrangements. Her tough demeanour showed that she didn't suffer fools gladly, but unlike Melissa Stone she seemed prepared to tolerate measures designed to keep her students safe. I glanced around her office as she spoke. The room was in one of the building's turrets, with octagonal walls, and a direct view of the Albert Hall. I peered at the lead tracing on the concert hall's domed roof, ornate as icing on a wedding cake. The students must pass it each day, dreaming that one day they might perform on the venue's stage.

Tania and I reached Stanley Yacoub's office on the third floor a few minutes late. The man who opened the door looked more relaxed that his boss. A rangy black guy in his late thirties, dressed in jeans and a crisp blue shirt, his office almost filled by a grand piano, with wooden chairs pushed back against the walls. But there was something remote about the way he greeted us, grey eyes unfocused when he gestured for us to sit. I put his distant manner down to the shock of losing his colleague.

'Sorry this place is a tight squeeze.' Yacoub had a soft American accent, as if he'd lived in the UK so long, he'd lost touch with his roots. 'You want to talk about Gareth, don't you?'

'I'd be grateful to hear about Adrian Stone first.'

His gaze failed to connect with my face. 'He saw more of Gareth than me. I helped him with composition and written work, in this very room.'

'What was he like?'

Yacoub's smile faded. 'A trapped bird, beating its wings against the window.'

'How do you mean?'

'By fifteen he had more technical skill than most concert pianists ever achieve, but always wanted more. He was frantic to master the classical repertoire. I felt sorry for him; it made me think he was unhappy at home.'

'Why?'

'Child prodigies are caught between a rock and hard place. Kids don't accept them, neither do adults. Something drove him to outperform: fear, or the need to please someone.'

'Personality disorders often make people obsessive.'

'It was more than that. Would you like to hear one of the pieces Adrian wrote as a boy? It might explain what I mean.'

'You still have the sheet music?'

He shook his head. 'These days I play from memory.'

When Yacoub made his way to the piano, his vague gaze finally made sense. He ran his hand along the piano, head tipped back as he seated himself, never looking at the keys. It had taken me ten minutes to realise that he was blind, but his lack of sight didn't reduce his skill. Once he began to play, his description of Stone as a caged bird made sense. There was a wild energy in the movement of Yacoub's hands across the keyboard, notes chasing each other, tempo so rapid it assaulted my senses. Whatever evils Stone had committed, it was clear he had an exceptional gift. The music seemed to affect Tania too, her face rapt with concentration as the piece ended.

'Adrian completed his first orchestral score at age twelve,' Yacoub said. 'He was incredibly versatile. His jazz compositions are extraordinary too.'

'What would Stone have done, if he hadn't committed his crimes?' I asked.

'He'd be playing at the best venues across the world.'

'Do you know much about the nocturnes Chopin wrote, here in London?' I asked.

He faced the piano again, playing a few bars of the music Stone had left at the first murder scene. 'Chopin had planned a grand concert tour across Europe, but he was too weak to perform. He was dying from consumption when he arrived in London. If you listen carefully you can hear his despair in every chord.'

Yacoub's words stayed with me as Tania closed the interview. Why had Stone chosen a location where a musical genius had been so unhappy? Maybe he was proving his theory about the relationship between music and pain. Everything I'd read about Chopin suggested that his life had been shaped by suffering: exiled from his home in Poland, he always reminisced about his homeland. But what had Stone been missing? There must be some part of his life that he believed had been stolen.

I had little time to debrief with Tania, before she raced back to the station. Reg issued a lecture on personal safety on our drive to Covent Garden; he and his colleague insisted on following me to the café where I was meeting Lola. My suggestion that they wait in the car drew a fierce look from my bodyguard.

'The DCI told me to stick to you like glue.'

Luckily Lola was too busy peering at wedding brochures when I arrived at Paul's café on Floral Street to notice policemen loitering outside. Neve lay in her pram beside the table, fast asleep. I kissed Lola, then leant across to admire my nine-month-old goddaughter.

She had the same auburn hair as her mother, long coppery eyelashes fluttering over milk pale cheeks. I was tempted to pick her up, but the look on Lola's face warned me not to wake her. It was clear that my friend was having a bad day.

'There's been a disaster of epic proportions,' she said.

'What?'

'The florists have cancelled. Help me, before I crack up.'

I suppressed a smile. While I chased a mass murderer, my closest friend was in meltdown over floral displays. We spent the next hour debating over types of buttonholes and bouquets, allowing me to slip back into normality. After a second cappuccino I was about to say good bye, but Neve was waking up. Lola scooped her out of the pram and dumped her in my lap, eyes still heavy with sleep, small fists curling round my fingers. I leant down to inhale her scent of talcum powder and innocence. But when I straightened up again, Lola's feline stare fixed on me.

'You should have one of your own, Al.'

'Not any time soon.'

'Why not? Burns is crazy about you, and you'd get great maternity leave.'

'I'd rather play with yours, then hand her back.'

She looked amused. 'Liar. I've never seen anyone broodier.'

I didn't have the heart to explain that my work wasn't compatible with motherhood; she had enough worries in the run up to her wedding, but her suggestion lingered when I left the café. Reg was waiting in the squad car to escort me back to the station. Proof positive that ordinary comforts like marriage and kids had no place in a life like mine.

19

Stone sits on a garden wall, concealed by shadows. He has spent the morning observing his aunt and uncle's house in Chiswick for signs of activity. The property is prim and well-maintained, coated in flawless white paint. He's certain that the Volvo on the drive belongs to his uncle, but there's no other sign of him. The only people he's seen are a postman dragging his trolley down a tree-lined avenue, dog walkers, and a woman pushing flyers through doors.

The need to find his sister is growing more urgent, frustration mounting as the morning ebbs away. He's about to leave when a silver Toyota pulls up on the drive; even from a distance his aunt is easy to recognise. Emma Stone is tall, with a cap of short dark hair, movements rapid as she removes shopping bags from the boot then locks the car. His fists tighten in his pockets as he watches her. It's a relief that there's no sign of a security here yet. He feels certain that Melissa will visit soon.

'I can wait for you,' he mutters, before walking away.

Strangers' conversations pulse in his ears on the train back to town, a soft drumbeat accompanying his thoughts. When he reaches Soho, he checks his appearance in a shop window. Dressed in black jeans, a white T shirt, and casual grey jacket he blends into the crowd perfectly; a tourist or young professional on a late lunch break. It's only when he gets to Frith Street that his pulse quickens. The neon sign outside Ronnie Scott's jazz club is announcing opening hours from six-thirty p.m. to three a.m. Inside the basement entrance the walls are the colour of strong red wine, a sea of chairs grouped around circular tables. A woman of indeterminate age is leaning on the bar, gazing at her tablet. Long chestnut hair is scooped back from a face that looks designed to scowl, black rings of mascara circling her eyes; she's wearing high heels and a tight blue dress. Her frown stays in place when she finally notices him.

'We're closed, love. Come back tonight.'

'I'm looking for the manager,' Stone says.

'You found her. Nancy Morris, how can I help?' Her voice sounds like it has been roughened by a thousand cigarettes.

'I'm a pianist, looking for work.'

She gives a grating laugh. 'Do you know how many musicians walk through my door?'

'Just let me play for ten minutes, please.'

'Send me a CD, sweetheart. I'm busy'

'Five minutes, that's all I ask.'

She rolls her eyes. 'Then you'll leave?'

'Sure, if you don't like what you hear.'

She sits close to the stage not bothering to conceal her impatience. Stone strokes the keys slowly at first, then lets the city's hectic pace stream through his fingers, violence and dreams converting into a rhapsody of sound. When he finishes, the woman's bored expression has been replaced by grudging interest.

'Classically trained, aren't you?'

'Years ago. I've been in the US ever since.'

'What's your name?'

'Seth Rivers.'

'You're in luck.' Her eyes narrow. 'One of my house pianists is sick. Get here by midnight tomorrow; play for an hour as my guests leave. Musician rates, plus tips.'

Stone is grinning when he returns to the afternoon's cool light. The meeting gave him the perfect outcome: his talent will be recognised at last.

20

The senior team briefing began at two p.m. It would have been a challenge to assemble four more disparate individuals in the station's meeting room: Angie was an elfin chatterbox, cheeks loaded with freckles, her pillar box red hair standing up in dense spikes, Tania svelte and unflappable at her side. Pete Hancock was keeping himself apart, his thatch of white hair in need of a cut, black eyes glowering. Sitting at the head of the table, Burns towered over them all, like the sole adult in the room. His skin was paler then before, eyes shadowed, his shirtsleeves rolled up, as if he was preparing for a brawl. He studied each of us in turn, his gaze unblinking.

'Stone escaped three days ago, but there are no solid clues yet. All we know for sure is that Matthew Briar's actions caused the death of his colleagues. There's no hard evidence that someone else helped him set up the escape, even though Briar gave us a hint. Since he got free Stone has killed his former piano teacher in the most barbaric way imaginable, by removing his heart, and he's just hitting his stride. He won't stop till we catch him. Tania, let's have your update first please.'

She looked up from her notes. 'Road cameras and footage from local train and bus stations haven't given anything. We know someone helped him vanish, sorting out a car, or train ticket. It could have been Matthew Briar acting alone, but he's still in hospital, refusing to talk.'

Burns gave a crisp nod. 'What about you, Angie?'

'I've been at Rampton, checking staffs' alibis, in case they were involved, but so far they're all in the clear. My team's arranged security for the relatives, and at the music college. We know Stone hurts people close to him, especially if he feels let down. Given that he's killed three family members, Melissa Stone and her aunt and uncle are especially vulnerable. Right now they're staying together in the couple's Chiswick home. The girl's refusing personal protection, but we've got covert surveillance.'

'Alice, can you predict what he might do next?' Burns asked.

I returned his gaze. 'Most psychopathic violence is rooted in childhood experience, but for Stone it's also linked to his melophilia.'

Angie stared at me. 'What's that exactly?'

'An obsessive love of music. Stone has played and composed constantly since childhood. He thinks it's his destiny to be recognised as a musical genius. If anyone questions that dream, he reacts with violence. I think he cut out his former teacher's heart as a punishment for his lack of faith. He may be keeping it somewhere, as a memento, or he'll choose somewhere with a personal meaning to leave it. I imagine he'll have recruited a helper by now, probably someone submissive, like Matthew Briar; the person could be male or female. He'll choose someone to reinforce his grandiose delusions.'

'How about the clues he's leaving?' Burns asked.

'The music at the first scene signalled where the next body would be found. Chopin was staying in Dover Street when he wrote it, at the exact spot where Stone left his tutor's body. The fragment of music in Gareth Keillor's hand is from Mozart's first symphony, written in seventeen-sixty-four here in London, when he was eight years old.'

'He was that young when he wrote a symphony?' Tania looked astonished.

'Stone was a prodigy too, but didn't get full recognition. It's likely he'll try to realise some of his dreams now. He's telling us about his own experience with each piece he leaves.'

'Do you know where it was composed?'

I flicked through my notes. 'Mozart spent that year touring with his father and sister; they stayed at different addresses around London. The ones I've found so far are at Cecil Court, Frith Street and Ebury Street, but there may have been more.'

'Where do you think he'll strike next?' Burns asked.

'Stone kills anyone who disrupts his plans. Gareth Keillor spoiled his dream of becoming one of the world's youngest concert pianists. He may change tack and kill one of his remaining relatives, for failing to believe in him. Or the next victim could be a teacher, or mental health professional who got in his way.'

'Like you or Ian Carlisle?' Burns kept his eyes on my face.

'We must be on his list.'

His face darkened. 'Make sure you stick to the security plan.'

Talk shifted to the next topic, but the team's discomfort lingered, everyone reluctant to meet my eye. The meeting ended with Hancock describing the forensic evidence from the Nottingham attack and Professor Keillor's car. While Stone had used only his bare hands to kill his guards, the attack on his tutor had been systematic. The professor had been driven to Dover Street, then locked in the boot. Hours later Stone had returned with a nine-inch blade to cut out his heart. Facts floated past me without registering. For the first time it dawned on me that I might be next; Stone could outsmart even the most sophisticated security. I let my panic surface, rather than keeping it locked down, aware that psychological manuals warn against ignoring your fears. My best chance of staying alive was to focus on finding Stone, before he found me, even though his musical calling might be a false trail.

'I need to see Matthew Briar again tomorrow,' I said, as the meeting closed. 'He must have more information. If we can find his helper, it could lead us to Stone.'

'I'll sort it,' Tania said. 'But he's keeping his trap shut.'

'He'll crack sooner or later,' I replied.

Burns gestured for me to stay behind when the meeting ended, his mobile ringing before he could explain why. His body language stiffened as he fielded a call from Scotland Yard. The deputy commissioner's gruff baritone was audible from three metres away, insisting on another news conference, to appease the press. Burns's expression was thunderous as he stuffed the phone back in his pocket, mumbling curses.

'Trouble upstairs?' I asked.

'They love putting their oar in.' He turned to me again. 'We've had a lead on the helpline. A woman from the street where Stone killed his family says her kid saw him there Tuesday afternoon. Do you think it's worth a visit?'

'Is she credible?'

'She's a science lecturer at London University.'

'Let's make the trip. Killers often return to their murder sites; it's where they feel most powerful.'

Burns was subdued when we reached his car, easing his hulking frame into the driver's seat. I couldn't resist leaning over to kiss his cheek. He responded by gripping my hand hard enough to make my knuckles ache, then concentrated on punching digits into his sat nav. He seemed to be managing his tension by staying on task, but part of me wished we could drive straight to Heathrow, and catch a plane to an exotic location that no one could find. I plugged my phone into his car stereo as we left the car park. Burns looked startled at first, then listened in silence as Mozart's first symphony filled the car. I'd been expecting a virtuoso piano solo, but it was a simple blend of oboe and strings, the main melody picked out on a harpsichord. I gazed out of the window as genteel suburbs flickered past. It beggared belief that a child of eight could have written music that was still celebrated two hundred and fifty years later. But why had Stone chosen it for a calling card? Thousands of classical pieces had been composed in London; this one must have a personal meaning. I gave the melody my full concentration, eyes still closed when the car came to a halt.

'The mother's in a state,' Burns said. 'Her son's hardly left his room.'

'Let me talk to him.'

He frowned. 'I've got two boys, remember? I won't scare him.'

'Trust me, Don. Most of my training was with traumatised kids.'

The tension between us thickened as we approached the house. It was a turn-of-the-century cottage, set behind a low wall, the grass neatly cut. Whoever lived there seemed more committed to the garden than the property. Clematis had been carefully trained across the wooden porch, but paint was peeling from window frames and the doorbell didn't work. Eventually someone responded to Burns's hammering on the door. The woman who greeted us was around my age, dressed in a dark blue sari, black hair hanging over her shoulder in a long plait. I could tell she'd been crying, her eyes glossy with tears.

'Dr Gupta?' I asked.

'Anita, please. I'm grateful you're here; I've been so worried about Sanjay.'

She led us to a small, neat living room. A figurine of Krishna smiled down from the mantelpiece, almost hidden by photos of her son in school uniform. She gestured for us to sit, but remained on her feet, hands clasped in front of her waist.

'Can you tell us what's wrong, Anita?'

'My son saw Adrian Stone.' She fiddled with the thin gold bracelets on her wrist. 'Sanjay's always truthful. He's a quiet boy, studious; but now he's refusing to go to school.'

'Could I speak to him, please?'

'If I can stay in the room.'

'Of course.'

Dr Gupta led us past her kitchen door. The aromas of chocolate and caramelised sugar carried on the air, hinting that she'd been baking delicacies to tempt her son downstairs. When she reached the landing Anita tapped lightly on the door, but no sound came back. Burns waited on the landing when I finally entered the room. It was half-lit, the air stale. A child huddled on the bed, face pressed to his knees, clearly terrified. I settled myself on the edge of the divan, staying silent until he registered my presence.

'My name's Alice,' I said quietly. 'Can you tell say why you're upset, Sanjay? It'll help you to talk about it.'

At first there was no reaction. The child's thin frame didn't move an inch, but after five minutes, he finally lifted his face. He must have been eleven or twelve, huge brown eyes gazing into mine.

'That's a really good start.' I smiled at him. 'Now why don't you tell me what you saw?'

'He was leaving the haunted house.' His voice trembled as he spoke. 'I knew it was him straight away.'

'Why are you so sure?'

'No one goes there after dark. I saw him on the news; his hair's brown now and his eyes are blue, but it was him. He bumped into me so hard, he almost knocked me over.'

'Did he do something to scare you?'

'Maybe he'll come back to hurt me, like he said.'

I shook my head firmly. 'He just wanted to see his old house. It was bad timing, that's all. Nothing can harm you now.' I pulled a piece of paper from my pocket, which held Adrian Stone's image. 'You're sure it was him?'

The child shuddered when he studied the photo. 'That's the man I saw.'

'You've been very brave, Sanjay. Come downstairs now and eat some of your mum's food. It smells wonderful.'

Burns followed me back downstairs, leaving the boy being comforted by his mother.

'What do you think?' he asked.

'It sounds like Stone's revamped his image.'

'How can you be certain the kid's right?'

'Body language, eye contact and intonation. He's a hundred percent certain of what he saw.' I remembered the conviction burning on the boy's thin face. 'I'd like to see Stone's house while we're here.'

Light had faded by the time we left the Guptas' home. Burns was busy calling in instructions while we walked to a large property, fifty metres down the street. I could see why local kids believed it was haunted: the house stood behind a high brick wall, only the top storey visible from the street, black glass shimmering in empty windows.

'What happened to you here?' I muttered to myself.

'Sorry?' By now Burns had caught up with me.

'Nothing. Is it okay to enter the grounds?'

'We'd better wait. Pete's team are on their way.'

I used my gloved hand to push the heavy wooden gate open and peer inside, a few wet leaves brushing my face. The house must have been unoccupied for years, overgrown trees turning to shadow in the dying light. Wood pigeons were calling to each other, their voices so low and mournful, it was a relief to back away.

21

Stone is passing time in the library on Cromwell Road, elated by the afternoon's success. He's imagining the joy of playing in a prestigious venue, after being denied so many chances. When he glances at the nearest desk, a young girl is studying her laptop, images from a news website flashing across her screen. He catches sight of himself and almost chokes on his coffee. A police illustrator has adjusted his mugshot, tinting his eyes blue, and darkening his hair; somehow they know about his disguise. Stone rises to his feet, pulling up his hood as he leaves. It doesn't take long to buy an electric razor and glasses with clear lenses from a local chemist.

He's waiting outside Lily's flat when she finishes her shift. The girl looks pale and tired in her nurse's uniform and ugly flat shoes, but he produces a smile as he hands her a bunch of bright pink roses.

'I've been thinking of you all day,' he says.

'They're lovely, Seth.' Emotion flares across her face as she kisses his cheek.

Stone returns the gesture, an unfamiliar feeling stirring in his chest. The girl's devotion triggered a sensation he hasn't experienced in years. It's been so long since he felt connected to anyone, the sensation is edged with panic.

Once they get inside, she takes a shower, then wanders back into the bedroom dressed only in a towel. As she walks by he pulls her into his lap.

'I could keep you prisoner here,' he says, kissing her shoulder.

She laughs then wriggles free. 'My friends are coming to the pub. They're dying to meet you.'

'I'd rather stay here.'

Her face falls. 'But I said we'd go.'

'That was stupid, Lily.' His grip tightens on her wrists. 'Never make promises without asking me first.'

Stone watches the girl flinch, before dropping another kiss on her shoulder, like she has nothing to fear.

22

I waited on the street as Hancock's team searched the grounds of Adrian Stone's former home in their white suits, setting up arc lights. They allowed me inside once plastic sheeting had been laid across the path. I can't explain why the place made the hairs rise on the back of my neck. Tiredness, or the knowledge that a teenage boy had launched a brutal murder campaign there, was affecting me more than I'd realised. Burns loomed out of the dark, making me catch my breath.

'Don't creep up on me like that.'

He smiled. 'So you do get jittery after all.'

'I was shocked, not scared. Can I see inside the house?'

'We don't have a key.'

'Since when did that stop you?'

'I can give it a try.'

Burns ran his torch over the front door. It took him several minutes of fiddling with a credit card and skeleton key to make the mechanism click open. 'You won't find anything; the place is empty.'

'I'm looking for atmosphere, Don. A nuance you might not understand.'

He rolled his eyes before loping away. The air inside the house felt colder than the garden, lights flickering as I touched each switch. Recent occupants had tried to deny the past by covering the walls in pastel shades suitable for a child's nursery, but the facts lingered. I climbed the stairs to the landing, recalling the crime scene photos. Stone had killed his mother and father here, then his older sister had paid the ultimate price for defending her parents. If Melissa had opened her bedroom door, she would probably have met the same fate. There was no evidence now of the carnage Stone had left behind. The carpet was a tasteful light grey; the bedrooms too had been redecorated, wardrobes standing empty, long curtains gathering dust. The place had the tasteful neutrality of an upmarket hotel, yet the air in my mouth tasted sour as I wandered from room to room. I'd never believed in ghosts, but the place tested my scepticism, particularly when the floorboards creaked loudly, making me spin round to see if someone was following.

It was only when I returned downstairs that part of Stone's personality announced itself. The small room beside the kitchen had held his piano; when I pushed the door open, the silence was almost too thick to penetrate, the overhead light refusing to work. My eyes strained against the blackness, as I tried to imagine a young boy, spending countless hours on a hard wooden stool, perfecting his technique. I was still standing there when shouting began outside.

'I need more light over here.' The Newcastle accent belonged to Hancock; his discovery must have been important. It was rare for his excitement to show.

Pete was surrounded by SOCOs on the far side of the house when I arrived, looking like a company of spectres in their white suits. Burns was beside them, peering at the ground.

'What have you found?' I asked.

'Freshly turned earth, covered in size ten boot prints.' Hancock replied.

Burns's face was sombre. 'Someone fetch a shovel. Let's see what's under there.'

After five minutes of steady digging a fist-sized plastic package was pulled from the ground. I stood back as Hancock laid it on a plastic tray, keeping my eyes averted as it was slit open. The sight of the youngest SOCO retching onto a nearby bush let me know what it contained. Stone had returned to Richmond, to bury his grim memento, in the gardens where he'd played as a child. I wondered why he'd risked carrying his former tutor's heart half the way across London. Maybe he was immune to personal danger, or it was a bizarre gesture of respect. He had chosen a key personal location for Keillor's shrine.

I watched the SOCOs taking photographs, then the plastic tray with its blood-stained package was carried to their van. Adrian

Stone's capacity for violence was increasing, yet it was Sanjay Gupta who stayed in my mind. Such a close brush with violence was bound to leave its mark on a sensitive child. The killer's face would inform his nightmares for months to come.

23

At two a.m. Stone is restless. Lily is asleep beside him, too innocent for nightmares. He rises from the bed in silence then goes to the bathroom, the low buzz of his electric razor humming as he shaves his scalp. Once he's finished, he studies his appearance in the mirror, trying on the thick-framed glasses he bought from the pharmacy. They turn him into a bald-headed intellectual, ten years older, bearing little resemblance to the dark-haired young man the police are seeking. The change fills him with relief, yet his thoughts don't settle.

He paces the kitchen floor. It's been too long since he practiced, hands itching to touch a keyboard, converting his churning emotions into sound. He pulls composition paper from his rucksack, scrawling notes across the stave, each phrase as personal as a signature. The sky outside lightens as he works. When he raises his head once more, a seamless harmony flows across twelve pages of his notebook. He can hear the timbre of each note, the orchestra's heartbeat behind the piano's hectic rhythm. It occurs to him that he's composing the best music of his life, strengthened by the girl's faith in him, the concerto almost complete. Lily seems to understand that his talent must be fulfilled, but only one pianist is skilful enough to play the central duet with him. It will take luck and careful planning to capture her.

Stone stands in the bedroom doorway, staring at Lily's sleeping form, aware that he will have to kill her if she learns the truth. She's a true innocent, blinded by fake romance, but it's too soon to test her. He slips back under the covers, longing for the new day to start.

24

Friday 25th March

There was no sign of my police escort the next morning, only Burns's black Audi parked in the alleyway. I watched him emerge from the car, big and shambling in his dark grey mac, oblivious to the spring sunshine. His hunched shoulders and slow movements revealing that he'd had little sleep. Our conversation about the future had slipped to the back of my mind. The stress of working together was taking its toll, yet I couldn't imagine either of us resigning. My job still fascinated me, and walking away would be professional suicide, for both of us.

Burns's expression made me forget about our personal dilemmas, his tense frown signalling bad news.

'What's happened, Don?'

'Is that your best welcome?' He leant down to kiss me. 'I need coffee first.'

My anxiety mounted as he followed me into the kitchen, watching in silence while I rooted in the fridge for milk. Normally he just spat out the facts without hesitation, but this time he took a long gulp from his mug before speaking again.

'We've got CCTV of Stone leaving Richmond station on Tuesday, but he'll have changed his look since then. The bloke's a chameleon.'

'Something else is bothering you, isn't it?'

'Matthew Briar topped himself last night. He hung himself from a sheet tied to his bedframe.'

'That's why you're upset,' I said, studying his face. 'It's not your fault.'

'The bloody hospital had him on suicide watch.'

'He acted fast then. He must have been determined.'

'We've been through his phone records and bank statements. There's nothing at his flat to suggest that he'd spent money arranging Stone's getaway. The only unusual thing is that he made a cash deposit of three grand into his savings account six weeks before the escape.'

'You think someone paid him to free Stone?'

'We can't prove there's another accomplice, now Briar's dead.' He glanced down at his mobile. 'My phone's going nonstop. Hospital staff have leaked details to the press.'

There was no point in rubbing salt into his wound by stating that the suicide would have a negative impact on the case. Briar had taken the killer's motives with him to the grave and Stone was proving that he could kill victims without lifting a finger, the guard's suicide raising his tally even higher. Briar must have spent his time in hospital contemplating his long prison sentence ahead, and how he would be vilified. Now it would be even more difficult to track down the person who had given Briar money, but I decided to concentrate on practicalities instead of dwelling on the latest fatality. While Burns dealt with his phone messages I sliced bread, then laid rashers of bacon under the grill.

He looked surprised when I passed him a plate. 'What's this?'

'Breakfast, obviously.'

'God, I adore you.'

'Does unexpected food always make you romantic?'

'Only bacon sarnies.' His grin flickered into life.

Burns seemed more relaxed as we headed for the station, even though his car radio spewed out a barrage of messages. I avoided the clamour of the incident room, heading for a quiet office to read Adrian Stone's case notes. The Board of Psychiatry had finally released them as evidence, after my boss at the FPU had intervened. The thick manila files dated back nine years. When I opened the first folder, it was clear my task would be time consuming. Dr Frances Pearce had made copious notes on the initial consultations, her handwriting small and constrained. I flicked through the pages, noting that she had focused on teaching him cognitive behavioural techniques to reduce his violence, as well as managing his drug regime. When he arrived at Rampton he had been heavily tranquillised, but she had slowly reduced his medication. I flicked back to their first meeting and found the description chilling. When asked about his crimes, the teenaged Stone had simply stared at her in silence. The one subject he had discussed freely was his desire to continue playing music. He seemed to view his incarceration as a temporary setback to his professional development, asking for a better piano in the music room and permission to practice for six hours a day. When his requests were denied, the seventeen-year-old had hurled himself at a window in the refectory, injuring himself badly enough to spend three days in Rampton's infirmary, with a dislocated shoulder and bruised ribs. It interested me that the notes from subsequent meetings were very brief, listing medication changes and summarising Pearce's clinical approach in a few sentences. She had included little detail about her therapeutic strategy, or whether Stone's obsession with music had reduced, but the thing that interested me most was her failure to expose his motives for violence. Despite frequent questions, he had never revealed why he had killed his family.

I sat back in my chair, wondering how Pearce had maintained her calm through years of frustration. The grim reality of Stone's crimes would have been impossible to forget. She had spent more time communicating with him than anyone else at Rampton: it was possible that he had found her weak spot, just like Briar. I dismissed the thought almost as soon as it arrived. Angie had done background checks on all staff at the secure unit, and psychiatrists were trained to spot signs of manipulation. Even if Pearce had developed loyalties towards Stone, they had never been alone; a guard always stationed outside the room during the consultations. Two years after arriving at Rampton he was still considered high risk, requiring full restraint whenever he was moved between cells. Tania appeared as I deciphered the psychiatrist's minute script.

'You'll get a migraine reading those.' She peered over my shoulder at the notes. 'Do you fancy making a house call?'

I rubbed the back of my neck. 'I could use a break. Who are we seeing?'

'Melissa Stone, like you asked. She's not thrilled about another meeting, but she'll do it, provided her aunt and uncle are present.'

'Do you know much about them?'

'Only that they raised her, after she was orphaned. He's a retired accountant and she works part-time for a kids' charity.'

Tania gave me details from the previous night's work as she drove. More information had emerged about Stone's actions. He had packed the professor's heart in layers of cellophane before burying it, the cool ground preserving the organ in good condition. It was easy to visualise him methodically completing the task, yet his motives escaped me. His desire for vengeance was obvious, but I sensed that he was driven by more complex emotions. There was a look of distaste on Tania's face as she described the details. Remembering the autopsies we'd attended together, I knew she was even more squeamish than me, so I tried to distract her.

'How's your daughter these days?' I asked.

'The same as ever. A teenage bitch most of the time, with odd bouts of sweetness.'

'Does Sinead like your new man?'

She cast me a look. 'Who said I had one?'

'Your body language mainly. Go on, tell me about him.'

'Geography teacher, divorced, no connection with the Met, thank God.'

'Lucky you. What's he like?'

She cast me a smug look. 'Interesting, and seriously fit. The guy does triathlons for fun. I'm still pinching myself.'

'You deserve some luck, Tania. It's great news.'

By now we'd parked on a quiet Chiswick lane, her smile replaced by her professional mask. We agreed that this time Tania would ask the questions, giving me a chance to observe Melissa Stone's interactions with her aunt and uncle, to assess her mental state. The couple's address was less than two miles from the house in Richmond where Stone committed his original crimes; Melissa had spent her teenage years a stone's throw from the scene of the tragedy. When we left the car an odd sensation travelled across the back of my neck, as though someone was watching me, but the street was empty, apart from a woman pushing a buggy. The house was an elegant Edwardian semi, with tall sash windows, front door gleaming with fresh green paint. The woman who greeted us looked almost as well-kept as her home, around fifty, with a slim tennis player's build, chestnut hair cut into a no-nonsense crop. She was dressed in capri pants and a fitted blue shirt, ideal clothing for a lunch date in a smart restaurant, but a muscle ticked in her cheek when she tried to smile.

'Melissa's not herself today,' she explained. 'She's reluctant to talk, I'm afraid.'

'Thanks for letting us come,' said Tania. 'Could we see you and your husband first?'

Emma Stone's kitchen showed a softer side to her personality. It was a typical family room, surfaces cluttered with recipe books and utensils, a golden retriever rising from his bed to sniff our shoes. A man of around sixty strode through the French doors just as I was leaning down to stroke the dog. David Stone's appearance was unsettling; he had the same light blue eyes and high cheekbones as his nephew, as if I was confronting the killer forty years down the line, his skin weathered, hair turned steel grey. His expression was grave when he shook my hand, which was unsurprising. He must have taken years to recover from the loss of his brother, only for the same horrors to repeat themselves. I stayed silent while Tania explained that Adrian had returned to Richmond, and it was suspected that he had killed again. There was a moment's silence while the couple collected their thoughts, then David Stone stared at Tania.

'Why in God's name haven't you caught him yet?' His voice was icy.

'A huge team are working on it, Mr Stone. It's only a question of time.'

'My niece was putting her life back together, then you let him escape. Your incompetence is staggering.'

Emma touched his wrist. 'It's not their fault, darling. He escaped from the psychiatric unit.'

'Someone should take responsibility.' David Stone shot us both a furious look, before rising from the table and stalking away, leaving his wife with head bowed.

'I'm sorry,' she said quietly. 'My husband worries about Melissa terribly; he feels responsible.'

'In what way?' Tania asked.

'He's thinks we could have stopped Adrian, if we'd spotted the signs. The piano connection upsets him too.'

'Sorry, I don't understand.'

'My husband's musical too, he was tremendously proud when Adrian got into the Royal College. I think that's why he's never turned his back on him. David's visited Adrian regularly, right from the start, even though it upsets him.'

My alarm bells rang immediately. Despite his nephew's killing spree, David Stone had remained loyal. Was he so emotionally invested that he had wanted him set free? Before I could arrive at an answer, Melissa Stone appeared in the doorway. Her appearance was as ethereal as before, wavy blonde hair covering her shoulders, blue eyes a fraction too wide as she joined us at the table. She listened in silence while Tania described her brother's recent exploits, omitting the most disturbing details.

'You need twenty-four-hour protection, until Adrian's caught. We can't risk your safety,' Tania said.

'I won't have a bodyguard.' The girl's voice wavered.

'Can I ask why?'

'He ruined my life. My brother's crimes shouldn't affect me now.'

'Better to be safe than sorry. The guards will protect your aunt and uncle too,' Tania said.

Melissa stared straight ahead. 'But it's me he's after, isn't it?'

'How do you mean?' Tania asked.

'He won't be happy till he's wiped out his nuclear family. Other people will keep on dying till he catches me.'

'That's just a theory, Melissa.'

She shook her head. 'It's true.'

I was about to comfort her when a blast of music penetrated the air, a few loud bars of a rock anthem I couldn't name. The sound fell silent instantly and I guessed that David Stone had switched on a radio by accident in a distant room. But it was his niece's reaction that fascinated me. She had covered her ears with her hands, cowering in her seat, obviously petrified.

'Calm down, darling,' her aunt said, touching her shoulder. 'Let's get you to your room.'

Tania looked on in amazement as the girl was led away, but her symptoms made perfect sense to me. Anyone might develop irrational fears, after the tragedy she suffered, her phobia of music becoming disabling. I wondered how she dealt with it at work; maybe she had found coping mechanisms to help her tolerate lessons when her pupils sang and danced.

Emma Stone looked uncomfortable when she returned. 'She's not normally this bad. Her anxiety's worse than ever.'

'How long has Melissa been afraid of music?' I asked.

'Since she lost her family. Hearing it suddenly often starts a panic attack. She's convinced Adrian broke out of Rampton to kill her; she blames herself for all the other victims.'

'The news reports must terrify her,' I replied. 'Can you tell us what her family situation was like, before Adrian committed his crimes?'

'We knew something was wrong from the kids' behaviour. They were subdued, and her parents hardly ever invited us round, apart from Christmas and birthdays. Lawrence was always remote; his wife was the same.'

'How do you mean?'

'We popped round sometimes, when the kids were small, but they never made us welcome. We wanted to be involved, because we didn't have children of our own. It was Lawrence who had that high wall built, like a moat round a castle. My husband gave Adrian music lessons when he was small, but there was no other contact.'

'Did the kids seem close?'

She bit her lip. 'Melissa hero worshipped the older two, but they were so busy. Jenny seemed unnaturally grown up.'

'What about Adrian?'

'My husband was closer to him than me. The boy seemed locked in his own world, but that could be hindsight talking.'

'How often did your husband visit him at Rampton?'

'Every month, like clockwork. He believes Adrian's ill, not evil, but I'm not convinced.'

'Thanks for your time, we'll let you take care of Melissa.' I gave her a sympathetic smile. 'You've been very helpful.'

The tension in the house was palpable as Emma led us back down the hall. Melissa Stone was hanging on by a thread, battling a chronic case of survivor guilt, her uncle desperate to protect her, while his wife struggled to hold the family together. Adrian hadn't just deprived his sister of her closest relatives, he had dismantled her confidence, so that a few notes of music could make her unravel. My time with the family had made my urge to find Stone even stronger than before.

25

By mid-morning Stone has tracked down Dr Carlisle, using a computer at Kensington public library. The address of the psychiatrist's private practice appears on his website, and it takes him less than an hour to reach Stoke Newington. The sight of the pleasant house overlooking the park increases his anger: Carlisle has lived in luxury, while his last decade has been full of suffering. Stone loiters at the edge of the park, surveying the property through the railings. He waits until the doctor and his wife emerge at one o'clock, well-dressed and relaxed. When the couple get into their BMW then drive away, Stone smiles to himself, a dark sedan following in its wake. The Met is being vigilant, watching those at risk.

'Wrong strategy,' Stone whispers to himself.

Now only a small white Fiat is parked on the drive, no police guards in sight; the person he wants to see is still inside the Carlisles' house. Stone emerges from his hiding place to saunter across the road. He stands in the porch for a few seconds before pushing the bell. When the door swings open, a young girl surveys him. She's about the same age as Lily, but with few other similarities. Her brown hair is shot through with highlights, skin glossy with make-up, a knowing expression in her eyes.

'I'm here to interview Dr Carlisle,' he says, smiling.

'He's out, I'm afraid. He won't be home for another hour.'

Stone pulls his phone, pretending to check his calendar. 'He must have forgotten our appointment. Pity, I was looking forward to hearing about his practice.'

'You're a journalist?'

'For the Standard, I'm writing about mental health issues in the city. Sorry to waste your time. Could you tell your husband Seth Rivers called? I'll email him for another date.'

The girl laughs, her manner suddenly thawing. 'He's my dad, not my husband. Wait for him here, if you like. I'll make you tea.'

'Are you sure?'

'Positive, I'd like to hear about your job. I just finished an English degree.'

'That's good timing, we're taking on interns. What's your name?'

'Sacha.'

Stone's smile widens as she admits him to the hallway. The girl is already so at ease when she leads him into the lounge, she makes the mistake of turning her back. The room contains everything he requires: a piano, a fine music collection, and a young woman with no sense of personal danger.

26

I spent the afternoon at the FPU, my police guard parked on the forecourt outside. It was a relief to swap the feverish atmosphere of the incident room for the quiet of the country's headquarters for forensic psychology. After an hour poring over my psychological summary of Stone's crimes, I still had no clear picture where he would strike next. My best option was to seek out Mike Donnelly, hoping that the Irishman's decades of experience might shine fresh light on the case. I found him gazing at his computer screen, calm and rotund as ever, white beard in need of a trim.

'Can I pick your brains, Mike?'

'If you make me a brew. The kettle's just boiled.'

He heaped endless spoons of sugar into his tea. Donnelly seemed to do little physical exercise, apart from taking the stairs to his first-floor office, where he survived on caffeine and doughnuts. Yet despite his poor diet his mind was always razor sharp; he'd dealt with more juvenile criminals than I'd had hot dinners.

'Stone's calling cards are confusing me,' I admitted.

His shrewd eyes observed me over the top of his mug. 'What have you got so far?'

'He's never explained his motives, but the family home was a time bomb. The parents were obsessive hard workers, insular, rarely socialising. The massacre happened the day Stone learned he was being forced out of music college.'

'The end of his dreams. The younger sister's alive, isn't she?'

'Melissa's at breaking point. She had therapy as a teenager, but this is bringing it all back. She believes her brother's got her in his sights. I found out today that since Stone attacked her family she's developed melophobia.'

'She associates music with violence?'

'It's her brother she's scared of, not a song on the radio.'

'Others must have been close to Stone, if she won't talk.'

'He only targeted one staff member at Rampton, and never opened up to his psychiatrist.'

'Did he have visitors?'

I dug a sheet out of my folder. 'His uncle's the only one who saw him regularly. A journalist visited touting for a story, and three staff from the Royal College, including Professor Keillor, came a handful of times.'

'Who are the other two?'

'Stanley Yacoub, who taught Stone composition, and the college principal, Susan Weinman. They both visited, in the first year of his sentence.'

'One of them could unlock the calling cards for you.'

I took a swig of tea. 'Stone seems obsessed by London's musical history. He sees himself as part of a great tradition, on a par with famous composers.'

'That doesn't surprise me. When he was seventeen, he thought his talent made him immune to justice.' Donnelly studied me again. 'I'd follow the musical thread, but get his sister talking too, if you can. She could explain his primary motive. Violence starts in infancy, after all.'

Donnelly gave another gentle smile. I could tell he was concerned about my welfare as we flicked through the evidence notes together, but did my best to reassure him. Through his office window I could see Reg, parked outside the front entrance watching everyone who entered the building, reassuring me that it would be impossible to penetrate my security.

I was working in my room that afternoon when a shadow appeared in the doorway. My boss, Christine Jenkins had a habit of materialising, unannounced. She wore a pale blue dress, grey hair cut into a neat bob. I must have looked dishevelled by comparison, in black trousers and a plain white shirt, hardly any makeup. Christine's state of mind was impossible to read as she perched on the chair opposite.

'I'm surprised you're here, Alice. Burns seems reluctant to let you out of his sight. He's arranged security at his flat, if the safe house gets too isolating.'

'I came here for some thinking time. Stone left another piece of music with Keillor's body, to let us know he'll strike again, but there's been no more communication.'

She gave a slow nod. 'You'll figure him out.'

'He's trying to cement his place in history.'

'How do you mean?'

'Narcissism's his biggest motive. He wants to be seen as a musical genius, but if that's out of reach, being remembered as a prolific serial killer is better than nothing.'

'How are you coping with the pressure?'

'Reasonably, thanks, except Burns thinks one of us should resign.'

'Not you, I hope. No one else has your insight.'

I held her gaze. 'Do you ever wonder what it would be like do an easier job?'

Christine's smile reignited. 'I fantasise about running a yoga retreat in the Algarve at least once a week.'

When I opened my eyes again, she'd disappeared, making me wonder if I'd daydreamed the whole conversation. I rubbed my hands across my face, then focused again on the calling cards at each crime scene.

27

Stone's knife presses against the girl's throat, as he listens to her rapid breathing and whispered pleas.

'What instrument do you play, Sacha?'

'I stopped years ago.'

'Liar.' He twists the blade closer to her skin. 'Tell me the truth.'

'Piano.' The word emerges as a whimper.

'That's the right answer. Play this piece of Bach for me.'

'Don't hurt me, please. I'll give you anything.' Her hands tremble as he forces them onto the keys.

'All I want is musical entertainment. Start at the beginning.'

She delivers the first bars well, then loses tempo. The composition's quiet simplicity falls apart. The girl is destroying one of the most beautiful pieces ever composed. Stone watches her hands drop to her sides after a run of errors. She has failed the audition. He could give her another chance, or avenge her father's mistake immediately.

'Pathetic. Do you know what happens next?'

'Why are you doing this?' The girl is shaking as the blade hovers above her eyes. 'You don't even know me.'

A sudden movement takes him by surprise. She twists out of reach, a sharp pain in his left side as she makes a run for the door. He yanks her hair so hard that her head jerks back, eyes pooling with tears. His thoughts blur as instinct takes over. When his mind clears again, her body lies at his feet, bent and twisted as an abandoned rag doll. Her back is broken but she's still alive, breathing in shallow spurts, eyelids flickering wildly, blood trickling from a gash on her mouth onto the pale carpet. Her body twitches, but she's unable to move. Stone feels nothing except distaste, until he pulls up his shirt and sees the shallow wound she inflicted, droplets of blood staining his skin. He tuts angrily as he climbs the stairs. First he selects a bandage from the bathroom cabinet, taping it over the cut, then wanders through bedrooms, searching the wardrobes. Eventually he selects one of Carlisle's dark blue shirts, trying it on for size. It's important to look smart for his performance tonight.

Back downstairs he checks his watch. There's twenty minutes until the girl's parents will return. She's lying on the floor in the same position, injuries so severe she doesn't flinch when he steps over her to seat himself at the piano for a few minutes of practice. Releasing the first string of notes brings him even more pleasure than hurting the girl. Harmonies flow through his body, his hands a conduit for the countless melodies that resonate inside his skull.

28

I persuaded Reg to take me to St Katharine Docks to see my brother on the way back to the safe house, by promising to remain indoors for the rest of the evening. Houseboats were lined up in the marina, like pencils in a box, the Bonne Chance's red paint gleaming. Will and Nina had rented it from a friend, but seemed to enjoy beautifying their temporary home. I asked Reg and his deputy to wait in the car. My brother's bipolar disorder made him prone to paranoia; the sight of my bodyguards would trigger his anxiety. But when I walked closer, he looked perfectly relaxed, a carbon copy of my laidback older brother, before his illness began; slim and rangy, dark blond hair a little too long. He stood on the roof of the boat, watering planters full of herbs. Luckily he didn't seem to notice anything unusual when he welcomed me.

'Hello, stranger.'

'Not by choice,' I replied. 'Life's been hectic.'

'You always say that.' He slung his arm round my shoulder. 'Come inside and tell all.'

'Where's Nina?'

'Teaching an evening class on Keats and Wordsworth, she'll be sorry to miss you.'

I ducked my head to enter the galley kitchen. It smelled wonderful, as always. My brother had a talent for concocting perfect meals from leftovers, which I'd always envied. We sat on the small sofa, surrounded by mismatched furniture that had been salvaged from skips, vivid enamelware hanging from hooks on the wall.

'What have you been up to?' I asked, as he poured me some wine. It was always easier to ask about his life, avoiding the complexities of mine.

'Making changes. My new job starts on Monday.'

'You've left the juice bar?' Since his breakdown my brother had worked behind a counter in Covent Garden, despite his raft of qualifications.

'I've got a trial as a sous chef at the Pont D'Or. It's something I've fancied doing for ages. They'll train me, if it goes well.'

I hugged him. 'They won't need to, you're already a brilliant cook. How do you feel?'

'Shit scared,' he said, laughing. 'But it might be fun.'

I studied him in amazement. Somehow he'd reconfigured the broken pieces of his life into a picture that made better sense, but the structure was still fragile. My stomach muscles tightened when his face darkened again.

'There's bad news too,' he said.

'What?'

'Lola wants me to give a wedding speech. I don't know what the hell to say.'

I released a shaky laugh. 'Anything, you're a great raconteur.'

'Seriously, Al, I need guidance.'

We spent the next half hour quibbling over anecdotes to set the right tone; affectionate and amusing, mixed with a dash of embarrassment. My fears about the case faded under so much distraction. It was only when I reached for my coat that he finally broached the real reason for inviting me round.

'Mum's getting weaker. She was frail when I visited her.'

My mother's Parkinson's had progressed rapidly, which hardly seemed fair. She'd survived marriage to a violent alcoholic, only to be levelled by a devastating illness in her early sixties.

'I'm seeing her on Sunday. Let's talk about it next week.' I stepped out onto the jetty, then kissed him good bye. 'It's great news about your job.'

Will held my gaze. 'Give my best to Don. He called by for a drink last week.'

'He kept that quiet. How did it go?'

'We had a few beers, and he pumped me for information.'

'About what?'

'You, of course. He likes to make plans.'

'He should talk to me, not my brother.'

Will looked amused. 'Sounds like I've landed the poor sod in trouble.'

My brother's laughter rang in my ears all the way back to the safe house. He had improved his life, making my own seemed chaotic by comparison. I admired how little he needed to survive. He'd abandoned the high-pressure lifestyle that had done him damage, for a simpler one with no mortgage or bills to juggle. I wandered through the unfamiliar rooms of the flat, suppressing my urge to kick the wall. When I had worked at Guy's hospital, watching patients rebuild their lives had given me plenty of satisfaction, but forensic work needed different skills. It relied on analysis and supposition, with none of the pleasure of seeing someone heal. The stakes were higher too; failing to understand a criminal's motives could result in another murder. I stood by the window, trying to forget the reality that Stone might already have taken a new victim.

There was no sign of Burns's car in the alleyway. I thought about his unexpected visit to my brother. The fact that he'd been digging for information behind my back made me grit my teeth in irritation. I'd been open with him from the start. My previous relationships had been short and simple, with no room for recriminations. Now my feelings were deeper. Sooner or later they needed to be resolved, for both our sakes, but that would require a massive leap of faith. My parents' bitterly unhappy marriage wasn't something I wanted to repeat. I considered phoning him, but decided against it. London's jagged horizon was visible outside the window, the Shard pointing its sharp finger at the sky. No doubt Burns was still out there somewhere, hard at work. He was the most dogged man I knew, yet his chances of locating Stone remained slim. It would take luck as well as graft to flush a highly motivated psychopath to the surface.

29

Lily waits with Stone at the side of the stage at Ronnie Scott's, preparing for his set.

'Do I look okay?' he asks.

'Very smart,' she replies. 'But I wish you hadn't shaved off your lovely hair.'

He smiles. 'I's my spring ritual. It'll soon grow back.'

'You still look handsome.'

Stone kisses her cheek then pulls back the curtain and enters the spotlight's glare. He focuses on the music alone; it's midnight before he looks up from the keyboard again, to see his audience talking among themselves, a handful listening with rapt attention. Lily has found a seat close to the stage. She's made an effort tonight, almost beautiful in a black dress and red lipstick, her hair drawn back from her face. He feels a wave of anger when a middle-aged man approaches her table. She's flirting with someone right in front of his eyes. He fights his impulse to jump down from the stage to teach her some respect, but nothing must interrupt his playing. Soon Nancy Morris signals from the side of the stage and he finishes his improvisation of Rhapsody in Blue, then closes the lid of the piano. Applause circulates the room, people raising glasses to toast him.

The manager offers a narrow smile. 'Very classy, Seth. I'll use you again.'

'I'll call by soon for another booking.'

'You prefer cash, right?'

'Perfect.' Morris passes him an envelope, then returns to the crowd by the bar.

Lily is alone once more when Stone returns.

'Ready to go?' he asks, frowning down at her.

'You were amazing,' she gushes. 'Can I finish my drink first?'

His fingers close around her arm. 'We're leaving now.'

'I need my coat and bag first.'

He lets her collect her things before putting his hand in the small of her back, propelling her to the exit. 'Who were you talking to earlier?'

She looks blank. 'No one, I was by myself.'

'I saw him, Lily.' Stone stares down at the girl's face, bleached pale by streetlight. His grip tightens round her wrists. 'Some guy was hitting on you.'

'He wanted you, not me. I promised to give you his card; he loved how you play.'

Some of the pressure rises from Stone's chest when the girl hands him a gold-edged card, imprinted with the words United Artists. The man was just an agent, looking for clients. He laughs out loud.

'It's my lucky day, Lily. This could change everything.'

He picks the girl up, spins her in a dizzy circle, but her laughter is tinged with fear.

30

Saturday 26th March

Something woke me at five a.m. My eyes wrenched open, mouth so dry it felt like I was choking on dust. My phone was buzzing on the floor beside my bed. When I picked it up Burns's voice sounded gruff with tension.

'Can you come to Ian Carlisle's house?'

'What's wrong?'

'His daughter's missing.'

'I thought they were being protected.'

'We're watching Carlisle, not his family,' he explained. 'Security trailed him and his wife on a shopping trip yesterday afternoon.'

'I'm on my way.'

Reg had been relieved by a middle-aged WPC and a plain clothes officer who looked like he'd just left school, but thankfully they kept silent as the car drove north. The city was empty as we crossed London Bridge, the sky turning pink as the river twisted east towards Canary Wharf. If Carlisle's daughter had been taken, Stone's MO was moving from quick impulsive attacks, to premeditation. Killing the girl would be a horrifying retribution, causing her parents a lifetime of psychological pain.

'You think you're invincible,' I murmured to myself.

We passed through Bishopsgate, into neighbourhoods once dominated by the cloth trade. It was a far cry from Savile row, but street names revealed the district's origins as I gazed from the window: Clothier Street, Silk Court, Weaver Street. One of the things I loved about the city was the layers of history trapped inside its skin, and Stone shared my fascination. While I noticed architectural details, he obsessed over buildings occupied by his musical heroes.

The front door of Ian Carlisle's house hung open. Pete's team of SOCOs were treating it as a crime scene, even though no body had been found. I waited on the path while an officer scribbled my name on her pad, then allowed me inside. One of the forensics team was kneeling on the lounge floor, using minute scissors to cut fibres from a stain on the pale carpet. The blood was oxidising already, turning from red to brown. I watched his painstaking work, trying to imagine Stone's feelings on entering the house. He must have been jubilant about causing the psychiatrist so much distress.

I found Burns sitting with Ian Carlisle in his kitchen. On the other side of the room a striking woman with short ash blonde hair stood by the window, gabbling into her mobile. Burns gave me a warning look as Ian greeted me.

'Thanks for coming, Alice. None of this makes any sense.'

'Can you tell me what's happened, step by step?'

The woman finally abandoned her mobile. She was wearing a red T shirt, and black jeans, her face gaunt with shock. 'I'm Miriam, Ian's wife,' she said, her voice trembling as she spoke. 'Ian had the afternoon off, so we drove to Islington, to pick up a handbag I'd ordered for Sacha's birthday. We expected to get back in an hour but bumped into friends. I sent her a text saying we'd be later than we'd planned.'

'What time did you get home?'

'About six. Sacha's car was gone. We didn't worry at first; she often pops out to see people, but lets us know when she'll be home. She's always been considerate.' Her words petered into silence, Carlisle's face growing paler as he studied the table's surface.

'Are you okay?' I asked.

'We should have chosen protection,' he replied. 'If I'd agreed, my daughter would be safe.'

'Sacha didn't take her phone, so something must be wrong,' Miriam interrupted. 'She never goes anywhere without it. We've called all her friends, but we didn't notice the blood stain for hours, it was covered by a pile of books.'

'There's no clear proof she's in danger,' I replied.

'My daughter's asthmatic, she needs her inhaler,' Miriam said. 'She left it in her room.'

The Carlisles were reacting to the trauma in different ways: Ian had withdrawn into silence, while his wife seemed fuelled by anger. Her rage towards her daughter's attacker hot enough to scorch paint from the walls. Sacha Carlisle sounded like a free spirit, keen to start a new career. She was twenty-one years old, newly graduated from London University, looking for work as a travel journalist. The kitchen was filled with evidence that the trio were close, photos tacked to the fridge with brightly coloured magnets. One showed the family on holiday, standing under a palm tree, arm in arm. Beside it was a picture of a pretty, dark haired girl on graduation day, giving the camera a mocking smile. When the doorbell rang it was a relief to escape the anxiety that was stealing oxygen from the air.

Millie Evans stood on the doorstep, one of Burns's most experienced family liaison officers. I had worked with her on several cases and always admired her direct approach; she was a plump woman of around fifty, dressed in a jacket and jeans, round face marked by laughter lines. Millie's presence was as comforting as a favourite aunt, but today she looked concerned.

'I've had the lowdown already, Alice. When did the girl go missing?'

'Yesterday, afternoon or early evening.'

'And they think Adrian Stone's responsible?'

'It looks that way.'

Millie frowned. 'God help her then. I've been following the news.'

The papers were both a blessing and a curse. The information they printed made people vigilant, but their portrayal of Stone as the worst serial killer on record would fuel his confidence. I showed Millie through to the kitchen and watched her at work. She could defuse even the tensest situation with her sympathetic manner. Her skill lay in reducing people's stress, through common sense and kindness. It interested me that Ian didn't argue when she advised him to rest upstairs, following her instructions straight away, while Millie looked after his wife. After ten minutes Burns and I left her alone with the couple. Two squad cars drew up outside, but it seemed clear that security had arrived too late.

Burns and I ended up in a Turkish café on Church Street, drinking the strongest tea imaginable, his hand gripping mine under the table.

'What else do you know?' I asked.

'He's using her car. Angie's got CCTV footage of it driving south, towards Islington. It looks like a man at the wheel, not a woman, but the image is blurred.'

'Maybe she was in the boot.'

'Just like Keillor.' His disgust showed on his face. 'What's he playing at?'

'Revenge, and his MO's getting more sophisticated. There's a new element of psychological torture; hurting Ian's daughter would inflict more pain than killing him.'

'Do you think the girl's still alive?'

I shook my head slowly. 'His victims never last more than twenty-four hours. If he intends to kill, nothing changes his mind.'

'We're focusing on CCTV. If I can get a clear image, we'll have something for the next news bulletin.'

'Have your team checked the addresses where the last piece of music was composed?'

He nodded. 'There's no sign of Sacha's Fiat near any of them.'

'Let's look again.'

Burns's face was gloomy as we got back into his car. He didn't share my outlook, but I felt certain Stone had left the fragment of Mozart's first symphony at the last crime scene for a reason. I stared out of the window as we set off, remembering the panic on Miriam Carlisle's face.

31

Supermarkets have changed during Stone's incarceration; self-service tills, and a dizzying range of products. He watches Lily loading bags with fruit and vegetables, thrilled to buy food for them both. Provided he keeps up his charade, she will camouflage him for as long as he needs.

'I should visit the library after this,' he says. 'I want to contact some agencies, in case United doesn't work out.'

'That's a good plan. I'll make a lasagna while you're out.'

'My favourite.'

Stone carries the shopping to her flat, then returns alone to the High Street. It doesn't take long to locate what he needs on a public access computer. Dr Alice Quentin's photo appears beside her profile on the FPU's website. The woman looks just as she did three years ago, when she and Carlisle condemned him to a life in captivity. Her delicate face is unsmiling, green eyes staring straight at him. He jots down the address of her workplace on a slip of paper. His resentment mounts as he scans her profile; the psychologist is an expert on psychotic behaviour and violence disorders.

'Clever little bitch, aren't you?' he whispers.

Quentin bears a passing resemblance to his sister Melissa, but he puts the thought aside. There's a hierarchy to follow; the least important victims will be dealt with first. He uses his phone to capture Quentin's image. In the next half hour he focuses on finding more of his enemies, scribbling down phone numbers and addresses. He clears his browsing history from the computer's memory then rises to his feet. Stone gives the library assistant a courteous smile on his way out.

Soon he will need to return, to research more details of his victims' lives. It's important to plan every step; a single mistake could put him back behind bars.

32

Burns's bad mood had worsened when we walked down Charing Cross Road, and I could understand why. A young woman had been abducted, yet I was leading him round London on a wild goose chase, determined to investigate the killer's latest calling card. The pavements thronged with weekend strollers, buying tickets for that afternoon's matinées, others heading to Trafalgar Square to visit Nelson's Column. Cecil Court turned out to be a narrow pedestrian street which had stayed true to the area's tradition of bookselling. Each shop specialised in a different form of literature, from first editions, to poetry, crime writing and translated novels. Number nineteen's green exterior had been freshly painted. It was called Watkin's Books, a sign in the window explaining that it had been an independent bookshop since 1894, specialising in philosophy and spirituality. A poster by the door stated that healing, counselling and divination services were available on site.

'Great,' Burns sighed. 'Let's have our palms read.'

I studied the building's facade, imagining how it might have looked in Mozart's day. The Regency buildings would have been brand new in 1764, elegant red brick terraces, with tall sash windows.

'We're wasting time, Alice.'

'Let me see the back of the building, then we can leave.'

The alley contained only empty cardboard boxes, cigarette stubs littering the ground, the air soured by overflowing drains. My vigilance seemed to be leading us nowhere. It was unlikely that Stone would risk bringing a victim's body to a central London location that was overlooked from all sides.

Burns was taciturn when we arrived at Ebury Street. Although the road would have intrigued classical music fans, it was even less promising than Cecil Court. The row of houses had been renamed Mozart Terrace; a statue of the child prodigy playing a violin on the junction with Pimlico Street, a blue plaque marked the building where he and his family had stayed. One hundred and eighty Ebury Street was just a well-proportioned three-storey building, hemmed in by affluent Westminster mews. I gazed up at it, trying to work out why it might have fascinated Stone. Two hundred and fifty years ago, the infant Mozart would have run out into open fields, unaware that centuries later police would be hunting for a murderer in the teeming streets nearby.

By the time we reached the last location on my list, Burns's ill-humour was set to explode. I could see it in his tense jaw and the way his hands clenched the wheel, but it was too late to back down. Number twenty Frith Street stood in the heart of Soho, and even the most audacious killer would have struggled to leave a body on such a busy thoroughfare. The road was filled with cafés and bars, a neon sign flickering above Ronnie Scott's, even though it was the middle of the day. The only clue that Mozart had stayed in a neighbouring house was another plaque, stating that the original house had been demolished.

'The sodding place doesn't exist anymore.' Burns's phone rang as I studied the words imprinted on the sign, his expression thunderous. 'The girl's car's been torched; it's on a building site in Westminster.'

I stared at him. 'Was she inside?'

'The fire investigators are just arriving. I should be there.'

'Let me check the back alley first.'

'Didn't you hear me? We need to leave.'

'Two minutes, Don, please.'

I left him on the pavement, barking instructions into his mobile. By the time I reached the alley I felt foolish. Sacha Carlisle's vehicle had been found several miles away, yet I was obsessing over irrelevancies. Stone was smart enough to send us in the wrong direction, changing his MO yet again. I cast my eyes along the narrow passageway, scarcely any sunlight falling onto the stained cobbles. Through barred ground floor windows I could see into restaurant storerooms as I reached the back entrance to number twenty. A bicycle was chained to a drainpipe, a cluster of wheelie bins pressed against the wall, half-hidden by shadows. It irked me that I would have to eat humble pie for wasting Burns's time. I lifted the lid of one of the bins hurriedly, but found nothing. But opening the third bin made me stumble backwards suddenly, my fingers clenching into fists. I leant against the wall to regain my balance then fumbled for my phone.

'I found her, Don. She's right here.'

The girl's body had been packed tightly into the bin, brown eyes gazing up at me. Death had turned her lips a dull blue, a chain of bruises circling her throat. A pair of headphones covered her ears, as if she had crawled into the bin to enjoy her favourite music undisturbed. The next thing that crossed my mind was her parents, waiting at home; Millie Evans would have to inform them that someone matching their daughter's description had been found. Their nightmare would deepen when they identified her body at the mortuary. Burns's footsteps were growing closer, beating a heavy tattoo on the concrete.

'Are you okay?' His arm closed around my shoulders.

'I'll live. Is Pete on his way?'

'Breathe, sweetheart, you're white as a sheet.'

'Stop fussing, Don. I need to know what music's on that iPod.'

'Leave that to me, a squad car's taking you to mine.'

'Why? I can go to the safe house.'

'Jesus, you're hard to help.' His fingers tightened round my arm. 'Do you think I'd leave you alone after this?'

On any other day I'd have argued, but finding the girl's body had weakened my defences. Sacha had just graduated, yet Stone had stolen her future. Why would he leave her corpse outside a house where a world-famous composer had stayed as a child? Maybe it was because he too had been a prodigy, the weight of adult expectations smothering him whenever he played. Suddenly I felt out of my depth. I had always enjoyed classical music, but my knowledge was limited. I would need expert help to decipher the information Stone was using to taunt us.

The location was becoming a crime scene in front of my eyes. Uniforms were unwinding black and yellow tape across both ends of the alley, turning away vehicles and pedestrians. I was still puzzling over details when Hancock and his team arrived. The white Tyvek of their suits contrasted with the stained cobbles when they set to work. Hancock tapped my shoulder as he passed, the gesture of support bringing an unexpected lump to my throat. The last thing I needed was to weep at a crime scene. Crying in public was unacceptable in the Met's macho world, so I swallowed hard. It could have been the girl's youth that upset me, or the fact I knew her father, but it was a relief when Reg and his juvenile sidekick finally appeared. Burns stared at me from the other side of the alley before I turned away.

For once Reg made conversation during the journey, instead of delivering a lecture. 'Find the body yourself, did you?' he asked.

'That's right.'

His gaze met mine in the rear-view mirror. 'You'll feel better once you're indoors.'

The old timer told stories of corpses he'd discovered during the drive. It sounded like he'd had more than his fair share of grisly adventures in his thirty-year career, including visiting a fly-infested flat where the resident had died, weeks before. On any other occasion the anecdotes would have turned my stomach, but his gruff monologue was a reminder that we were members of the same club, unwilling witnesses to the death of strangers. For once I didn't argue when he trailed me upstairs to Burns's flat.

'I'll be right outside, if you need anything,' he said, before leaving me alone.

Silence pressed in from the walls of Burns's untidy living room and the tears I'd been bottling came out in angry sobs. After my crying fit ended, I slumped on the sofa and surveyed the mess. A cluster of half-empty mugs stood on the coffee table, Burns's outsized trainers parked by the door. The sketchbook that lay open on an armchair was a reminder of the year he had spent at art school, before joining the police. I rose to my feet, unable to stay still. Traffic buzzed along Southwark Bridge Road, a steady flow of commuters escaping the city, like rats from a fire. In an ideal world I could dash to Lola's flat nearby, forget about my troubles for a while. Instead I closed the curtains, flicked on the TV and lay down on the settee, but the picture failed to calm my nerves. Adrian Stone's image smiled back at me from the latest news bulletin, confident that he had the upper hand. I gave the off button on the remote a hard jab with my thumb to make him disappear.

33

It's early evening by the time Stone reaches St James's Park. He walks through quiet avenues to Dacre Street, to find the Forensic Psychology Unit in darkness, apart from a single light above the entrance. No sign announces the work that takes place inside the tall brownstone.

'Cowards,' he mutters to himself.

Stone studies the building's exterior, wondering which storey holds Alice Quentin's office. A sophisticated intruder alarm is flashing by one of the second-floor windows. He can't risk being found on the premises when there's still so much to achieve, but challenges always appeal to him; entering the building will be like mastering a complex sonata, after weeks of practice. He scans the street to make sure no one is looking, then circles the building to photograph the fire escape on his mobile.

His mood is buoyant when he returns to Kensington, to find Lily queuing outside the Albert Hall. An unexpected warmth rises in his chest when he sees her. The girl's expression is so guileless, it looks like she's never had a bad thought in her life. It crosses his mind to walk away and leave her unharmed, but she's already spotted him.

'Where've you been, Seth? I waited at home for ages.' She steps forward to kiss his cheek.

'Looking up an old contact.'

'A girlfriend?'

'Just someone I used to know. Sorry I'm late.'

The girl babbles about her day, arm linked through his as they cross the foyer. She's still glued to his side as they climb the stairs to the cheap seats in the gods.

'I've never been to a classical concert before,' she says.

'You'll enjoy it. Mahler's first symphony's a favourite of mine.'

She looks up from her programme. 'Why?'

'It follows the cycle of life. The first movement's about creation, new life coming into flower in the andante, passion ripening in the scherzo. Then the second movement's a downward spiral. It ends with an outpouring of longing for everything death takes away.'

'I love how you describe it, but it sounds so sad.'

He shakes his head. 'The funeral march is exquisite.'

The lights have faded, the orchestra poised for the first note. Stone feels a surge of hatred for the Japanese woman seated at the grand piano, occupying his rightful place. Her name is Asako Mori; she was his only serious rival at the Royal College. She has benefited directly from his suffering. He's fantasised about hurting her for years, but when the first bars of music play, his resentment fades. She is the only one who could deliver the second part in his duet, although it will take time and effort to make her follow his wishes. Now the other instruments announce themselves in a surge of glory. When the music overtakes him the girl at his side ceases to exist, vanishing along with the building and the city around it, into a maelstrom of sound.

34

Burns arrived that evening with a takeaway from my favourite Vietnamese, while I was immersed in checking the progress log from the case. Sacha Carlisle's face still haunted me; it felt better to stay busy than let my mind wander back to her suffering. Burns greeted me with his usual gesture, arm slung round my shoulders as he steered me towards the kitchen table.

'Christine Jenkins called,' I said. 'She wants me back at the safe house.'

'There are guards outside. You'll be fine here.'

'If Stone follows me, you're in danger too. Isolation's the best policy.'

He grunted his disapproval. 'You're my girlfriend, not an infectious disease. I'll take a shower then let's eat.'

The food was good enough to lift anyone's spirits: hot and sour soup, duck with plum sauce, noodles with wild mushrooms. Burns had abandoned his suit in favour of worn out Levis, a sweatshirt with paint stains on the sleeve, feet bare. Despite his relaxed appearance I could tell he was preoccupied, neither of us able to switch off in the middle of a case.

'Want to talk it out?' I asked.

'Let's clear our brains for half an hour first.'

I refilled his wine glass and we sat together on the sofa, until his phone buzzed loudly on the coffee table.

He threw me an apologetic look. 'Sorry, I'll have to take it.'

His footsteps battered along the hall, deep voice rumbling through the wall. I cast my eyes round his lounge again. Burns had painted the two landscapes on the opposite wall years ago, granite islands rising from the sea into a glare of winter light. I was still admiring them when he settled beside me again, his hand on my thigh.

'Do you ever miss painting?' I asked.

'Often, but I've forgotten everything I knew. A break would be good though. Jobs like mine have a shelf-life; plenty of senior cops hit the bottle, get sick or go crazy.'

'We could both use a holiday after this. What was the phone call?'

'They've identified the music on the girl's headphones. It's from a Glenn Gould piano sonata written in the Fifties. The volume was set at the highest level.'

'He made her listen as she died?'

'The police surgeon thinks the cause of death was asphyxiation, but we need the autopsy to be sure. The bastard broke her back too.'

I winced. 'The team need to check whether Glenn Gould ever visited London.'

'They're already on it.'

'I saw a documentary on him once. It's not surprising Stone chose him.'

'Why?'

'Gould was another child prodigy, but his life wasn't easy. He suffered from mental illness and died young.'

'Another tormented bloody genius,' he muttered. 'All I want is the address he stayed at in 1959.'

'Stone knows we'll be looking for the location; there may be another clue inside the music this time. He won't make it too easy.'

Burns rubbed his hand over his five o'clock shadow. 'There's bugger all we can do now. Let's call it quits for the day.'

'There's something I should check first,' I said, opening my lap top.

He frowned at me. 'We can't keep working this way, Alice. When this is done we have to make changes.'

'So you keep saying.'

'You're still not sure about me, are you?'

'That's ridiculous. We're together all time.'

His tone hardened. 'You're a closed book. I don't even know if you want the normal things, like marriage and kids.'

'Is that why you talked to my brother?'

He stared back at me. 'I just want to know where we're heading, Alice.'

'Why not just ask?'

'You always shut me down. I need to know what goes on behind that game face of yours.' He touched my cheek, then his fingers closed around my wrist.

'I've never felt this way before. It's a bit daunting.'

'Come to bed.' He reached over to shut down my laptop.

When he pulled me to my feet, and I made no attempt to resist. Sex between us had never been a problem, it was the prospect of what came after that frightened me. My skin burned under the weight of his touch, our clothes abandoned in a heap on the bedroom floor. Reality only crept back into the room afterwards, as my body cooled. Streetlight filtered through the curtains, a woman's cackling laugh rising from the street below, reminding me that Adrian Stone was still out there, revelling in his adventure, like the murders were a glorious joke.

35

Stone is still buzzing from the night's music, melodies coursing through his veins. None of the images on the TV can flatten his euphoria. Lily appears in the doorway, dressed in her bathrobe. When she settles beside him he inhales her scent of shampoo and innocence.

'Coming to bed, Seth?'

'Soon, I'm just winding down.'

'The music really affected you, didn't it?'

He puts his arms round her shoulder. 'Didn't you feel anything?'

'It was beautiful, but I didn't really understand it.'

Suddenly her attention is distracted by the news bulletin. Stone's stomach twists, it's too late to switch channels when his own face fills the screen. The girl watches intently, making him hold his breath; if she recognises him, he'll have no choice but to kill her.

'People like Adrian Stone fascinate me,' she says quietly. 'I know he's evil, but he must have suffered terribly to act like that. Don't you think?'

'You could be right.'

She returns his gaze. 'You look a bit like him. The shape of your face is similar.'

'Thanks, sweetie.' He forces out a laugh. 'So I bear a passing resemblance to the worst serial killer in recent memory.'

'Your eyes are different. Dark brown, instead of sky blue.'

'That's reassuring.'

The girl drops her gaze. 'Seth, can I ask a favour? You don't have to say yes.'

'Fire away.'

'Would you come to church with me tomorrow? I promised to go with dad. It would make his day to meet you. He loves all kinds of music.' The girl's voice peters into silence.

'I'm not keen on religion.'

'Didn't you go to church as a kid?'

He nods. 'It means nothing to me now, but I'll go, just for you.'

'Then it's even more special that you'd come with me.'

She flings her arms round his neck, then leaves him alone. His pulse steadies, but the news story was a reminder that his security is fragile. He watches the rest of the bulletin in silence. They must have found Sacha Carlisle's body; the chase intensifying every day. Now a tall man steps in front of the camera, staring directly into the lens, eyes hard as coal, threatening to track him down. The man's name and rank flash across the bottom of the screen: DCI Burns, senior investigating officer. His appearance brings a contemptuous smile to Stone's face; the detective is built like Goliath, far too big and lumbering to win the fight.

36

Sunday 27th March

Sunday morning began with a trip to Covent Garden. Reg was off duty, so two monosyllabic uniforms drove me to Floral Street to meet my mother. Will's concern about her health was still in my mind when I reached Bertorelli twenty minutes early, the squad car parking at a discreet distance. I sat in a window seat, while young girls traipsed past, loaded with shopping bags. Despite the cool temperature they were dressed for summer, in short skirts and espadrilles. The sight of them filled me with nostalgia for weekends when Lola and I would scour the neighbourhood for bargains, buying retro jewellery and clothes from vintage shops.

My mother arrived in a black cab. The cost of travelling from her home in Blackheath must have been extortionate, but her tenacity was admirable. I quelled my urge to run outside to help her indoors. Her pride wouldn't tolerate intervention, even though she crossed the pavement at a snail's pace, leaning heavily on her stick. She was dressed in an ivory coloured mac, which emphasised her pallor. Her usual elaborate makeup was missing, and I understood why. The tremor in her hands would make applying lipstick and mascara impossible now, but her silver-grey hair looked elegant, combed neatly into place.

'Good to see you, darling.' She kissed the air directly beside my cheek.

'You too, mum.' Her Parkinson's had grown more pronounced, words vibrating as she spoke. Her hands shook violently as she sipped from a glass of mineral water. 'Are you off coffee?' I asked.

'Doctor's orders, which is a damn shame. I miss it more than a decent glass of brandy.'

'Have you seen the specialist lately?'

'My health is too boring for words, I refuse to discuss it. Tell me about that handsome man of yours.'

'He's still working hard, struggling to switch off.'

Her shrewd grey gaze met mine. 'Don't let him get away, Alice. Men like Donal are few and far between.'

'Only you ever use his full name.'

'Donal McIntyre Burns. It's fine title.'

'You're a fan, aren't you?'

'I may steal him. He's taking me to the Surrealism exhibition at the Tate next month.'

I produced a laugh on cue, but the idea of Burns and my mother on an outing brought mixed emotions. He'd won her trust instantly, even though my relationship with her had always been fragile.

'How's Elise?' Mum's long-suffering assistant cooked her meals and cleaned her flat, five days a week.

'Monosyllabic, overpaid and easy to offend.' She reached across the table. 'Don't change the subject, darling. I came here with news to deliver. I'll forget it if you distract me.'

'Go ahead.'

'I've got some cash for you and Will. My holiday fund's useless to me now; you may as well find something to spend it on.'

'Don't be silly, mum. We don't need your savings.'

'Your brother can't live on that draughty boat forever.'

'Give it all to him then.'

'Ingratitude is such an unpleasant trait,' she said, scowling. 'If someone offers a gift, you should accept graciously.'

'It's kind of you mum, but I already own a flat. Will and Nina would be thrilled by your gift.'

My mother shook her head. 'You may regret turning it down.'

'What will you live on, if you give away your savings?'

'I'm selling my flat and moving into sheltered housing; there's a place in Greenwich with charming gardens.'

The untrained eye would have missed the change in my mother's expression. One of the cruellest symptoms of Parkinson's is the way it freezes the facial muscles, until feelings are hidden, but her eyes gave her away. She was terrified of losing her independence.

'You could use your cash to pay for carers, mum.'

'No, darling. I've given it a lot of thought.'

'Greenwich is a great choice,' I said quietly. 'You love the market and the park, and you'll be near your friends.'

'Exactly.'

We kept the conversation light and breezy after her announcement. It was only when mum said good bye that her frailty showed itself again. For once she let me flag down another cab, her hand trembling on my arm. She smiled as the taxi pulled away, then gave an unsteady wave. I don't know why that small gesture made me want to sit on the kerb and weep. Maybe it was the fact that no one was waiting for her at home, even though she'd chosen solitude since my father died. She and Lola had both championed Burns since our relationship started, as if he might cure my fear of commitment, once and for all.

There was no time to clear my mind before making my next visit. Dr Stanley Yacoub had agreed to let me call at his home in Pimlico, the squad car depositing me on a narrow street of mansion blocks one street back from the river. I wanted more information about the music Stone was leaving at each crime scene, but when I pressed his doorbell there no answer, making me wonder if the academic had forgotten our appointment. It took several minutes before the entrance door clicked open. Yacoub's flat was in the basement, when I approached with one of the uniforms in tow. The tutor's smile was tentative, as though he was waiting for events to unfold before deciding whether to be happy or sad. His movements were more relaxed than they had been at the Royal College; maybe his blindness was easier to handle at home, where the territory was familiar.

'Thanks for letting me visit on a Sunday. My colleague will wait for me in the lobby, if that's okay.'

'You're saving me from the hell of marking the first years' compositions,' he replied.

'They're not promising?'

'Most of them are trying too hard; I listen to each one on headphones, so it takes concentration. Can I get you a drink?'

'Tea would be great, thanks.'

Yacoub left me alone in his living room. The interiors of people's homes had always fascinated me; the academic's flat carried plenty of evidence of his personality, but the windows admitted little light from the street above, even though it was early afternoon. I remembered that Yacoub's blindness would have made him oblivious to the gloom. A sheaf of blank paper lay on top of an upright piano in the corner of the room, closer inspection revealing that each page was imprinted with minute dots and dashes of braille. The professional challenges Yacoub faced every day would have been staggering, in an environment where his students had the advantage of sight. When I scanned the room again photos of cityscapes, as well as portraits of smiling relatives and friends, lined the pistachio green walls.

'You're wondering how I decorated this place, aren't you?' Yacoub had reappeared, balancing cups and saucers in his hands.

`How did you guess?'

'People always ask. My ex-wife chose most of the furniture, leaving it behind when she went back to the States as a goodwill gesture. I've only been blind ten years; my sight faded slowly, so I remember how the place looks, right down to that Manhattan skyline beside you.'

There was something unnerving about the fact that he could locate me so accurately, from the sound of my voice. I couldn't possibly have found him with my eyes closed. It was only when we sat at his table that our conversation turned to Stone's escape.

'I need to understand the clues he's leaving, Dr Yacoub.'

'Call me Stan, please. And I believe you're Alice?'

'That's right. If I can figure out the meaning of each piece of music, I might be able to predict his actions. So far he's left extracts from one of Chopin's London Nocturnes, Mozart's first symphony, and a piano sonata by Glenn Gould.'

Yacoub looked thoughtful. 'The composers were all child prodigies, like Adrian, playing public concerts at age five or six. But in sound terms, they couldn't be more different.'

'How do you mean?'

'The nocturne's quiet as a lullaby, the Mozart's loud and triumphant and the Gould is abstract jazz. The pieces come from three different centuries.'

'Were they all composed in London?'

He shook his head. 'Gould only visited once. He never composed here.'

My head spun. There was little unity between Stone's calling cards, his MO changing with each crime. 'So the only link is that they were written by men who began their musical careers early, and were acknowledged as musical geniuses during their lifetime?'

'Suffering could be another link, I suppose,' Yacoub replied.

'Sorry?'

'Chopin was dying when he wrote the nocturne, and his affair with Amantine Dupin had just ended. Mozart was pitifully homesick for Austria. His father wanted to show off his talent to the English court, but he was just a young boy, longing for his mother.'

'What about Gould?'

'His life was toughest of all. His mental illness worsened as he aged; he had to retire at thirty-one.'

'Gould was bipolar?'

'I don't think he was ever diagnosed. He wouldn't shake people's hands, and obsessed about performances. The guy would practice sixteen hours a day, always using the same chair when he gave concerts, until it fell apart.'

'Sounds like OCD, or Asperger's.'

Yacoub gave another wry smile. 'A touch of madness helps in my industry. You have to be crazy to lock yourself away with only a musical instrument for company, sixty hours a week.'

'That sounds calming to me. It's human beings that make life complicated.'

He laughed. 'Sign up for my course; you've got the right attitude.'

I studied Yacoub's face in the dim light of his apartment. He was classically good looking, with high cheekbones, coffee-coloured skin, dark eyes permanently fixed on the middle distance. But something in his stance revealed his loneliness as clearly as the tremor in my mother's voice. I would have hated being exposed to others scrutiny, without vision to help me to interpret their reactions.

'Have you got security here, Stan, in case Stone pays you a visit?' I asked.

'The police offered it, but Adrian wouldn't harm me.'

'How do you know?'

'I argued his corner. Everyone at college thought he needed time to mature except me.'

'You were his advocate?'

Yacoub nodded. 'The piano was all that mattered to him, a few years delay wouldn't have changed that.'

'Stone has a track record of hurting people he respects, as well as enemies. You should take care.'

'Believe me, my self-preservation instinct is alive and kicking.'

Yacoub seemed unconcerned as he accompanied me down the dark corridor. When I looked back he was still standing there, wearing his unreadable smile, my footsteps echoing on the hardwood floor. The man's isolation and unwillingness to acknowledge danger made me concerned for his safety as I walked away, with my police guard at my side.

37

At three p.m. Stone approaches the stage door of the Albert Hall. He's wearing blue overalls, a baseball cap low over his eyes, clutching a toolbox in his hand. The old woman guarding the entrance glances up from her knitting.

'I've come about the lights,' he announces.

'No one told me.' She checks her clipboard. 'I'm not expecting anyone.'

'I should have been here yesterday, but I was snowed under. There's a problem in one of the dressing rooms.'

'All right, love. Do you know where you're going?'

He nods. 'I've worked here before. Will it disturb anyone if I need to drill?'

'Not today. The place is empty, apart from the pianist rehearsing.'

'Thanks, I'll get started, but if it's a big job I'll have to come back tomorrow.'

'Fine by me.' The woman's knitting needles are clicking again as he walks away.

Stone's heart lifts as he navigates the corridors. As a student he used to sneak into the hall, when no one was looking; he knows every nook and cranny of the vast performance space, and the labyrinth of rooms below the stage. The air smells the same as ever: grease paint, dust and excitement. In the distance he can hear someone playing an avalanche of scales at breakneck speed.

It doesn't take long to locate Asako Mori's dressing room. The door is unlocked, which makes his task easy. He hides himself in the closet. Through the narrow gap he can inspect every inch of the space; the walls painted green to sooth performers' nerves, posters and reviews pasted around the mirror, as reminders of past glories. When he closes his eyes, he can remember how Mori looked when they were at college, waifish with long black hair, a smile sweet enough to cloy. She was the only classmate with a talent to rival his own. But people viewed him with suspicion, while she ingratiated herself, making no enemies along the way.

His body is stiff with tension by the time she returns. The twist of the doorknob makes his pulse accelerate. But when Mori enters the room, the old woman from the stage door is close behind, her walkie-talkie releasing a crackle of sound.

'Sorry to make you leave early, dear. I have to lock up. The electrician didn't disturb you, did he?'

Mori shakes her head. 'All I heard was my own mistakes.'

The doorkeeper laughs. 'Nonsense, you're getting great reviews.'

Stone curses under his breath. The minutes tick by slowly until Mori and the old woman finally leave, then he emerges from his hiding place and hurries back down the corridor. He peels off his overalls in a public toilet before going back to Lily's flat, reminding himself that the biggest prize will take time to reach. His freedom matters more than anything, without it his dream will never be achieved. He leans over one of the basins to splash his face with cold water, rinsing his anger away, humming to himself as he emerges into the light.

38

Sunday afternoon shifted me back to normality. My police guards dropped me outside St Pancras Old Church, which looked much as it would have done two hundred years ago, with an ornate stained-glass window above the porch. Lola and Neal had chosen a picturesque spot for their wedding, the cemetery filled with ancient gravestones, daffodils blooming by the elm trees that flanked the gates. The only thing disturbing the building's peace was a whisper of traffic in the distance, as if the city had suddenly drawn closer. Lola stood by the entrance welcoming friends and relatives to the dress rehearsal, and it finally hit home that my wild child friend was getting married in a week's time. I had always assumed that she'd stay single forever, scraping by as an actress, attending endless parties, but the mile-wide smile on her face proved that she'd made the right choice. Neal looked happy about taking the plunge too, despite being ten years younger, he had the smug appearance of a man who had landed on his feet. His hug was so enthusiastic, my feet temporarily lifted from the floor.

'Can you take the baby, Al? Lola's mum's panicking.'

Stella Tremaine was ushering people into the church with a serious expression on her face. Clearly her mother-of-the-bride duties were weighing heavily as the run-through began. Neal deposited his sleeping daughter in my arms, offering me another quicksilver grin before hurrying inside.

The church's interior was simple and unadorned, two dozen mahogany pews lining the knave. I sat alone in the back row, my goddaughter's warm bodyweight resting on my knee. It gave me the chance to admire her coppery ringlets and flawless skin, her small hands curled into fists. The atmosphere of the place was so restful I could have closed my eyes and slept for hours. Churches always make me wish that I was a believer, but my scepticism refused to budge. I watched Lola arranging people, while the elderly vicar waited for the commotion to die down. The interval gave me time to imagine being in Lola's shoes, but my past had provided few clues about how to make a relationship last forever. My parents' marriage had caused both of them pain. Dad's alcoholism increased his violence, yet my mother stayed with him, despite regular beatings. When he succumbed to a stroke that left him speechless and paralysed, she had employed carers to look after him at home, her independence restored, until he died. I lifted my head to watch Lola, flirting with her fiancé, tall and beautiful, in the afternoon sunlight that filtered through stained glass. I felt certain her marriage would be a success, happiness imprinted on her DNA. I found myself reaching for answers about my own future but finding none, my personal life as frustrating as the case. All I knew for sure was that regret washed over me when someone removed Neve from my arms, so I could join the rehearsal. The next ten minutes were spent following my friend up and down the aisle, slowing my walk to the dignified pace expected of a maid of honour.

When the practice ended, Lola applauded all of her guests. She caught up with me outside, revealing her first sign of nerves as we loitered on the church path.

'It's really happening, Al.' She gave a shaky laugh. 'I keep pinching myself.'

'You'll be fine. The Greek God's perfect husband material.'

Neal was standing close by, charming everyone within touching distance.

'Don't tell him,' she said. 'His ego's already out of control.'

From the corner of my eye, the headlights of the waiting squad car flicked on as the dusk thickened. My guards wanted me back in the safe house before darkness arrived.

'Are you coming to the pub?' Lola asked.

'Sorry, sweetheart, I can't. Work's crazy right now.'

'I've hardly seen you in days. Come with us, please.'

'It's not my choice, Lo. I wish I could.'

She narrowed her eyes. 'Don't let me down on the big day.'

'Have I ever?'

'There's a first time for everything.'

I gave her a final hug then wrenched myself away, but my footsteps felt heavy as the church gate clanged shut behind me.

39

Stone can't escape his obligation. Lily and her father are waiting outside St Michael's church on Ladbroke Grove, the building grand and imposing. Mr Roberts is a watchful, grey-haired sixty-year-old, his stooped frame making him look older than his years.

'It's Seth, isn't it?' Sunlight reflects from his thick glasses as they shake hands, a trick of the light reducing the old man's eyes to the size of pinpricks.

'That's right, Mr Roberts. Glad to meet you.'

'Call me Patrick, son.' He glances at the people hurrying up the steps. 'We're late, the service starts soon.'

Lily is holding her father's arm. For reasons Stone can't identify, their intimacy irritates him. He's still brooding when they sit at the back of the church. It's years since his parents forced him to attend mass, the environment grating on his nerves. The air is sticky with incense and damp, the organ grinding out a tune, a semi-tone out of key. When the worshippers' voices rise for the first hymn, their singing is so discordant he's desperate to leave, but Lily's gaze pins him there. She looks pathetically grateful, as if he's the only man to show her kindness, apart from her father.

Once the service ends Stone follows the pair to a busy Turkish restaurant on Portobello Road. The old man looks out of place, among the young diners, a flurry of teenagers racing past the window.

'I hear you worked on a cruise ship, Seth,' the old man says, his voice subdued.

'I was a pianist on a liner for a while.'

Roberts's small eyes peer at him. 'I was in the navy, before Lily's mother died. Where did you sail?'

Stone gives a slow smile, aware that he must risk making a mistake. 'The Mediterranean, all the usual ports.'

'Which cruise company?'

'Stop it, dad!' Lily intervenes. 'You're interrogating poor Seth.'

'I'm curious, that's all.' The old man gives an awkward laugh.

'Lily says you did a great job raising her, on your own,' Stone says, to deflect his questions.

'She never gave me any trouble. What about you? Are your parents in London?'

'They died when I was in my teens.'

Suspicion is quickly replaced by pity in the old man's eyes. 'Sorry to hear it, lad. That's a bad time to lose your family.'

Stone chooses to remain silent, letting Lily and her father steer the conversation, while he runs through names in his mind, considering risks and strategies. Anticipation rises in his chest as he decides his next step.

40

Monday 28th March

The team briefing was scheduled for eight a.m. in the station's meeting room. People's faces looked grey when I arrived; all leave had been cancelled, detectives getting by on coffee and adrenalin. Burns looked preoccupied, skin pale as candlewax as he thumbed through a report, making me wonder how long since he'd breathed fresh air. An internal window offered a view of the incident room, and denied us privacy. We had an unspoken rule about avoiding physical contact at work, making me suppress my urge to walk into his arms for a shot of comfort.

'How are you doing?' His gaze lingered on my face.

'Fair to middling. When's the last time you slept?'

'A while back, but we're making progress.'

'Any news?'

'I'll fill you in when the others arrive.'

When I returned to the incident room to collect a hot drink, new photos had been pinned to the evidence board. The images turned the clock back forty-eight hours to the moment when I opened a bin in Soho, to find Sacha Carlisle's body discarded like a piece of trash. The Met's scenes of crime photographer had documented the girl's death thoroughly. Her knees were folded tight against her chest, head tipped back, like she was gagging for air, pristine white headphones covering her ears. Her life meant nothing to Stone, but the music was all-important. He wanted it playing at full volume, with perfect sound quality, as she drew her last breath.

'Does anyone matter to you?' I muttered.

'Chatting to yourself is the first sign of madness.' Angie appeared at my side, bearing a tray of takeaway coffees. 'These are for the meeting. Pour that drink down the drain; the shite from the vending machine tastes like diesel.'

Angie's perky smile was still in place. Her enjoyment of her job seemed to be a permanent feature; I marvelled at her joie de vivre during a frustrating manhunt. My own work still intrigued me, Stone's campaign was the most complex I'd witnessed. My sense that the roots of his violence lay in childhood events was growing stronger. Psychopathic murderers were often abuse victims themselves; to risk returning to his childhood home to bury Keillor's heart proved that Stone had unfinished business. Despite his sister's vulnerability, I would need to interview her again, to discover what she was hiding about their shared past.

The atmosphere in the meeting room was focused when the senior team gathered. Tania was drumming her biro on her notepad in a restless tattoo, clearly eager to get back to work, Hancock's black gaze fixing on Burns's face when he began his briefing.

'Stone's getaway car's been found in the car park at Romford station. He picked it up at the edge of the forest, then drove it straight down the A1. It's an old banger, covered in parking tickets. Can you tell us any more, Angie?'

'My lot are chasing ownership documents. The car wasn't sold through a garage, or it'd be on the DVLA's database. It must have been a private sale, recently. The number-plates show it was manufactured in London, but that doesn't help much.'

'It's more than we had before.' Burns's eyes glittered. 'What was inside?'

'An iPod loaded with music,' she said, scanning her notes. 'Bach, Sibelius, Mozart…'

'All classical?'

'Jazz too. There was nothing else.'

Tania shook her head. 'Why would Briar go to the trouble of downloading Stone's favourite music, if he planned to leave it behind?'

'To begin their new lives on the right note. He thought they'd live together incognito, united by a shared passion for music,' I said. 'But it may not have been Briar who bought the car. Someone else could have helped him.'

'Like who? Briar may just have been trying to spread the blame. The other staff at Rampton have clean alibis.'

'He could have contacted someone from Stone's childhood; psychopaths often have a lasting impact on people they meet. I'm going to see his closest friend from college this morning, but we need to look at anyone he knew before killing his family.'

I listened carefully to the other team members' updates. Hancock had been busy at Sacha Carlisle's crime scene; his work had revealed that Stone had made no effort to cover his tracks. The headphones jammed over the girl's ears were loaded with fingerprints. She had suffered agonising injuries, but her death was caused by slow strangulation. The thought of Stone throttling her as music blared in her ears filled me with anger. His need to punish anyone who stood in his way coupled with psychopathic violence made him incapable of empathy. The meeting was wrapping up when I finally voiced my thoughts.

'He'll try to perform again,' I said quietly. 'Stone believes his destiny is to dazzle the world with his talents. He won't be satisfied with second rate venues; he'll aim for at least one big performance before he's caught.'

Burns looked surprised. 'You think he'd risk his freedom for a moment of glory?'

'Playing the piano is his raison d'etre; it sustained him through his time at Rampton. It's as natural to him as breathing. Right now he'll be planning how to pull it off.'

When the meeting ended Burns motioned for me to stay behind, his expression serious. 'Would you do something for me?'

'Depends what it is.'

'Sacha Carlisle's parents are refusing to leave the station. The mother's in bits; maybe you can calm her down.'

'I'll do my best.'

The walk to the interview room with Angie felt uncomfortable. If I had insisted on Carlisle taking full protection, Sacha might still be alive. A raw noise hit me at the end of the corridor; someone crying, the sound high and plaintive. Miriam Carlisle was slumped across the table, eyes sealed as her sobbing increased. My former colleague looked like a shadow of himself. His clothes were dishevelled, face hollowed by anxiety. He was kneeling beside his wife, but comfort wasn't working. The first stages of grief affected people in different ways, as disbelief turned into rage. Ian's numb expression showed that his daughter's death hadn't yet hit home. I reminded myself that he was a senior psychiatrist, not a patient or a suspect, then reached out to touch his hand.

'What can I do, Ian?'

'Miriam can't rest till she knows how Sacha died. She won't leave till someone explains.'

His wife's eyes were puffy with tears, skin blotchy from hours of weeping. Her voice was raw when she finally spoke. 'I need to know if she was in pain. It's all I can think about.'

'I don't think she'd have been conscious. Sacha probably wasn't fully aware of what was happening.'

The lie slipped out easily. Normally I made a rule of telling the truth, but on this occasion it would have done too much harm. The Carlisles weren't ready for the full horror of their daughter's death. Angie remained silent when we left them to grieve, but her irrepressible high spirits had vanished. Her jaw was gritted, as if witnessing the Carlisles' misery had hardened her determination to track down their daughter's killer.

Tania accompanied me on my next visit. We left the station by the back entrance to avoid the journalists thronging on the front steps, hungry for details to flog to the tabloids. She looked calm and polished as her car entered the mid-morning traffic. The river appeared between buildings, glinting with sunlight as we cut east through Wapping. I would have preferred to sit in a quiet pub for an hour, allowing its steady tide to rinse away my memories of the Carlisles' distress.

'How did you find this mate of Stone's?' Tania asked.

'Stanley Yacoub told me a guy called Ben Wrentham was close to him, from the start of his course. He had his contact details.'

'He's teaching at my old school, poor sod. I hope his pupils aren't as bolshie as me.'

We pulled up outside a secondary school in Tower Hamlets. The building was a square Seventies monolith with few distinguishing features, more like a prison compound than a school. The atmosphere improved once we got inside; colourful posters and artwork filling the walls, a welcome video running on continuous loop. We found Ben Wrentham in a portacabin behind the main building, the air stale, condensation streaming down the windows. The teacher was screwing a pair of cymbals to the base of a drum kit. He must have been around thirty, shirt buttons straining over his developing paunch, a haystack of sandy hair crying out to be cut. He straightened up to give us an awkward smile.

'The kids love dismantling things,' he said. 'I spend hours putting them back together.'

'Thanks for seeing us, Mr Wrentham. Are you sure this is a good time?' Tania asked.

'Of course, my sixth formers are in the library. Is this about Adrian?'

Wrentham stood in the middle of the room, his hands clutched tightly together, skin shiny with anxiety. Stone had seemed far more poised during my meeting with him. The teacher would have been even more gauche ten years ago, his manner piquing my curiosity, making me wonder what had drawn them together.

'We'd like a clearer picture of Stone's time at college,' I said. 'Do you remember much about him back then?'

He nodded vigorously. 'He was already a virtuoso, with an incredibly broad repertoire. It was impossible not to be impressed.'

'Is that why you became friends?'

The teacher's gaze dropped. 'Adrian tolerated me, but we never really socialised.'

'Staff at the Royal College said you were close.'

'I was hoping to learn from his technique. Sometimes I'd hang around, watching him practise. We ate together in the refectory, but he was very private, even though people were intrigued. He just wanted to be left alone.'

'Did he spend time with anyone else?'

Wrentham hesitated then shook his head. 'Only our teachers.'

'He didn't see any girls?'

'Only briefly in his final year. Her name was Bella Sanderson, a first-year violinist.'

'Was it serious?'

'Not for him.' Wrentham gave a sheepish smile. 'Girls were queuing up to educate the boy genius, if you know what I mean. I just watched from the side-lines.'

'Do you have Bella's contact details?'

'Sorry, we lost contact.'

I nodded. 'Would you say Adrian was competitive?'

'It goes with the territory; thousands apply of musicians apply for every vacancy in a national orchestra. But Adrian was in a league of his own.'

'No one else came close?'

He rubbed his hand across his forehead. 'Not that I remember. It feels like a lifetime ago, to be honest; I try not to think about it much.'

'It must have shocked you, hearing what Adrian had done.'

The teacher nodded. 'I knew he was obsessive. To reach that level of skill, you have to sacrifice things, but I'd never seen him be violent. If something got to him, he just walked away.'

'Did you carry on performing after you left college?' I asked.

He gave a quiet shrug. 'I'm better at flogging kids through their GCSEs. It's chaos here most days, but it suits me.'

'Did you have any contact with Stone, after he was sentenced?'

'None, I couldn't imagine what to say.'

Tania nodded. 'Thanks for giving us your time.'

We were halfway to the door when Wrentham spoke again. 'Adrian never liked a student called Asako Mori. He was furious that the staff gave her the solo slot at our graduation show. I still see her, she did a recital at the school last year.'

'She plays for a living?' Tania asked.

He let out a laugh. 'She's a classical megastar. Asako was young musician of the year before she graduated.'

'Can we have her number, please?'

Wrentham frowned in concentration as he transferred Mori's details from his phone. I wondered why Stone had tolerated the teacher's company at college, when he'd shunned so many others. Wrentham's modesty could have been the deciding factor, content to bask in the younger pianist's limelight. It was a reminder that Stone was a true narcissist, only tolerating people who acknowledged his superiority. I felt sure he would have acquired another acolyte by now; someone to obey his instructions, without question.

Tania made a phone call once we left the building. I listened as she arranged to have Bella Sanderson tracked down immediately. She tried to call Asako Mori as we returned to her car, with no reply, giving a frustrated curse as she slipped her mobile back into her pocket.

'She's probably practicing scales somewhere.'

Ben Wrentham emerged from his portacabin as we left the school's car park, his expression subdued. Only a handful of music students in his year had achieved success, the rest drifting away from the limelight. It surprised me that the teacher had shown no bitterness, even though he'd sacrificed years pursuing his dream.

'I'd like to know more about Wrentham,' I said. 'He hero worshipped Stone, and still sees him as a tormented genius, rather than a murderer. It's possible he's involved in some way.'

Tania seemed surprised, but gave a brisk nod as the car pulled away. She looked sceptical about a mild-mannered soul like Wrentham being implicated in a brutal series of murders, but I was clutching at straws.

41

Stone flashes his fake ID at the doorman at the Albert Hall. This time he's disguised as a young executive, in a crisp black suit and shiny Oxford brogues, skin darkened by fake tan, eyes brown instead of blue. He keeps his head up as he strides towards the stage, passing cleaners, janitors and sound technicians in the busy corridors.

It's eleven a.m. when he conceals himself beside the empty stage. Stone's gaze drifts over the ranked seats of the stalls, past the royal box, up to the gods. It gives him pleasure to observe the huge sound-shields hanging high above the auditorium, softening the timbre of every note, making this one of the best venues in the world for piano acoustics. He is destined to fill this place to the rafters, dazzling the audience with his skill, but it's Asako Mori who crosses the stage to claim the huge Steinway as her own.

When she starts to play, his anger simmers. She displaced him once before; he can't let it happen again. She deserves to suffer indefinitely. Stone waits until his calmness returns. Once he's fully in control he emerges from his hiding place, coming to a halt beside the piano. Mori looks up in surprise. It's clear that his disguise is working; there's no hint of recognition in her eyes.

'Sorry to interrupt you, Miss Mori. I work for your agent, Simon Colbert. I'm afraid your father's unwell.'

'What's happened?' The pianist's face reveals her panic.

'He collapsed at your hotel.'

'I should be with him,' she says, stumbling to her feet.

'Simon wants me to take you to the hospital.' Stone gives a sympathetic smile. 'I told the stage manager today's rehearsal's cancelled.'

He places his hand under her elbow to lead her from the stage, guiding her down a twisting corridor at a rapid pace. Mori is so shaken by his news, she doesn't ask a single question.

42

Burns drove me to Chiswick that afternoon, the atmosphere subdued as the car edged west through London's wealthiest suburbs. Neither of us mentioned the elephant in the room; if Ian Carlisle's family had been targeted, my own name must be high on Stone's hit list too. His warped logic was easy to interpret. I shared equal responsibility for thwarting his destiny; anyone who had held him back faced retribution. Carlisle's punishment seemed cruellest of all: although his life had been spared, his happiness had been destroyed forever. I was still trying to predict where Stone would strike next when Burns turned to me. We were stuck in traffic, miles from our destination, his nonchalant tone of voice indicating that he was trying to distract me.

'How's Lola getting along?' he asked.

'She's obsessed by veils and seating plans.'

'They're going the whole hog?'

'A white Rolls Royce, designer dress, and London's entire acting community in attendance.'

Burns glanced at me. 'Ever considered tying the knot yourself?'

I shook my head. 'Big weddings aren't my idea of fun.'

'What about small ones?'

'I don't believe in public statements. It's how you act in private that counts.'

He released a low grumble of laughter. 'You've never been asked.'

'I have, actually. Not that it's any of your business.'

'Openness is your most attractive quality, Alice.'

Attack seemed like the best form of defence. 'What was your wedding like?'

'A quick dash to the registry office. Not exactly wild romance, but it was all we could afford. Julie was pregnant with Liam; it seemed the right thing to do.'

The conversation made me uncomfortable. Marriage didn't appeal to me, but the idea of Burns belonging to someone else felt worse.

'We agreed not to talk about the future before the case ends,' I said.

He smiled innocently. 'I'm just chatting, while we're stuck in traffic.'

'My arse.'

'What about kids? You must have thought about having one.'

'God, you're relentless.'

'Sooner or later you have to tell me what you want.'

'I don't honestly know.'

'You're a shrink for god's sake. I bet you've got a five-year plan, filed away somewhere.'

'Let's wait for a quieter moment to discuss this.'

He pointed at the stationary traffic. 'It doesn't get much calmer. Tell me if you've ever wanted kids, then I'll quit.'

'I thought about it in my twenties, but work took over. If it was going to happen, I'd have had one then.'

'There's still time.'

I stared at him. 'How would that work?'

'You never know,' he said, smiling again. 'Things might change.'

I wanted to ask what he meant but the traffic was moving again, new messages blaring through his police radio. The conversation left me stranded in unknown territory, but Burns was the most dogged man I knew. He would keep pursuing the topic, treating me like a case to be cracked. I pushed the thought aside as we approached Chiswick Bridge. Three wide arches spanned the river, a group of men sitting on the bank in the pale sunlight, clustered round a single fishing rod. I was tempted to join them. It felt like months since I'd spent time relaxing, with no threat hanging over me.

When Burns parked the car outside Stone's aunt and uncle's home, the place still looked neat and prosperous, with tulips blooming in tidy circles. It seemed like the last place a killer would target, situated on a quiet, tree-lined street. The only giveaway that the house's occupants were in danger was the squad car parked on the drive. Burns paused to speak to the patrol officers before I rang the doorbell.

'How do you want to play this?' he asked.

'I need to win Melissa's trust. She can help me understand her brother's actions.'

'Let's call it a family support visit.'

David Stone's disapproval was easy to read when the door finally opened. I thought he might slam it in our faces, but he stepped back to admit us. It was only once we reached his kitchen that his anger spilled over.

'My niece has suffered enough already. You people only come here with bad news.'

I kept quiet to let Burns placate him; faced with two opponents Stone was likely to go on the attack.

'We want to support Melissa, Mr Stone. We know the strain your family's under, I need your cooperation to keep you fully informed.'

'She might come down, but it's unlikely.'

'Before you go, can you tell us about Adrian's piano playing?' I asked.

He blinked rapidly. 'What do you want to know?'

'His parents didn't own a piano originally, did they? Melissa told us that he was six, before they bought one. Did he come here to play right at the start?'

'I found him in the music room, one Christmas, when he was four or five. I showed him how to play a few scales.' His face softened at the memory. 'I collected him from school a few times a week after that, brought him back here. It was clear he had a special talent.'

'Did you teach him for many years?'

He shook his head angrily. 'My brother ended it, a few months later. He employed a qualified tutor, in case the boy developed bad techniques.'

'That must have been hurtful.'

'Why waste time discussing ancient history? I'll see if Melissa will speak to you.'

David Stone stalked out of the room, arms swinging like a sergeant major on parade. I'd spent enough time working as a psychologist to know that stress manifested in many ways: aggression in some patients, hyper-anxiety, insomnia and loss of appetite in others. David Stone's anger was typical disassociation. Casting blame on others deflected his guilt for missing the signs of his nephew's violence. When he finally returned, Stone appeared calmer, but there was no sign of his niece. At close proximity his craggy features were etched with worry, pepper and salt hair sticking in uneven clumps.

'I'm sorry for snapping,' he said quietly. 'Melissa still believes Adrian wants to hurt her more than anyone; I've never seen her more fragile. She'll see you, but please don't keep her too long.'

'I know you're just protecting your family,' I replied. 'I'll try not to upset her,'

Anger and suspicion still shimmered in his eyes. 'If you do, I'll make a formal complaint.'

Melissa Stone appeared five minutes later. She had lost weight since her ordeal began, cheekbones sharper than ever. The grey shadows under her eyes revealed that she'd been having trouble sleeping.

'Thanks for seeing us again,' I said. 'We wanted to check you're okay.'

'Not exactly.' She gave a shaky laugh. 'Nothing feels quite real anymore.'

'Melissa, we're certain Adrian is being helped by someone. It could be a childhood friend or a contact from college; it would help if you can talk more about life when you were kids, but I know that's difficult.'

Her eyes were unfocused. 'I didn't question it at the time. Mum worked long hours, so we spent a lot of time at home with dad. My sister was always in her room studying, Adrian's music filling the house. At the weekends he was often away performing, when I was at primary school.'

'Your parents pushed him hard?'

147

'They expected all of us to succeed.' She gazed down at her hands.

'What did you do while Jenny and Adrian worked?'

'Painting or drawing, but I never had much talent.'

'Was your dad a good father?'

'It feels wrong to judge him now.'

'Did he show much physical affection?'

Her cheeks flushed. 'If one of us did well, he'd make an announcement over dinner. My sister and Adrian won most of the compliments.' Melissa's phone buzzed loudly in her pocket before she could complete her statement. 'It could be someone from work. Do you mind if I take this?'

'Not at all, go ahead.'

Melissa kept the phone pressed to her ear, but it was clear something was wrong. Her face blanched, then she pitched forwards, eyelids fluttering. Burns helped me make her comfortable, a soft moan emerging from her mouth as she came round.

'It's me he wants,' she whispered. 'No one else.'

While Burns comforted the girl I listened to the message. There was a loud click, followed by a burst of piano music, complicated rhythms overlapping. It was the pace that disturbed me most, an erratic heartbeat, notes tumbling out in a frenzy. Stone's chaotic melody seemed designed to warn us about his state of mind.

43

Stone leans against the wall, breathing the damp air. The tunnel seems to go on forever, its echo whispering back every sound, no light except his torch beam, cutting a swathe through the blackness. He lights a pair of candles, their flickering light falling on dozens of abandoned musical instruments, pianos standing side by side. They have been left here to rot, but he has brought two of them back to life, tuning them to perfection. Asako Mori is seated on a piano stool, arms limp at her sides, a chain cinching her waist so tightly, she's struggling to breathe. The young woman tries to stand, but it's impossible. Restraints yank her back into place, hands clattering on the keyboard.

'Don't stop,' he says. 'Practise, till you get it right.'

'I need a break, Adrian.' Her voice is proud, refusing to beg.

'I'll film you tomorrow, let the world know you're still alive.'

'You always hated me.' Mori's eyes gleam with anger. 'No one else challenged you, did they?'

Stone's hands clench into fists. 'Stop whining and get to work.'

'Let me go, you bastard.'

'Shut up and play.'

When he steps closer, Mori flinches, then her hands touch the keys once more. Stone gradually relaxes as notes wash over him. It may take days for her to learn the duet's full cycle, but he's in no rush. No one will find her here. London is playing its hectic tune above their heads, a cacophony of sirens and engine noise, but down here the silence is perfect.

It's the ideal practice space, a vault deep below the city's surface; the only other occupants are rats that have colonised this place for centuries.

Soon Stone leaves Mori in darkness, only the pianos and vermin to keep her company. His next task will require thorough planning; he considers details as he walks towards Mayfair, his bag slung over his shoulder. It's only when he reaches a quiet shopping street that he slips down an alleyway, checking that no one is watching before stepping behind a hoarding to remove the glass bottle from his bag. He pulls on rubber gloves then pours battery acid into shallow bowls, positioning them over a doorway and basement windows. The next person to visit this place will be rewarded by excruciating pain. He replaces the bottle in his bag then walks away. Soon Alice Quentin's knowing smile will be wiped from her face, once and for all.

44

It took an hour to calm Melissa Stone down. I felt certain her phone message had come from her brother: no one else would play such a cruel joke, but it raised the question of how he'd found her number. Burns looked preoccupied as he drove through back streets to the station on St Pancras Way, breaking the speed limit. Tania was waiting for us when we arrived, her expression sober.

'Asako Mori's missing,' she said. 'She left her rehearsal this morning in a hurry; two sound technicians saw her leave the stage with a guy in a suit. No one's seen her since.'

'Has she contacted anyone?' Burns asked.

Tania shook her head. 'Her management's cancelled tonight's performance at the Albert Hall.'

Burns swiped his hand across his face. 'He's got her in a lock up somewhere. It could be her playing on that recording he sent his sister.'

'This explains his last clue,' I said. 'Glenn Gould only visited London once, to perform at the Albert Hall.'

I listened in silence as operational details were agreed. Statements from staff at the concert hall were being verified, CCTV and road camera film footage was being checked, patrols hunting for witnesses. My frustration mounted as the evening progressed; the incident room bubbled with activity, but I could only listen to the helpline's phones jangling. A publicity shot of Asako Mori had appeared on the evidence board. Coal black hair was swept back from her attractive, ivory-skinned face, her makeup flawless. Two more stills had been downloaded from security cameras as she strode towards the Albert Hall's main entrance, a slim figure in jeans, trainers and sweatshirt, her expression determined. The images proved that behind her sophisticated stage image lay a normal young woman, coping with a hectic schedule. A film flickering on a computer screen nearby showed Mori performing at a charity gala, dressed in a glittering silver gown. The sound was muted, fierce concentration on her face. For once I felt glad to have no musical talent whatsoever. Being a professional performer seemed to require a willingness to abandon your private life to perfect your craft. I could only hope that Mori's tough self-discipline would help her cope with Stone's violence.

Angie appeared at my side, her smile missing for once. 'Do you think she's alive?'

'It's possible. He might treat a classmate differently.'

'You wanted to see Stone's ex-girlfriend, didn't you?' She offered me a photo. 'This is Bella Sanderson when she was at the Royal College nine years ago, at the time of their fling.'

The picture showed a pretty dark-eyed girl clutching a violin, her smile innocent.

'She'll let us interview her today?'

Angie nodded. 'We can go there now, but be warned, her answers were really vague on the phone. Maybe she was shocked to hear Stone's name after so long, or she could be a nutcase.'

Journalists were still crowding the front of the station, so we slipped out the back exit. News of Asako Mori's kidnapping seemed to be common knowledge, even though no public announcement had been made. Once we escaped the car park, our journey to Bella Sanderson's home took just ten minutes; she lived on the border between Pentonville and Islington, a low grind of traffic from the Grays Inn Road greeting us as Angie parked her car. Half a dozen small bungalows huddled together, simple grey boxes with slate-tiled roofs, overshadowed by apartment buildings, no trees or greenery in sight. The location didn't seem glamorous enough for a graduate from the country's most prestigious music college.

Angie and I waited in the porch, but no one arrived. We were about give up when the door finally swung open. Bella Sanderson looked nothing like the bright-eyed girl of her college days: she could have been anywhere between thirty and forty, small red-rimmed eyes peering out from a tangle of mousy curls, a shapeless grey dress falling to her ankles.

'You're not here to arrest me, are you?' She gave a quiet laugh.

My concern rose as we followed her down the hallway. She was significantly overweight with the shuffling walk of a much older woman, her breathing laboured. Sanderson's lounge turned out to be a feline kingdom. Half a dozen cats gazed back at us from worn out furniture; a thin Siamese rose from an armchair, hissing loudly before slinking away.

'I hope neither of you have allergies.' She laughed again, as if the idea was hilarious.

'Thanks for giving us your time,' I said. 'Did the duty officer explain our visit to you?'

'It's about Adrian, isn't it?' Sanderson's body language grew more agitated. She perched on the edge of the settee, twisting a lock of hair around her forefinger, while two long-haired tabbies prowled at her feet.

'Can you tell us about your relationship, when you were at college?'

Her shoulders gave a nervous shrug. 'Adrian was sixteen, I was eighteen. We weren't together long.'

'Ben Wrentham says you saw a lot of him in his last year.'

'I was renting a flat near college with another girl, but she was always at her boyfriend's place. He came round sometimes, after practise.' Her voice tailed into silence.

'We need to build a picture, Ms Sanderson. Any details you give could help find him.'

'What do you want to know?'

'Can you say what happened between you?'

A dreamy look came into her eye. 'It was my first year at college. I'd never had a proper boyfriend before; it didn't bother me that he was younger, there was something ageless about him.'

'How did it start?'

'Adrian spoke to me at the bus stop. He was this genius everyone talked about, the tutors said he had a special talent.'

'You became close?'

Sanderson angled her face away. 'I thought so, he even said he loved me once or twice.'

'Did he ever stay at your flat?'

'You're asking if we had sex. Of course we did, we were teenagers.'

'How long did you see each other?'

'Four months, in secret, because he didn't want his parents to know. He came here a few times a week, but never stayed long.'

'When did it end?'

'The day he was arrested.' She gazed down at her hands.

'Did you know he'd been unhappy?'

'It seemed unbelievable; he was this quiet, teenaged genius and then he was gone. I wanted to know why he'd done something so awful, but my parents never let me visit.'

'You've had no contact since?'

Sanderson finally met my eye. 'Didn't Ben tell you what happened?'

'He said very little.'

'I didn't want anyone to know we'd been a couple, or the papers would have door-stepped me. Hiding my feelings got too much; I found it impossible to concentrate, so I dropped out of college, went back home for a while. My multiple sclerosis started kicked in five years ago, I haven't worked since.'

'It sounds like you've had a hard time.'

Her hands bunched into fists. 'Adrian never wrote to me. I needed him to explain what he'd done.'

'It's not in his makeup to consider other people's feelings.'

'It sounds mad, but I missed him for months afterwards.' Her voice had dropped to a low monotone.

'Psychopaths can be very seductive. They say what you need to hear, the truth's not important to them.'

'He wanted to be worshipped, that's all.' A tear rolled down her cheek.

'Would you like to see a counsellor, Bella? Looking back must be upsetting for you.'

There was a pause, before Sanderson shook her head. She gave the impression of someone who could easily succumb to depression, illness increasing her vulnerability.

'Is there a chance Stone could find you?' I asked.

'I've moved five times since then.' A spasm of terror crossed her face. 'You don't think he'll come after me, do you?'

'He'd struggle to track you down,' Angie said.

Our visit seemed to have sapped Bella's energy. We saw ourselves out after saying goodbye, and for once Angie fell silent, only speaking again once we reached her car.

'I can't believe she's pining for a bloody serial killer,' she said.

'There was no closure. One minute they're having a sweet teenage romance, then the papers were calling him a monster. He singled her out because she was naïve, and I bet the person helping him now is just as innocent.'

Angie shoved her key into the ignition. 'Capital punishment's too good for bastards like that.'

The solution was more complicated for me. Stone's violence was a feature of his psychopathy, triggered by past events that were still a mystery. I looked back at Bella Sanderson's small grey home as we pulled away, wondering how many more lives he would devastate before he was found.

Lily appears in the hallway as Stone removes his coat. One of her best qualities is that she never asks questions, even though it's midnight, and she has no idea where he's been. The warmth of her smile floods his system with unfamiliar emotions.

'You look pleased with yourself.' He leans down to kiss her cheek.

'Shut your eyes, I've got a surprise for you.'

Stone has always hated losing control, but he lets the girl lead him into the lounge, eyes closed.

'You can look now,' she says quietly.

The furniture has been rearranged, table and chairs pushed under the window. It's only when he turns round that he notices the piano in the corner. The instrument is at least fifty years old, scratches marking its walnut frame, ivories worn thin by use. He picks out a scale in C Major, assessing its cadence.

'Will you be able to repair it?' she asks.

'It'll sound as good as new.' Stone touches the dark wood again, then turns to Lily. 'Why did you buy it for me?'

'Because you're so talented. You deserve a Steinway, but it's all I could afford.'

When Stone stares down at the girl's face something shifts in his chest, a door opening that should remain closed. No one has ever given him a present before without asking anything in return. The kindness in her expression almost makes him feel ashamed.

Tuesday 29th March

Reg was monosyllabic when he collected me, but even he couldn't cast a shadow over the morning. It was so crisp and sunny, I felt like deserting my duties for a walk by the Thames. People were sitting outside cafés by London Bridge, bus-boats ferrying commuters upstream to Westminster. The city seemed oblivious to the fact that a killer's violence was increasing every day. I was on my way to meet Asako Mori's father, aware that he must have been watching the news, the media obsessed by Stone's campaign.

We pulled up on Park Crescent in Marylebone. I admired the Georgian terrace's elegant curve as I stepped onto the pavement; two hundred years ago wealthy merchants would have lived there, a stone's throw from Regent's Park. The hotel Asako Mori's father had chosen was adorned with gleaming paintwork, marble tiles in the hallway and a lavish chandelier. Burns was waiting by the reception desk, looking irritable and dishevelled, suit jacket creased, but none of that mattered. I still wished we could check into a room, then hang a 'do not disturb' sign on the door for the rest of the day. The tension on his face soon banished my fantasy.

'The old man wouldn't come to the station. He plans to wait for his daughter here.'

'Fair enough,' I replied. 'We need to hear him talk about Asako. She may have revealed details he didn't pick up.'

'I'll get the procedural stuff out of the way, then you can take over.'

Burns summoned the lift, but peering through its doors made me back away. It was so tiny and airless the ride would have triggered my claustrophobia, so we took the stairs instead. Burns was panting by the time we arrived, but the view from the penthouse level was stunning. The green expanse of Regent's Park unrolled into the distance, flowerbeds rioting with colour. When I turned round Mr Mori was waiting on the landing. He was in his late fifties, small and immaculately dressed in a black suit, grey hair neatly combed. At first sight he looked like any other businessmen on his way to work, but there was no hint of a smile when he shook my hand.

'Please come inside,' he said. 'Thank you for helping my daughter.' His voice was formal, with a soft Japanese accent. He gave a slight bow as he ushered us through the door.

Mr Mori's suite must have cost a fortune. The living area opened onto a sun terrace, overlooking the park, dark wooden furniture in the living space contrasting with long white settees.

'Do you often stay with your daughter when she performs, Mr Mori?' Burns asked.

'Always, now I've retired. We rent rooms near each venue. Last month we were in Prague, next week it's Dublin.'

Mori's voice tailed away, as if he'd only just realised his daughter might not return. I listened in silence as Burns updated him on the hunt for his daughter. A huge team were chasing every lead, from her mobile phone records, to sightings of her car.

'Do you recognise this number, Mr Mori?' Burns asked, showing him a slip of paper.

'Let me check.' Mori pulled reading glasses from his pocket to inspect his own phone, then shook his head. 'It's not familiar, sorry.'

'It's the only number we can't match. Someone called her twice this week, around midnight. Does Asako have a partner?'

'A boyfriend, you mean?' the old man asked. 'I wish she did. She travels from country to country, never resting.'

'It sounds like she's made sacrifices,' Burns replied.

'Asako wants to be number one pianist in the world. She never complains.' The old man's voice was thick with suppressed tears.

'How well did your daughter know Adrian Stone?' Burns asked.

Mori frowned. 'Asako is very competitive; she got upset if he won a prize, or did better in an exam. It annoyed her that he was younger, but so talented.'

'She must have been shocked by his arrest.'

'It was a tragedy for his family, but it launched her career.'

'How do you mean?' Burns looked up from his notebook.

'Stone was about to tour with the Philharmonic; Asako took his place. She got great reviews.'

The reasons for Stone's hatred were growing clear. Not only had Asako been his strongest competitor, she had benefited from his incarceration. When Burns finished checking information, I leant forwards to catch her father's eye.

'You seem devoted to your daughter, Mr Mori. Is she your only child?'

'My son is married, living in the United States.'

'And your wife died last year?'

'She told me to keep Asako safe; my wife worried about her working too hard.'

'Music's a demanding discipline.'

He nodded in agreement. 'It's an addiction, not a normal life.'

I studied Mori's face again. 'Did your daughter do anything unusual in the last fortnight?'

'She had breakfast early each day, then went to rehearse. We spent evenings together when she didn't have to perform.'

'Nothing struck you as odd?'

He looked thoughtful. 'We got back late once from dinner. Someone had pushed an envelope under the door. She said it was a welcome letter from the hotel management, but didn't show me. Normally she lets me deal with such things.'

'Could I see Asako's room, please?'

The old man hesitated. 'She's a very private person. Is that necessary?'

'It could help find her.'

'Then please go ahead.'

The room showed how pressurised Asako Mori's life had been. Sheet music was stacked on the chair beside her bed, an electric keyboard under the window. She must have practised in the hotel, as well as the venues where she performed. Her wardrobe was filled with evening dresses, jumbled with T shirts and leggings she wore in her downtime. The only personal item was a print tacked to the wall, of a Tokyo street filled with cherry trees in bloom. I closed my eyes and inhaled the room's chemical odour of hairspray and expensive perfume. Asako Mori had been working nonstop to make the world acknowledge her talent. With luck her strength would keep her alive, but time was running out. I turned towards the bed and opened the drawer of her nightstand, finding it empty. It was only when I searched the chest of drawers that I found an envelope, tucked under the lining. Stone's odd forward-sloping handwriting was instantly recognisable. His audacity was extraordinary; it would have taken a strong nerve to deliver the letter personally. My hand trembled as I pulled out a glossy sheet of paper. It was a publicity flyer, promoting a new museum. The information explained that the composer George Frideric Handel's home had become a museum, with musical events for the public to attend. There was nothing else inside the envelope, sending my frustration into overdrive. Wherever Stone was hiding, he was doing a great job of sending us in circles.

47

Stone is tense as he retraces his steps. Lily is to blame for his confusion, lodged in his mind like a burr. Even when they're apart her loyalty and gentleness are hard to forget. He mutters to himself as he follows the busy Kensington street, hood raised to conceal his face. He stops on a street corner to ask himself the vital question. Will he be able to kill her, when the time comes? It takes him a full minute to decide. If she discovers his identity, he will have no choice. For once the idea of ending someone's life brings no pleasure at all.

He waits until no one is watching before slipping through a narrow opening between two outbuildings to find the trap door. He lifts the rusting hatch and climbs down the metal ladder. Despite the mid-morning sun, no light penetrates this hidden place. He follows the tunnel's blackened walls, with only his torch to guide him, anger rising with each footstep. Asako Mori has stopped playing; all he can hear is silence. Stone finds her slumped over the keyboard, the sharp smells of urine and fear filling the air.

'Why did you stop?' he snaps.

'I practised for hours but the candle ran out.'

Mori's expression angers him. He's in control, yet she's unwilling to accept instructions. The challenge makes him determined to break her will.

'You're filthy. There's a bucket of water in the corner. Wash yourself, then start over.'

'You're crazy. You know that, don't you?'

Stone's answer is a hard slap, leaving a red imprint on Mori's cheek, yet she doesn't make a sound. He unlocks the padlock, then removes the chains binding her to the piano. He watches in distaste as Mori splashes her face with water from the bucket. He may have to wait days for her to perfect her part in the duet, but after their performance he can kill her at last. Other names on his list will receive their punishments in the meantime.

48

I stared at the flyer from the Handel museum again, once I reached Burns's car.

'There was nothing else in the envelope?' he asked.

'Maybe she destroyed his note.'

Burns stared at me. 'You think she'd bin a letter from Stone without telling anyone?'

'To protect her dad, but she's done Stone a favour. He knew we'd find the envelope.'

'So the message is for us?' Burns turned to face me.

'It's another musical clue. Something must be waiting for us at the museum.'

'You think Asako's been left there?'

'We should check,' I replied.

'I'll get a team on it, then we'll take a look.'

Burns had to return to the station for a press briefing. His strategy was to offer snippets of information, to stop journalists chasing every squad car he despatched. Intense media speculation would only raise public concern to fever pitch. I stood at the back of the room while he held court, giving the camera his no-bullshit stare. It was a reminder of the qualities that had attracted me to him at the start; he was always the truest thing in the room. Burns was as focused on finding his culprit as Asako Mori had been on perfecting her piano skills. When the briefing ended he was called to an unexpected meeting at Scotland Yard, his expression irritable as we said good bye. There was nothing he hated more than humouring his seniors.

It was Tania who drove me to Mayfair at midday. We parked at the end of Brook Street, then walked north to the Handel House Museum. The area was dominated by designer clothes stores, shoppers loaded with bags from Gucci and Mulberry. We stood outside number twenty-five Brook Street, admiring the tall regency townhouse. A sign explained that Handel had lived there until his death, another blue plaque marking the house next door. It announced that Jimi Hendrix had lived there between 1968 and 1969, a span of a hundred and fifty years separating the musical geniuses' lives.

The head curator greeted us inside the museum. Ruth Jenner's grey hair was pinned back from her face, spectacles dangling from a cord around her neck, her expression startled.

'This is unexpected,' she said quietly. 'We're closed for refurbishment. I've had to send the contractors away.'

Tania gave her a look of sympathy. 'Our search shouldn't take long.'

Uniforms were combing each room, carrying evidence bags, which so far hung empty.

'Things have been eventful recently.' Dr Jenner said. 'Someone tried to break in on Tuesday night, but nothing was touched, so we didn't report it. We thought it was kids on a dare.'

'What time?'

'Around two a.m., I think.'

I took a step closer. 'Would you mind showing me the house, Dr Jenner?'

My intention was to keep her out of the search team's way. They had specific instructions to hunt for memory sticks, sheet music, handwritten notes, but as soon as she led me up the stairs, my interest deepened. Jenner described each room in detail, as though I'd paid for a tour.

'Handel moved here in 1723, when the house was brand new. He was a court composer, writing music for the king. As a foreign national he couldn't buy a property, so he rented it until his death. At the height of his career, his rent was thirty-five pounds a year.'

I laughed. 'You couldn't buy lunch in Mayfair for that now.'

'How times change. This is where he composed.'

The room she showed me had been restored to its original condition. The walls were a soft, duck egg blue. A trio of oil paintings revealed men in powdered wigs, and pink-cheeked women wrapped in lace and ermine, fancy clothes at odds with the simplicity of the room. The window seats were lined with green baize cushions, where the composer would have sat alone at his harpsichord, testing new melodies. I followed Jenner through the other rooms, admiring the composer's four poster bed, with its long crimson drapes, gleaming oak boards covering the floor. Upstairs the servants' garrets were airless and low-ceilinged.

'Handel employed a cook, a butler and two maids. At the end of his life he relied heavily on his servants.'

'Was he ill?' I asked.

'His sight was failing. He'd been blind for years when he died in 1759.'

I was about to ask another question, but a voice echoed up the stairwell. My time as a medical student had taught me to recognise a cry of genuine pain; I chased downstairs to the basement, following the sound. A young WPC was crouching beside a puddle of liquid and shattered glass, clutching her hand. The air was acrid with sulphur, red welts blossoming across the girl's palm.

'Come here,' I said. 'We need to wash that off fast.'

She screamed when I held her hand under the tap in the toilets opposite, but I carried on flushing the wound with water until Tania appeared in the doorway.

'Call an ambulance,' I said. 'Tell them it's a second-degree acid burn.'

The girl was silent now as shock kicked in, her face slick with sweat.

'What's your name?' I asked.

'Sam Wyedale.'

'All right, Sam, you're going to be fine. Thank God it didn't splash your face. Can you say what happened?'

'I opened the back door just now. I jumped back, but some caught me.' She pointed at places where acid had burned through her sleeve.

'Don't touch that liquid,' I told Tania. 'The dangerous substances team will clean it up.'

The curator found a plastic bag to cover the WPC's hand. Wyedale was white-faced but in control as the ambulance took her away. Once the building had been evacuated we stood outside on the pavement. The dangerous substance team were already searching the place in their protective suits, checking for more booby traps. Tania was busy debriefing her team on her phone, and my hands were shaking almost as badly as my mother's. Stone must have guessed that I would find the envelope in Asako Mori's room. The acid had been intended for me alone. When I closed my eyes, the raw faces of burns victims from my med school days appeared in front of me, features melting like candlewax. I forced myself to think rationally; the girl's burns were minor, nothing catastrophic had happened, yet my fingers carried on twitching in my lap.

49

Stone's face is concealed by a cap pulled low over his brow as he passes his aunt and uncle's house. An anonymous black sedan waits on the driveway, revealing that the police are unwilling to leave the property unattended. He loiters at the end of the block, past the officers' line of vision. Light is failing when a small red Nissan draws up, sending time into reverse. His sister Melissa is at the driving wheel, blond hair flowing over her shoulders. Her appearance hasn't changed since she was thirteen; still small and helpless, a rabbit trapped in the headlights.

'Here you are, at last,' he mutters.

Her slim form vanishes inside the house, the door closing too fast. The glimpse of her has been tantalising, but he will have to wait. It will be impossible to get near her today.

When Stone glances at his watch, he realises he will be late for his meeting. He jogs down an alleyway, retracing his steps to the train station, his sister's features locked in his mind. He switches on his iPod, listening to Esbjorn Svensson, half an hour of immaculate jazz diluting his frustration.

It's six p.m. when he reaches Covent Garden. The headquarters of United Artists Agency is in an office over the piazza, the young receptionist ushering him down the hallway to Jeremy Grayson's office like visiting royalty. The agent is leaning out of his window, puffing cigarette smoke into the early evening air.

'Filthy habit, but a bastard to kick.' He gives Stone an embarrassed smile. 'I was thrilled to get your call.'

Grayson is around fifty, smartly dressed, his smile worn thin. His teeth are a bleached unnatural white, filling Stone with distaste. Why bother with personal vanity when only talent matters? He has to force himself to be polite.

'Sorry I'm late, Mr Grayson.'

'Jerry, please. Look, I'll get straight to the point. You blew me away at Ronnie Scott's. I'd love to represent you.'

'I wasn't looking for an agent.'

The man's mud green eyes widen. 'We could build your reputation. Why not tell me how you got started?'

'I'm self-taught. I've been travelling for years, but plan to stay in London for a while.'

'Who can blame you? Your girlfriend's charming.' Grayson's smile flicks on again. 'If you sign with us, we'll take publicity shots and get you excellent press exposure.'

Stone frowns. 'I just want to play. I hate talking about myself.'

'That could work to your advantage. People love a mystery.'

'And I won't accept small venues.'

'What did you have in mind?'

'The Albert Hall.'

Grayson looks stunned, then releases a laugh. 'Fixtures like that only go to big names.'

'If you can fix it, we'll work together, Mr Grayson. If not, I'll look elsewhere.' He gives a pleasant smile. 'Now I must rush, I'm afraid.'

Stone offers a farewell nod, then slips away, disappearing into the horde of tourists wandering through the piazza.

50

The incident room's frenzy didn't encourage clear thinking that evening. Detectives were chasing from desk to desk, sharing information in loud voices. Nothing galvanised a police team like one of their own being attacked, the young WPC's injury sending tensions spiralling. Fortunately there had been good news from the hospital. Sam Wyedale would recover from her burns; rinsing the caustic liquid from her skin had saved her from a painful operation. When I looked down at my own hands, the shaking had gone, yet my anxiety lingered. If the girl had been slower calling for help she could have been permanently maimed. I needed to find the link between Stone's crimes, before Asako Mori received the same treatment, if she was still alive.

Tania approached me once she'd finished briefing her team, her expression sombre. 'We're having no luck at the Albert Hall.'

'CCTV isn't helping?'

'We think Stone must have left by a side entrance, then taken a pre-planned route, dodging street cameras.' She raised her hands in the air. 'It's like they've vanished into thin air.'

I left her to carry on her work, then went looking for Reg. The old timer was drinking tea in the station's café. He put down his mug abruptly when I asked him to drive me to the FPU.

'The boss wants you back at the safe house,' he said. 'I'll drive you there now.'

'It won't take long Reg. There's something I need to check first.'

He stuffed down the remains of his Cornish pasty then rose to his feet, grumbling. Fortunately he said little as the car wove through the dark streets. I gazed out of the window as we passed Bloomsbury's elegant garden squares, the white façade of the British Museum receding from view. It still wasn't clear why Stone had chosen the West End for his playground. He came from the suburbs, like me; the city's richest neighbourhoods probably appealed because they were glamorous and out of reach. Stone had frequented the heart of the city as a student, returning to its sleepy suburbs at night, but he knew these streets like the back of his hand. It was sobering to remember that he was out there now, always one step ahead.

At eight p.m. when Reg dropped me on Dacre Street, lights burning in the top floor windows of the FPU, proving that some consultants liked to work late.

'Be back here in half an hour,' he said, 'or I'll come after you.'

I gazed at him steadily. 'How old do you think I am, Reg?'

'Half my age, so do what I say. I don't care how many letters you've got after your name.'

'If I need longer I'll let you know.'

Reg got away with treating me like a kid because he was well-intentioned, but it felt like being locked in a caravan with a curmudgeonly uncle who disapproved of my every gesture.

My mood lifted once I tapped information into the computer. I started by inputting that day's location into HOLMES 2, using the Home Office's mapping software. I studied the screen until my eyes burned, forming a mental picture of Stone's hunting ground. The kill sites were located inside a small radius, with occasional visits to the suburbs to hunt for victims. Professor Gareth Keillor had been left in the boot of his car, on Dover Street, where the composer Chopin had stayed. Then Sacha Carlisle's body had been dumped in a rubbish bin on Frith Street, where Mozart composed his first symphony. Stone had booby trapped Handel's former home on Brook Street, then entered the Albert Hall and abducted Mori from a rehearsal, in plain sight. A jagged triangle stretched across my computer screen, connecting Mayfair to Soho, then north to Marylebone, the locations less than a mile apart. According to the predictive software, Stone was living near the centre of his zone of activity, in the heart of the West End. I pushed back my chair, trying to think straight. How could Stone be hiding in the city's most affluent district, where one night in a hotel cost hundreds of pounds, unless someone was helping him? I doubted that he was sleeping

170

rough. There was no sign of forced entry when Sacha Carlisle was abducted, and he had gone backstage at the Albert Hall without anyone raising an eyebrow, proving that he was smartly dressed. The person shielding him might be living less than a mile from my office. I walked over to stand by the window. Outside there was a flicker of streetlight, a stream of taxis conveying passengers to the drinking clubs hidden on back streets around St James's Park. The view gave me no clue whatsoever to Stone's hiding place.

Tiredness was getting the better of me, but I studied the map again. The Royal College of Music lay near the centre of Stone's zone of activity, the Albert Hall less than a hundred metres away, connecting his current violence to his original crimes. Stone had reacted to being ousted from the college by wiping out most of his family. Now he was at large again, having killed his former tutor, yet his targets extended further afield. Ian Carlisle's daughter had died because the psychiatrist had confirmed my verdict that Stone should never be freed. A wave of panic rose in my chest. Were the people I loved equally vulnerable, or would he aim straight for me? I still believed that his sister must be top of his list, but there was a chance he'd track me down first.

The latest file on my computer contained my analysis of Stone's musical clues. He had begun by leaving a Chopin nocturne in the mouth of one of his guards, then a fragment of Mozart's first symphony, followed by Glenn Gould's concerto. All three composers had been child prodigies, but further links were hard to identify. They came from different centuries, connected only by talent and the fact that they had spent time in London. My gaze wandered over the map of Stone's crime scenes. He was working at a frenzied pace, settling old scores before he was recaptured. Patterns were emerging but no clear answers; it was clear that I would need more expert help to understand Stone's calling cards. It bothered me that so little progress had been made in tracking down people who could have helped Matthew Briar spring Stone from Rampton. My last interview with the guard before his suicide still had me convinced that he'd used an accomplice.

I clicked on Wikipedia for more information about Asako Mori. The reviewer described her as one of the most talented young pianists of her generation. At twenty-nine she had already played in many of the world's most prestigious concert halls. There was no information about her private life, perhaps because her father's protectiveness had made relationships impossible. When the phone on my desk rang I felt sure it would be Burns, nagging me to quit for the day. I picked up the receiver without dragging my gaze from the screen.

'Hello?'

There was no sound at first, then I heard it. The piano was low and mournful, with a quieter sound behind it; the soft intake of air as Stone breathed into the receiver.

'I've been waiting to hear from, Adrian. You've been keeping busy.'

Words tumbled from my mouth but he didn't reply. It was essential to keep him on the line, so the call could be traced. My extension had been tapped days ago; someone at the station would be monitoring every word.

'Is that Asako playing, or is it a recording?' Suddenly the music came to a halt. 'You must be calling for a reason. I can only help if you talk to me.'

There was a loud peal of laughter as the line died.

It's midnight when Stone takes to the stage once more. The jazz club is busy tonight, his audience lingering over drinks, even though the main act finished an hour ago. He plays quietly at first, the sound slow and meditative. It's a relief to calm his racing thoughts as chords resonate around the room. The harmony echoes his life story: a calm beginning, followed by passion and chaos. When he glances down into the audience, Lily is alone. Two men at the next table are trying to attract her attention, champagne bottles littering their table. But Lily is so focused on him, she doesn't notice her leering admirers. His gaze fixes on her now, unwilling to look away, while sound streams from his hands. The manager congratulates him when he finally leaves the stage.

'You're popular, Seth. Punters keep asking for you.'

'Give me a Friday night slot then, Nancy.'

'Top billing goes to big names, you know that.'

He gives her a hard-eyed stare. 'This place is desperate for fresh talent.'

'Wait your turn, my friend.' Her face blanks as she passes him an envelope, then walks away.

Stone returns to the flat with Lily, hand in hand, stopping by the entrance to study her face. Her plainness no longer registers; all he sees is the delicacy of her skin and her wide-open smile.

'Let's stay like this, Lily. You and me against the world.'

The girl's eyes glisten. 'Do you mean that?'

'You're mine forever.'

She touches his cheek blindly, then fumbles for her key.

Wednesday 30th March

The morning began with an early visit to Lola's flat. It felt negligent to abandon work even for an hour, but there would have been hell to pay for bailing out. The Greek God was escaping when I arrived at eight. He kissed my cheek, before giving me a look of theatrical despair.

'She's got wedding fever, Al. Help her, please.'

'I'll do my best.'

Neal looked relieved as he sprinted for the stairs. The front door to their flat hung open, wedding outfits suspended from the picture rail on hangers, including Neve's tiny lace gown. A mass of papers was strewn across the kitchen tiles, covered in frantic scrawl.

'You look busy,' I said. 'What are you doing?'

Lola rose to her feet to greet me, long legs slowly unfolding. Even in ancient jeans and a ragged jumper, she was a poster girl for bohemian chic, auburn curls snagged back from her face by an electric blue scarf.

'Checking the seating plan. If it's wrong, there'll be hell to pay.'

'How do you mean?'

'Actors can be prickly. The right personalities have to sit together.'

'Is that why I'm here?'

'Nope.' She studied the list again. 'Breakfast first, then try on your dress.'

'I already did. It's fine.'

'It's been shortened since then.' Lola's green eyes narrowed. 'I don't want you tripping on the hem. Everything has to be perfect, Al.'

174

'How could I forget?'

Eating croissants together allowed me to admire Neve, who was doing vigorous aerobics in her Moses basket, throwing her arms in the air then grabbing her toes. Her mother seemed much less relaxed. It was the first time I'd seen Lola stressed since our A level year. Normally she treated life as a party thrown in her honour, but the wedding had flicked a switch I didn't know existed. She drummed her nails on the table as I emerged from the bedroom in my dark green silk dress.

'Can you walk in those shoes?'

'Of course I can. Stop fretting.'

When I looked at her again, her hands were pressed over her eyes, shoulders heaving. I put my arms round her, waiting for her sobs to subside. When she finally pulled back, her skin was blotchy with distress.

'What's wrong, sweetheart?'

She was still clutching my hand. 'I'm scared, Al.'

'Why? You wanted this so badly.'

'Neal's ten years younger than me, for Christ's sake.'

'Who cares? The question is, do you love him?'

'Heart and soul, that's the trouble. When I hit forty he'll leave me for a younger model.'

'That's absolute crap; Neal's adored you from day one. You can't ask for more.'

'Sorry, you don't need this.' Another sob gasped from her mouth. 'Tell me how your work's going, please. I need distraction.'

'I'm helping the police chase a psychopath, who thinks music matters more than life itself. If we don't find him, he'll keep on killing.'

Lola's tear-stained eyes widened. 'And all I've got to do is walk down the aisle.'

Her panic soon subsided. Emotions blew through her system like desert storms, quickly replaced by good humour. By the time I left she was making Neve giggle by blowing raspberries on her neck.

My phone rang as I returned to the patrol car. It took me a few seconds to identify the man's voice, with its muted American accent. The caller was Stanley Yacoub, asking me to visit him at the Royal

College of Music. His voice dropped even lower when he said that he would explain why at our meeting.

The atmosphere at the station was downbeat, detectives' faces grey and sleep-deprived. Pete Hancock was gazing at his computer when I arrived; his facial expression only lightened by a fraction when he saw me.

'You had a narrow escape,' he said.

'How do you mean?'

'There were booby traps of sulphuric acid over the basement windows at the museum, and the back door.'

'Where would he buy it?'

'It could be industrial drain cleaner, or he could have made it himself. Let water evaporate from battery acid for a few days, and it becomes a hundred percent caustic. You can leave it in the open for days, it'll still burn through anything it touches.'

I suppressed a shiver. 'Is there any news on last night's phone call?'

'The GPS is accurate to three hundred metres.' He shunted a piece of paper across the desk. It held a map from a network provider, tracking the phone's SIM card.

'He rang me from the heart of Soho?'

'Chances are he was on the move. The piano music could have been a recording.' Hancock carried on peering at his computer screen with rapt attention, like he was gazing into a black hole.

I studied the printout again. The map showed a blurry outline of Leicester Square and Covent Garden, the red dot falling between Frith Street and Soho Square. Stone had called me from the city's most raffish neighbourhood. It had smartened up in the past decade, with fewer massage parlours, Turkish baths and strip clubs, but it still knew how to party. The area flooded with students, tourists and office workers keen to have fun every night of the week. No one would have noticed a good-looking young man on his phone outside a pub, while a pianist tinkled the ivories outside, but it seemed unlikely that Stone could be holding Mori near where he'd dumped Sacha Carlisle's body. The area was crammed with pubs, restaurants and shops. It would have taken luck and a strong nerve to drag a reluctant victim through streets that never slept.

I felt a pulse of concern when Burns finally arrived, with Angie in tow. His face was paler than before, jaw clenched as he took his seat, but once the meeting got underway he threw me a quick, unguarded smile. There had been progress on finding an image of Adrian Stone from the CCTV at the Royal Albert Hall. The IT guys had provided a blurred shot of him crossing the car park towards the stage door, but Stone bore little resemblance to the young man I assessed at Rampton. He'd shaved his head and looked leaner and darker skinned, dressed in a smart blue suit. Stone was acting the part of a young professional, demonstrating his chameleon abilities. It frustrated me that he would have found a different disguise since the image was taken.

'This will be on every news bulletin tonight. Someone's got to recognise him,' Burns said. 'But we're still having no luck with pictures of him and Asako Mori. He must have taken her from exit six, down an alleyway to Kensington Gore. The guy did his homework; he'd have needed time and energy to plot a route with no cameras. We've had no sightings from pedestrians or cab drivers yet.'

The rest of the meeting contained plenty of leads, but no certainties. The bank accounts of everyone Stone had been in contact with were being checked to see if anyone could have given Matthew Briar cash, before Stone went missing, but no unexplained transactions had been found. Little progress had been made on the phone Stone had called me with the night before. It was a different pay as you go mobile from the one used to phone his sister. The GPS had tracked it to a side street in Mayfair which had been thoroughly searched. Stone had probably thrown the sim card down a drain after the call, then vanished into the ether.

I stayed in the room with Burns when the meeting ended. His hulking shoulders were bunched tight as he rubbed the back of his neck.

'The bugger's enjoying himself.' His voice was a low Scottish burr.

'Have your teams been watching Ben Wrentham and Bella Sanderson? If he's abducted one former classmate, they're vulnerable too.'

'We're keeping watch.'

'Both of them worry me. They've still got feelings for Stone, after all this time.'

'Neither of them has seen him for a decade.'

'If you fixate on someone, the feelings never completely die. There's a chance Briar would target Stone's old friends to enlist their help. Take a careful look at them.'

'Angie's checked already.' His eyes scanned my face. 'Pete told me about the museum. It bothers the hell out of me that you could have been covered in acid burns.'

'Thank God Sam Wyedale's recovering. She deserves a promotion for keeping a co0l head.'

He frowned. 'Nothing gets to you, does it? You're always so bloody rational.'

'That's not true.'

His fingertip grazed my temple. 'What's going on behind all that calm?'

'A will to survive.'

His face hovered inches from mine. 'I'll make bloody sure of it.'

Someone thumped on the door before he could continue. Reg stood in the corridor, his expression disgruntled as he explained that we needed to leave, or I'd be late for my next appointment. Burns was already back at his desk, thumbing through evidence reports. I tried to forget how tense he'd seemed on the drive to Mayfair, but concern nagged at me. Burns had regained his health since his heart bypass operation three years before, losing weight, exercising regularly and following his cardiologist's advice, but the strain of the case was punishing. The possibility of him getting sick again worried me more than the dangers I faced.

Reg insisted on escorting me upstairs to Stanley Yacoub's office when we reached the Royal College, a cacophony of instruments blaring from the practice rooms. It was only when we reached the third floor that my bodyguard stopped growling, eyes as alert as a Rottweiler's when he promised to wait by the main entrance. Stanley Yacoub seemed unruffled when he greeted me, his manner calm and urbane. He was dressed in a pale blue shirt with knife-edge creases, well-cut black trousers. I guessed that his friends kept his wardrobe stocked with classic items. He sat opposite me on his piano stool, long-fingered hands balanced on his knees.

'I don't want to waste your time,' he said. 'I thought of something, but it could be irrelevant.'

'It's okay, the trip here was a relief. I needed fresh air.'

'I listened to extracts from my archive. My students record essays, then submit them as sound files. It's easier than getting everything transcribed into braille.'

'Something caught your attention?'

'I've kept Adrian's essays. His voice is flat most of the time, but his final year project was on Chopin; suddenly you can hear the passion surfacing.'

'Is that relevant in some way?'

His vague gaze drifted towards me, settling a fraction wide of my face. 'There's only one other subject he talks about with the same excitement.'

'What's that?'

'The students had to pick their ideal venue. Some chose Sydney Opera House, or La Scala, but Adrian selected the Albert Hall. I can send you the recording of him reading his essay.'

'Can I hear the beginning now?'

'It's on my computer. Go ahead and open the file.'

It took me several minutes to navigate Yacoub's archive. An odd feeling tingled up my spine when Stone's teenaged voice filled the room, clear and confident.

'Queen Victoria commissioned the building after her husband died. We have to remember that the Royal Albert Hall is a monument to human suffering, as well as creativity. When the foundation stone was laid six years after Prince Albert's death in 1867, Victoria was still in mourning. She grieved for the rest of her life, but the monument to her husband's memory has hosted the world's greatest pianists and composers, from Wagner and Rachmaninoff, to Vladimir Horowitz.'

I pressed the off button, casting Stone into silence before he could list any more heroes. The teenager must have recorded the essay weeks before his killing spree, his belief in the connection between creativity and pain already established.

'What's the link?' I asked.

'It was his ambition to perform at the Albert Hall,' Yacoub replied. 'He missed two opportunities: I bet he's obsessed by the place.'

I looked out of the window at the huge concert venue, sunlight glinting from small windows that studded its domed roof. Adrian Stone would have gazed at it every day, imagining a packed auditorium, thousands of people giving him a standing ovation. I'd treated plenty of performers for depression and anxiety, all desperate for the next curtain call, but Stone's craving for an audience outdid them all. He was prepared to kill to keep the country's attention focused on him.

'Maybe you think I'm off track.' Yacoub's face was blank as he waited for my reply.

'Not at all. I was wondering if you could give me a tour of the concert hall.'

He nodded, smiling. 'My students rehearse in the Elgar Room, twice a week. I've got an entrance pass.'

'Could we go now?'

'Sure, I may stumble a few times, but I know the place back to front.'

Reg looked surprised when he saw me with Yacoub, my hand on his arm like sweethearts going for a stroll. He looked disapproving when I explained my plans, but I set off without looking back. The fact that Stone had abducted Asako Mori from the venue made me determined to understand why the place fascinated him. The teacher's gentle courtesy put me at ease, even though it felt odd to walk arm in arm with a complete stranger. Yacoub told me that the college had been subdued since the death of Gareth Keillor, some of the students in needing of counselling. Anger simmered in his tone of voice, revealing his desire to have his colleague's murder avenged.

I had visited the concert hall once before, as a child, for the last night of the proms. All I noticed then was the heaving crowd, wild cheering, and the chorus of *Jerusalem,* loud enough to raise the roof. The experience hadn't prepared me for the scale of the place when it stood empty, as I accompanied Yacoub to the front of the stalls.

'Pretty impressive, isn't it?' he said.

'Unbelievable.'

At eye level the curved stage was as wide as a football pitch, to accommodate performers and a full orchestra. Yacoub explained that the huge circular disks hanging from the ceiling were sound diffusers, made of fibre glass, to silence the domed roof's echo.

'The place holds five and half thousand,' Yacoub said. 'It was built for nine thousand originally, with seats going up another level, but health and safety won't allow that now.'

'Can we go on stage?' I asked.

Yacoub looked surprised. 'The steps are left of the stalls.'

My jaw dropped when I gazed out into the auditorium. Red velvet seats towered hundreds of feet above us, gold leaf adorning ornate plasterwork. It was a monument to Victorian excess, when the empire's wealth must have seemed limitless; the soaring lines reminded me of the grandeur St Paul's Cathedral, the place intended as a temple to music. Only Stone could connect such joyous architecture with human pain. Lighting engineers were completing a dry run while I admired the domed ceiling, patches of light appearing then dimming again at our feet. A grand piano stood centre stage, its frame gleaming under a single spotlight. When I touched a key, the note resonated with absolute purity. No wonder Stone believed the place was the ideal venue. It was jarring to remember that he had occupied the same spot only days before, intent on harming his new victim. It would have given him huge satisfaction to abduct his rival from a venue he longed to conquer.

'They say the place is haunted,' Yacoub said. 'A woman in a white gown drifts through the stalls at midnight.'

I scanned the boxes overhead, built for rich Victorians to observe the audience below. There were no ghosts now, except dust motes sparkling on the air, a few cleaning staff scouring the aisles, preparing for the evening performance.

'Why would this place haunt him?' I asked.

Yacoub turned in my direction, spotlight falling on his face. For an instant he could have been a principal actor, waiting for his cue. 'The greatest musicians have played here, for a hundred and fifty years. Adrian feels connected to them; performing here would have been another link in the chain.'

'The music he's leaving us has all been performed on this stage.'

My eyes scanned the auditorium again. The venue had been heavily guarded since Asako Mori was abducted. Reason told me that Stone could never return to carry out another crime, despite his fixation. He wasn't ready to lose his freedom, yet I felt sure his killing spree was linked to the place.

Yacoub showed me backstage after we descended from the stage. The maze of narrow corridors interested me as much as the auditorium. When I peered into a VIP dressing room it was small and airless, a narrow window illuminating the dingy interior. It amazed me that many star performers had used the space, including Caruso, Maria Callas and Pavarotti, in the days before celebrities required an entourage.

'Have you got time for a coffee?' Yacoub asked. 'There's a café on the first floor.'

'I never turn down a cappuccino.'

He seemed to have internalised the building's layout, only needing help when we climbed stairs or changed direction. The café turned out to be a smart tea room, tables covered in white linen, its windows overlooking Prince Consort Street. The teacher carried on discussing the building as we waited for our drinks, sharing his inside knowledge. The place had been used for boxing matches, circus events and political rallies during its long history. More recently it had hosted pop concerts, as well as classical ones, including visits by Elton John and Paul McCartney.

'But you're not interested in those, are you?' I asked.

He laughed. 'Do I seem that strait-laced?'

'I just assumed that pop and classical never mixed, like oil and water.'

'Here's my guilty secret: I brought my niece here, to see Kylie Minogue. She rocked the place. People were dancing in the aisles.'

'You strike me as the Beethoven type.'

'A change is as good as a rest,' he said, his smile hesitant. 'Are you married, Alice?'

The unexpected question left me floundering. 'My partner's a detective.'

'But you haven't tied the knot yet, so I'm in with a chance. Maybe we'll go to a concert someday.' His smile had only narrowed by a fraction. 'I like the sound of your voice.'

'It's a boring South London drone.'

'I don't agree, it's slightly husky. I find it attractive.'

I felt a moment's discomfort. We had spent the past hour arm in arm; making him wonder if I was available, even though I'd been so too focussed on Stone to notice his reactions.

'Stop charming me, before you turn my head. Is it okay to call you again, if I need help with the music Stone's leaving?'

'Any time. Is the investigation making progress?'

'We're getting there, but I can't give details.'

Yacoub gave a nod of agreement, then replaced his cup so precisely in the centre of its saucer, it was easy to forget that he'd been blind for years.

53

Stone is masquerading as a tourist today, a cheap camera slung from a strap around his neck, sunglasses and baseball cap concealing his face. He stands at the junction of Kensington Gore and Prince Consort Road. The view reminds him of everything he's lost, students spilling from the music college for their morning break, filling him with envy. If he could turn the clock back, he would practice until the janitor appeared at nightfall, jangling his keys.

He turns his head a fraction to watch the Albert Hall. Security has been reduced already. Yesterday three squad cars were parked on the forecourt, but now there are only two. Soon the police will shift their attention away from the site, believing that lightning never strikes twice. He should move on before anyone spots him, but his eyes keep being drawn back to the grandeur of the place. Classical figures adorn the walls, picked out in pale stone, spring sunshine turning the leadwork on the roof to silver. The building pulses with history. Stone can imagine a chain of legendary musicians and composers walking inside: Wagner, Bizet, Berlioz. He can't let another chance to follow them slip through his hands.

When Stone's gaze falls on the main entrance, his heartbeat stutters. A man and woman are walking towards him, arm in arm. He shields his face with the camera, framing them in the viewfinder, as the shutter snaps. Stanley Yacoub is being guided across the tarmac by Alice Quentin. It's a stunning act of betrayal, yet they look unafraid. The pair are only a few metres away. He could pull the kitchen knife from his pocket and finish the woman who destroyed his one chance of liberty in moments. Instead he turns away, as though he's taking another photo. They pass close enough for Quentin's voice to taunt him. His desire to make her suffer increases; he can picture her chained to a piano stool like Asako, with no prospect of escape. He lets another minute elapse before strolling away.

54

I could tell something was wrong from the mood in the incident room. The energy and noise had been replaced by quiet discouragement. Tania's shoulders were hunched as she checked phone messages.

'Has something happened?' I asked.

'Melissa Stone went to Richmond High Street with her aunt; they were shopping for food in Marks and Sparks, then she vanished. It happened so fast the guards didn't see a thing.'

'You think Stone's taken her?'

Tania shook her head. 'It doesn't look that way. Her aunt thinks she slipped away while she was paying.'

I blinked in disbelief. The last time I saw Melissa Stone, she had seemed petrified, yet she had fled from her aunt and uncle's protection.

'Survivor guilt's getting to her.'

'How do you mean?' Tania looked unconvinced.

'Imagine how you'd feel if one of your siblings wiped out your immediate family, leaving you sole survivor. She's convinced he broke out of Rampton to finish what he started, blaming herself for the other deaths. Melissa wants to be a sacrificial lamb.'

Tania shook her head. 'If my brother acted like Stone, I'd have him gunned down.'

'She was thirteen when it happened. The tragedy arrested her development; I'm not surprised she's regressing.'

'Don't use psycho-babble, Alice,' she snapped. 'I don't need it.'

'The trauma has made Melissa feel like a child again, with no defences, desperate to stop her brother killing. She's likely to go back to the house in Richmond.'

She gave a crisp nod. 'That makes sense. I'll get a team over there.'

'Call me, when she's picked up. She's very vulnerable.'

Tania was already barking instructions at one of the detectives. She kept her toughness concealed behind a glossy veneer most of the time, but glimpsing it made me admire her even more. Behind her sophistication was a dedicated cop who relished getting the job done.

I logged onto a computer and studied the map of Stone's murder sites on HOLMES 2 again, the locations forming a ragged triangle, at the heart of London's West End. My eyes scanned his stamping ground: from Brook Street to Kensington Gore, with the Albert Hall at its heart. I rubbed my hand across my eyes, afraid that frustration and tiredness were making me imagine things. Could Stone's sense of failed destiny be making him kill those who held him back, all of his violence centred around his favourite venue? When I looked through the window an hour later, Burns was holding court outside the station. His back was turned, but his body language was still easy to read; unlike most people, he never fidgeted under pressure. He looked immovable as a statue, ignoring the camera lenses thrust in his face. My first instinct would have been to back away, but he didn't flinch. I focused again on my computer screen, ignoring decisions that needed to be made, once the case closed. My personal life was on hold until Stone was caught.

I was still mulling over the facts when I left the incident room that afternoon, so preoccupied I didn't see Asako Mori's father waiting in the corridor, until he stepped into my path. He looked immaculate, the parting in his hair straight as an arrow, but his skin was ashen, eyes shadowed by lack of sleep.

'Could we speak please, Dr Quentin?'

'Of course, follow me. We can use an interview room.'

The man's anxiety grew more obvious once we were alone. Sounds drifted through the door as we sat down: an offender protesting about the state of his holding cell, a siren wailing in the distance, the low hum of traffic. Mr Mori seemed oblivious, his face solemn when he finally spoke.

'No one will tell me about Asako, but you seem honest. Please tell me the truth.'

'There's been no more progress. I'm sorry, I hope we'll have news soon.'

'My daughter's been gone forty-eight hours. Please tell me if she's dead or alive.'

'I wish I knew.' The desperation on his face forced me to carry on. 'Asako's case is exceptional, Mr Mori. I'm sure you're reading the papers, you know that Adrian Stone normally kills his victims fast. But there's no sign yet that she's been harmed. Her musical gift might help; Stone may give her special treatment.'

'You think my daughter's alive?'

'It's possible, yes.'

Mori slumped back in his seat, as if an elastic band holding him upright had suddenly been released. After a few seconds he regained his composure and produced a faded snapshot of a black-haired girl of five or six, standing in sunlit gardens, beaming at the camera.

'She was happy then, always singing and dancing,' he said quietly. 'How can she be in so much danger, when she hasn't begun to live?'

'I don't understand.'

'Asako has no husband or child, only her piano, and an old man to worry about.' His voice was raw with suppressed fear.

'Your daughter's lucky you care so much.'

His gaze locked onto mine. 'Find Asako, please. I promised her mother to keep her safe.'

Before I could reply, Mr Mori rose to his feet, inclined his head in a bow, then slipped away. It took me several minutes to control my emotions. Maybe it was because my nightmares were full of images of Gareth Keillor choking for air, and Sacha Carsdale's body folded into a rubbish bin. The old man would have little to live for, if his daughter died; his role as her protector would no longer exist. The passion in his eyes when he made his plea made me certain I was his last hope.

I'd intended to go to the FPU that afternoon, but the meeting left me shaken. I managed to persuade Reg to take me to Mayfair, despite initial moaning.

188

'I'm not a bloody taxi service.'

'My excellent company will keep you amused, Reg.'

'Don't bank on it.' He narrowed his eyes. 'An hour is all you get.'

'That should do it.'

He softened once we reached the car, describing his youngest grandson's passion for football. His gruff voice flowed past me as we circled Adrian Stone's territory. I was looking for buildings that would appeal to him, through a connection with music, but nothing revealed itself except the area's popularity. The streets thronged with tourists and diners leaving high class restaurants with smiles on their faces, as if the city was the safest place on Earth.

Stone can see his old rival is weakening. He left her chained to the wall by one wrist only, so she can drink from her supply of water, and piss in the bucket, to save him clearing up her mess. Her face is ghostly white in the flickering beam of his torchlight, but her expression shows that she's unbroken. He wants her to weep out apologies for everything she's stolen, but even though she's growing thinner each day, Mori still speaks to him like he's dirt on her shoe. He drops a packet of sandwiches into her lap, watching her claw at the cellophane.

'You're becoming an animal,' he says. 'Filthy and stinking.'

'Give me soap and water then. Let me wash.'

Stone shakes his head. 'Just play whatever I give you.'

Asako chokes down the last bite of bread. 'What do you want from me, Adrian?'

'We'll perform my duet, but only when you've perfected it.'

'Who will listen to a murderer's pathetic tunes?'

Her sneer makes him deliver a single blow to the side of her head, rage hardening the impact. Mori's body crumples to the ground; she doesn't respond when he tried to pull her upright. The sight of her lifeless form makes Stone panic. He needs her alive until the performance is complete. He leans down to shake her shoulders, the girl's head lolling on her chest.

I returned to Burns's flat, but by evening there was no still sign of him. After running flat out on his treadmill for an hour, I felt like a hamster on a wheel; the exercise had produced aching lungs and a hard sweat, but my frustration remained. At eight p.m. I called for an update, surprised that he picked up straight away.

'Where are you?' he asked.

'At yours. Why?'

'Melissa Stone's been found. She's being taken to Guy's hospital in an ambulance; the paramedics can't calm her down.'

'I'll be in the parking area, behind casualty.'

I grabbed my coat and ran downstairs at full pelt, to find Reg half asleep in the patrol car. Driving down Southwark Bridge Road gave me time to gather my thoughts. I had worked as a clinical consultant at Guy's for years, so it felt like a return to familiar ground. I put through a call to my old head of department, Dr Hari Chadha, as the car neared London Bridge, relieved that he was on night duty. The regency buildings of the hospital's campus pressed in on me as I jogged across the quadrangle.

Hari was waiting in the docking area, hands buried in the pockets of his white coat. He wore a saffron turban with matching tie, beard neatly trimmed, his appearance much the same as when he'd offered me a job a decade before. When he reached out to hug me, his dark eyes were calm and unblinking.

'You sounded upset, Alice. Are you okay?'

I explained that Melissa Stone had been found wandering an hour ago. It had been judged necessary to bring her in for acute mental health care. Hari's eyebrows rose.

'She might be better with a CPN at home.'

His statement made perfect sense, community psychiatric nurses provided a good service, and acute mental health wards were frightening places. All of the patients admitted for short in-patient care suffer from delusions, psychosis or mania, but it was clear the paramedics had made the right call. Melissa Stone huddled inside the ambulance, babbling to herself. When I approached her, she lashed out, hands curled into claws. I stood back to let Hari work his magic. He climbed into the van, sitting opposite her, not moving a muscle.

'You've been brought here to rest, Melissa. Why not come inside and we can talk?'

I couldn't tell whether she'd heard, but her frantic hand gestures slowed. After twenty minutes Hari had coaxed her from the ambulance into a wheelchair.

'I'll take you inside,' he said. 'You're perfectly safe.'

The girl's wild-eyed panic was still there as the wheelchair spun away, but at least she was accepting medical support. Once she was admitted, Hari instructed the nurses to give her another milligram of Lorazepam, to top up the sedative the paramedics had administered, explaining that diagnosis could wait until she'd calmed down. Afterwards we sat in the canteen, Hari's face contemplative as he sipped mint tea.

'You didn't tell me you were forensic lead on the Adrian Stone case, Alice.'

'It's taking its toll. Melissa's not in a good way, is she? Hyperanxiety, disassociation and speech problems.'

'It could just be acute panic disorder.'

'She's got good reasons to be afraid. Her brother's out there somewhere, butchering his friends and enemies.'

Hari's calmness faltered. 'She's lived through the worst tragedy imaginable, poor girl. Let's check her NHS records.'

We spent the next half hour in his office studying Melissa Stone's notes, and discussing treatment options. She had been diagnosed with childhood anxiety, before her brother wiped out her relatives, proving my theory that the family home had been a tinderbox. The girl had experienced stress-induced symptoms from primary school onwards: attention deficit, speech problems, eczema.

Her condition had stabilised as she matured, but Stone had reduced his sister to breaking point again. When we returned to the psychiatric ward, she was in a single room, drifting in and out of sleep. Hari watched in silence before stepping outside.

'Let's not disturb her, Alice. What she needs now is rest; with luck we can avoid a section order.'

'She'll need police protection.'

'You think he's followed her here?'

'Stone's capable of anything, that's what worries me.'

He touched my shoulder. 'When this is finished, come back to us. I miss your light touch with patients. We'll have a vacancy for a consultant clinician in June.'

I gave a shaky laugh. 'That's very tempting right now.'

'Promise me you'll think about it.'

The patrol car was waiting on double yellow lines outside the exit, Reg chuntering about me running too fast for him to keep up. I glanced back at the hospital tower, dwarfed by the needle point of the Shard, trying to locate my old office on the twenty-fourth floor, but knowing it was pointless. Hari's offer had broken the spell once and for all. A quiet job helping people heal would no longer satisfy me; the white-knuckle ride of forensic work had become an addiction, and there was no turning back.

57

It's midnight when Stone emerges onto the street. Mori is barely conscious, but he feels no sympathy. She will spend the night in blackness so opaque, she might as well be blind. He's the powerholder now. She will exist in light or darkness, live or die, according to his will.

He stands in the shadows between two buildings, deciding how to proceed. There's a message he must deliver, but it's essential no one finds him. He takes a night bus north to the suburbs. At Manor Park he spots an internet café and keeps his hood raised so the cameras above the doors can't catch his face. The brightly lit café is filled with north Africans, sending messages home. No one raises their head when he seats himself at a computer. It doesn't take long to create a YouTube account under an assumed name, then transfer a film clip from his memory stick. He would like to watch it again, but the risk is too great. Stone thanks the man behind the counter, then heads down the street at a rapid pace, certain that by tomorrow the first stage of Asako's punishment will be complete.

Lily is still awake when he gets back, sitting up in bed with a book propped on her knees. She smiles, but doesn't speak until he lies down beside her.

'Are you okay, Seth? You look worried about something.'

'It's nothing, angel. Get some rest.'

'You haven't been yourself the last few days. Is it money?'

'I just need to find some decent work.'

Her cool hands touch his face. 'I could help you write letters. I'd do anything to help.'

'Anything?'

Her eyes shine with trust. 'Of course I will. Whatever you ask.'

58

Thursday 31st March

I found Burns in his office the next morning, wading through evidence reports, five o'clock shadow turning into a beard, yet the usual pulse of attraction hit me as he met my eye.

'Do you want the good or bad news?' he asked.

'Good, definitely.'

'Stone was spotted on a bus last night, leaving Mayfair. The bad news is we don't know where the hell he is now.'

'It's better than nothing.' I studied the shadows under his eyes. 'When's the last time you ate?'

'Yesterday, some time.'

'Come on, I'll stand you breakfast.'

'There's a briefing soon. I can't just leave,' he said, frowning.

'You're coming with me.'

We ended up with a compromise. He wouldn't quit the building, so we hunkered at a table in the canteen, watching traffic crawl down St Pancras Way. Our breakfast left a lot to be desired. The coffee tasted like it had been stewing since the night before, but at least Burns seized his chance to refuel. He ploughed through scrambled egg, bacon, and a mountain of toast while describing Stone's foray into north London. He listened closely to my update on Melissa Stone's anxiety disorder: she would need in-patient treatment before she could be discharged from Guy's, but was staying in the acute psychiatric ward voluntarily. The colour still hadn't returned to his face, so I tried a distraction tactic to give him a break.

'I couldn't sleep last night, so I did an internet search. What do you think of this?' I showed him a photo on my phone, of an old-fashioned cottage, with a narrow strip of sea unwinding in the distance.

'Looks peaceful. Where is it?'

'Cornwall, near St Ives. We can rent it for a fortnight, when this is done. You could paint there, and it's got enough rooms for the boys to visit.'

'How would you keep busy?'

'I'd swim, walk, catch up on sleep. We might even do some talking, if you insist.'

His smile lit up for the first time that day. 'You wouldn't survive two weeks outside London.'

'I'd give it a shot.'

The swing doors clattered open before he could agree. Angie rushed over to our table, cheeks flushed as she came to a halt.

'We've got CCTV of Matthew Briar near Ben Wrentham's flat, boss.'

'You're certain it's him?' Burns asked.

'Come and see for yourself.'

'Get hold of Wrentham. I'll interview him when he's picked up.'

'You've done a great job.' I leant forwards to catch Angie's eye. 'I need to witness the interview, for signs of cover-up. It'd be best to see him at home.'

I thought about Ben Wrentham as I paced back to the incident room. The only reaction the music teacher had shown when Adrian Stone was mentioned was reverence for his former friend's talent. He had come over as awkward and unassuming, but could have been hiding complex feelings about his time at the Royal College, and unfulfilled ambitions. Certainly there was no doubt that the man caught on CCTV outside his flats was Matthew Briar; a thin figure, slightly stooped, his beak-nosed profile easy to identify from photos taken before Stone's attack ravaged his face.

Burns and I made little conversation as we drove towards Tower Hamlets an hour later, but our thoughts must have been following the same lines. If the teacher had helped spring Adrian Stone from Rampton, he must have more information. Wrentham was our best chance of finding Asako Mori alive. My mouth felt dry with anticipation as we pulled up outside an old council block on the

197

outskirts of Wapping. The teacher was being released from a squad car, his tow-coloured hair messy, jacket strained tight over his paunch. His mild-mannered expression had been replaced by a scowl, eyes glued to the tarmac as the uniforms led him inside. The tower block looked neglected, rubbish bags dumped by the entrance, the floor grimed with substances I didn't care to identify.

'This is what a teacher's wage gets you in London,' Wrentham announced bitterly. 'The lift hasn't worked for months.'

The uniforms traipsed after us, as I followed him to the sixth floor, keen to enter the flat before he could hide evidence. When we finally reached the teacher's apartment, only Burns and I followed him inside. I knew immediately that he lived alone. Grey patches of mould bloomed along the skirting board in his hall, the air tainted by microwave meals, damp and loneliness. Only Wrentham's living room held signs of his musical interests: framed posters from classical concerts adorned the walls, alongside a lute, several violins and a banjo hanging from the picture rail, his vinyl collection arranged on shelves below. The teacher's affability had vanished when we sat down, his manner taciturn when he spoke again.

'Your officers had no right to humiliate me in front of my pupils.'

'That wasn't intentional,' Burns said. 'We needed to speak to you urgently.'

'Why couldn't it wait till the end of the day?'

'We've got questions for you, about Adrian Stone.'

'Like I explained, I haven't seen him since we were teenagers.'

'But you've spoken to his contact.'

'What do you mean?'

'Matthew Briar visited you six weeks ago. Can you explain why?'

Wrentham blinked rapidly. 'The guy turned up unannounced. I found his behaviour threatening, to be honest.' Words gushed from his mouth at a hectic pace.

'Take a breath, then tell us what happened, from start to finish.'

'I'd never met him before, but Adrian had told him about our friendship at college. Briar found my school's address, then conned a receptionist into saying where I lived. He was so pushy I felt obliged to let him in, but regretted it immediately.'

'Why?'

The music teacher looked flustered. 'Briar told me Adrian was having a bad time at Rampton. If I gave him money, his life would be more comfortable.'

'That's all he said?'

'I handed over a hundred quid, to make him leave.'

'How come?'

'He was agitated. I knew he wouldn't go till he got what he wanted.'

'Why didn't you inform us about the visit?'

'It didn't seem important.'

'You're joking.' Burns stared at him. 'What did Briar say about his plan to help Stone escape?'

Wrentham shook his head vigorously. 'Nothing. I'd have called the police straight away.'

'You expect me to believe that?'

'If you're going throw accusations around, I want a lawyer.'

'All in good time, Mr Wrentham,' Burns replied. 'I need your permission to search your flat first.'

The teacher's mouth flapped open. 'Why should I let you crawl over my property? I've done nothing wrong.'

Burns gave a loud sigh. 'Then we'll wait here till I get a search warrant. You're in a vulnerable situation, Mr Wrentham. The man who helped Adrian Stone escape was seen here; that looks like collusion to me.'

'Is that a threat?'

'It's a statement of fact. My investigation could take days; you may as well cooperate, if you've got nothing to hide.'

'I can't stop you.' Wrentham spat out the words. 'Go ahead, do what you want.'

'Dr Quentin will do a walk through now, but my team will check more thoroughly later.'

Burns handed me some sterile gloves and I beat a retreat from the tension between the two men, who were sizing each other up, like boxers before a prize fight. Wrentham seemed to be living quietly, fridge loaded with pizzas, convenience food, a six pack of beer. His bathroom showed a chronic need for DIY, cork tiles peeling from the floor. The bedroom was no different; the divan bed was pushed against the wall, his bedside cabinet holding only a reading lamp and a novel by Jeffery Deaver. But when I reached his office, my pulse quickened. The cramped space was dominated by a narrow desk, his pin board filled with photos and newspaper clippings. On closer inspection, it looked like the pictures were internet downloads. Neat rows of men and women in their twenties, the type of portraits people use on social media, with wide unquestioning smiles. Wrentham had written each person's name below their image. The articles from the internet related to musical performances, prizes or productions. When I returned to the living room, the two men were still glaring at each other.

'Can you explain the information on your noticeboard, please, Mr Wrentham?' I asked.

His cheeks flamed. 'It's how I keep in contact with old friends from college.'

'You're being very systematic. There's even a picture of Adrian Stone.'

'Some of my classmates have become famous, like Asako. It's just something I enjoy.' His voice tailed away.

'Do you see much of the people you studied with?'

'Asako visits, when she's in London.'

'No one else?'

His eyes failed to meet mine. 'Work keeps me busy. I don't get much time for socialising.'

Burns explained that the rest of the interview would be conducted at the station, my mind whirring as we stood in the car park, waiting for a squad car to collect him. The teacher's interest in his classmates' lives had seemed far too keen. Maybe his life felt so unfulfilled, reading about other people's successes gave him a vicarious thrill. One thing had become obvious during our visit: his body language and speech patterns had been highly defensive when Matthew Briar's visit was mentioned.

Burns let out a string of curses as we reached the car. He was gazing down at his phone, a stricken look on his face.

'What's wrong?' I asked.

'A film of Asako Mori's been posted on YouTube.'

'Is she alive?'

A muscle ticked in his jaw. 'She's being tortured.'

My first concern wasn't for the talented young pianist. It was for her father, alone in his hotel room, waiting for his only daughter to return.

59

The pub where Stone meets Jeremy Grayson is a quiet watering hole in Charing Cross, with bare floorboards, the lunch menu scrawled on the wall in coloured chalk. Tourists sit in clusters, too preoccupied by their itineraries to notice his arrival. Stone spots his new agent immediately. He's holding court at the bar, wearing an expensive coat, shoes polished to a high glitter.

'Good to see you again, young man.' Grayson shakes his hand with a flourish, like they're meeting for the first time.

The agent's insincerity sets Stone's teeth on edge. Anger surfaces so fast, he has to stop himself lashing out. 'Why did you invite me here, Jeremy?'

'All in good time, let's have a drink before talking business.'

They sit at a corner table. Stone studies the beer in front of him, without touching the glass.

'Venues are asking about you, Seth, but they need background info. I'm amazed you've found work without a CV and publicity shots.'

'My gigs come from word of mouth.'

'You're a tricky bugger, aren't you? Everyone needs a website these days.' Grayson looks amazed.

'The internet bores me.'

'You should be more flexible.'

Stone pushes his drink away. 'Like I said, I won't sign unless you get me a slot at the Albert Hall.'

'I'm making progress. They hold lunchtime concerts for new performers, the bookers are sure to agree once they hear a demo.'

Stone guards his thoughts in silence. A daytime slot won't fulfil his fantasy of playing to a packed house, but it could be a foot in the door. He's still listening to Grayson's endless chatter when a stranger approaches their table. The man is middle-aged with a heavy build, gazing at Stone with a fixed smile.

'Sorry to butt in, but do we know each other? Your face is so familiar I had to ask.'

Stone shakes his head. 'You're mistaken.'

'Have you been on TV?'

'I'm a musician. You may have seen one of my gigs.'

'That could be it. What's your name?'

'Seth Rivers.'

'I'll look out for your next concert, sorry for barging in.'

The man backs away, his expression confused. Stone's heart is pounding, and when he looks up again the man has disappeared; it's possible he's phoning the police already. He makes an excuse to Grayson then escapes from the pub, joining hundreds of pedestrians strolling past theatres on the Strand. He adjusts the visor of his baseball cap, eyes obscured by dark glasses. The encounter is a reminder that the city is on red alert. His best chance of freedom is to keep moving.

Stone is still shaken when he reaches Embankment Tube station. He picks up an old copy of the Metro, from a seat on the platform. His own story appears on the second page, telling him that his sister has been hospitalised. Her delicate face appears in his mind, tantalisingly close, but still out of reach.

60

Burns had assembled his detectives to watch the film of Asako Mori, and for once the crowd's banter fell silent. The incident room smelled of coffee, stale cigarettes and frustration. The team's faces looked exhausted, everyone desperate for sleep. The back wall was filled by YouTube's red and black logo as Burns stepped in front of the projector, commanding the group's attention simply by raising his hand.

'This film has been removed from the internet, but thousands have seen it already. Concentrate on details, please. Anything you spot could help us work out where she's being held.'

At first I could only see blackness, then a yellow glow of candlelight. The images were accompanied by a rapid musical refrain, endlessly repeated. When the camera swung closer, Asako Mori was seated an upright piano, her face dark with bruises, hands jittering across the keys. When the shot panned down, a thick chain coiled around her waist. It didn't take genius to know that Mori was playing for her life. Before I could process the idea, the room erupted in an angry babble. The sight of the pianist trapped inside a torture chamber had triggered everyone's outrage, but Burns's expression was impassive when he spoke again.

'Don't let emotions trip you up. Save them till he's caught.'

His low baritone resonated from the walls. The urgency in his voice made me wish that I had a practical skill to offer, but my work relied on analysing human behaviour. I needed a tighter handle on Stone's thought patterns to predict his next movements, even though there was little evidence of his strategy, apart from the music left at each scene. I slipped outside before anyone could stop me.

Reg was waiting in the car park. I had developed a liking for my dour bodyguard, but was glad that he stayed silent as the car headed for Guy's Hospital, letting my thoughts settle. The film proved that Stone's confidence was increasing. Not only had he abducted Mori from a public venue, he had recorded her humiliation. This time his calling card was more complex than before. The music Mori had been playing would offer clues, but it hadn't been identified yet. He wasn't just communicating with the police team; his message had been displayed to the entire world. I could only hope that Mr Mori wouldn't witness his daughter's suffering.

'Will you be long in there?' Reg asked, when we reached Guy's.

'I'll let you know. I'm seeing Stone's sister again, if she can face visitors.'

'Don't leave the building without me.'

'I wouldn't dare, Reg.'

He cast me a grudging look as I left the car, as if the trip was a massive inconvenience. When I blew him a kiss he made a show of rolling his eyes.

I made myself take the lift to the psychiatric ward, even though the stairs were more appealing. My claustrophobia always intensified when I was under pressure, the metal walls squeezing closer as it approached the tenth floor. My balance was unsteady when the doors finally opened, so I stood on the landing until the dizziness passed, the windows offering an immaculate view. London's skyline sprawled west for miles, punctuated by skyscrapers, the Thames unwinding into the distance like a thread of dark grey ribbon. I could have stayed there indefinitely, watching a cyclorama of clouds pass overhead, but the need to get information from Melissa Stone was becoming urgent. Even in her weakened state I felt sure she could reveal secrets about her brother.

Melissa was sitting up in bed in her small room, gazing out of the window, with a dead-eyed stare. The young woman's face was clear of makeup, making her seem more vulnerable than before. Even though she was sedated, one harsh word could shatter her into a thousand pieces.

'How are you feeling, Melissa?'

'I can't sleep properly. The doctors won't let me go home.'

'I'm sorry. You've been under so much pressure, haven't you?'

Her numb gaze latched onto mine. 'Has he hurt someone else?'

'Not yet, but he's holding a woman captive.'

A flicker of anger crossed her face. 'Do you still want to know about my family?'

'It would help, and it might release some of your painful memories.'

When she spoke again her words were as sing-song as a lullaby. 'My parents weren't like other people; they believed that you make your own chances. If you failed at something, there was no one else to blame.'

'That sounds punishing.'

'I got off lightly. Most of their attention was focused on my brother and sister, because they were oldest. Mum and dad made Adrian practice, once they realised he had talent; they locked him in the music room for hours. By the time he was seven or eight, he went in there willingly, to escape their nagging.'

'What about Jenny?'

'They pushed her to do science, even though she preferred English. After a while she copied them.'

'How do you mean?'

'Her emotions switched off, she became like a machine.'

'Did your parents hurt you?'

'The punishments were psychological, not physical. They separated us all the time, locking us in our rooms for hours, with nothing to do. We weren't allowed computers, or books; sometimes it felt like I was going mad. No one would have believed me, if I'd asked for help.'

'You didn't tell anyone?'

'They would have gone mad if I'd betrayed them.'

'Did Adrian feel the same?'

Her gaze slipped to the ground. 'He broke the rules behind their backs. We all had different strategies. I cowered in my room, Jenny mimicked their behaviour, Adrian lied and hid his feelings. He snuck outside sometimes to visit my uncle.'

Something about her statement rang my alarm bells. 'Was he close to David?'

'They had music in common. It united them.'

'Did your sister get any support?'

'She didn't need it. Siding with my parents gave her special privileges.'

'It sounds like a prison camp.'

'That's how it felt. We couldn't have friends round, and dad had an eight-foot wall built around the house.'

'Did Adrian ever talk about his future?'

She gave a rapid nod. 'He wanted to be a successful musician, so no one could criticise him again. He had this fantasy about playing in the best venues.'

'Like the Albert Hall?'

'That was top of his list.'

Melissa's words chimed with Stanley Yacoub's statements, my thoughts slowly clicking into place. I felt sure his ambition to perform had grown stronger over time. Even now he might be planning a strategy to return there, under a new disguise. He had already boosted his confidence by abducting Mori from the main stage in broad daylight, his narcissism blunting his sense of risk.

I was about to ask Melissa another question, when a loud crash came from the corridor; the sound of a trolley clattering against a door. The girl reacted as if a bullet had been fired into the room, hands shaking uncontrollably, but it was her expression that troubled me most. Fear was etched across her features so deeply, it reminded me of the soldiers I'd treated for PTSD. Her sanity would fall apart if her brother wasn't recaptured soon.

61

Stone is playing the piano when Lily returns. He ignores her footsteps tapping down the hall, too immersed in Chopin's final nocturne, its melody slow and elegiac. It's only when he turns round that he sees her, dressed in her nurse's uniform, eyes glistening.

'That's beautiful, Seth. Only your music makes me cry.'

'I hope that's a compliment.'

'You make it look so easy. Have you played since you were small?'

The question makes Stone flinch. 'I started at primary school.'

'It must have been wonderful having a special talent.'

'Not really, I took it for granted, like kids do,' he says, turning away.

Lily perches beside him on the piano stool. 'Why not talk about your past sometimes? I can see it hurts you.'

'Looking back's pointless, Lily.'

'Not if it sets you free.'

Her cool fingertips trace his brow, like she's trying to erase bad memories. Stone lets her sooth him, but his peace is soon shattered once more by the peal of the doorbell. He grabs Lily's wrist, keeping her at his side, remembering the man who approached him in the pub. The police may have followed him here.

'Leave it,' he whispers.

'But it could be important.'

'We're not expecting anyone.' His gaze locks onto hers. 'Let's not spoil the moment.'

Her dark eyes return his stare. 'Something's frightened you, hasn't it?'

'Just ghosts from the past. I'll need your help soon, Lily. Are you ready?'

'Of course,' she says, kissing his cheek. 'Please tell me what's wrong.'

'You'll have to trust me, even if you're scared.'

'What will I have to do?'

'People are looking for me. I want us to stay together, if I have to leave suddenly.'

The girl slowly nods her head, eyes full of silent questions.

62

I arrived at Burns's flat by early evening, too preoccupied to bother with food, even though I'd skipped lunch. The film of Asako Mori imprisoned in a darkened room had killed my appetite. There was no way to tell whether she was still alive. Stone was treating her differently from his other victims, making me cling to the hope that her talent could be protecting her from Stone's violence.

I opened my laptop and began to work. My first task was to check the information gathered on Ben Wrentham since his arrest. I scanned the report from the search at his flat, and the IT specialists' analysis of his browsing history. Wrentham's life seemed oddly solitary for a man in his twenties. He rarely socialised with work colleagues, his last relationship ending a year before. His flat had raised the search team's suspicions; it was too clean and tidy for a bachelor pad, as if he'd been expecting the police to visit. The only incriminating evidence was a keen interest in the lives of former classmates. He kept reviews of the musicians' performances in scrapbooks, filed in alphabetical order. Wrentham had also followed those who had not pursued musical careers, using social media to observe the minutiae of their lives. A folder in his office was stuffed with newspaper cuttings reporting Adrian Stone's retrial and the court's refusal to reduce his sentence. The teacher loved archiving the lives of his peers, but did his fascination implicate him? So far he had only admitted to giving Matthew Briar money, although his involvement could have been far greater. Burns's team were checking his bank statements, to see whether he could have financed Stone's escape.

I was still immersed in the reports when Burns's landline rang at eight o'clock. I considered letting his answer machine take it, but picked up, in case it was the station.

Reg's gruff voice greeted me. 'Family visitor for you, Alice. Shall I send him up?'

'Go ahead, thanks.'

It could only be Will, because no one else knew where I was, but when I opened the door, Burn's oldest son stared back at me. Under the boy's cocky exterior it was easy to see that something was wrong, his eyes reddened by tears. I smiled in welcome then stepped back to let him into the hallway.

'Is dad in?'

'Sorry, Liam, he's not back yet. Have you tried his mobile?'

'Loads of times.' Teenage anger bubbled behind his politeness. I wanted to offer comfort but knew it would be unwelcome; that privilege belonged to his real mother. It was better to keep the conversation matter-of-fact.

'Have you texted him?'

'He never answers.' His voice crackled with distress.

'Come in and wait. I can make you something to eat.'

'I won't stay if he's not here.'

'Maybe I can help?'

The muscles in his jaw formed a rigid line. 'All he does is work. He never thinks about us.'

'That's not true, Liam. He talks about you…'

My sentence ended abruptly when the boy slammed out of the flat. I had been about to explain that Burns spoke of his sons all the time; they were the reason he got of bed in the morning. I called after him, but there was no reply from Liam, apart from his footsteps battering down the stairs. I put through a hasty call to Reg, asking him to give the kid a lift home, then let off steam by pacing the length of Burns's messy living room. All of his contradictions were on display, from his atmospheric landscape paintings, to a mountain of work folders on the table, beside books on Scandinavian architecture. I came to a halt by a cluster of photos on his wall. My eyes landed on one Burns had taken before the case began, in Edinburgh visiting his sister. His sons shared their father's dark hair and strong features, but Moray was still round-faced and innocent looking. Liam had already developed Burns's unblinking stare. He would be a force to be reckoned with when he grew up, but right now he was just a thirteen-year-old kid, yearning for his dad. He seemed to believe that his parents' divorce could be blamed entirely on his father's obsessive work ethic, but that would never change. Burns's reputation for solving dangerous cases kept him in demand, the pressure of his role rarely easing.

I pushed personal concerns aside and kept my mind focused on the case. I was still working when Burns finally returned, just before ten. He stood in the doorway, wide shoulders blocking the light, a carrier bag from a Chinese takeaway in his hand.

'If that's dim sum, you're forgiven for being late.'

'It's here,' he replied. 'Plus noodles, Peking duck, and beef satay.'

'Call Liam before we eat. He came round earlier, pretty upset.'

'About what?' Burns face blanked. 'Jesus, what date is it?'

'The thirty-first of March. Why?'

He gave a sigh of disgust. 'It's his sodding birthday. How did I forget?'

Burns scrabbled for his phone, apologies flying thick and fast once the boy picked up. I watched him eat humble pie while I collected cutlery and rooted in the fridge for drinks. He sat with his head in his hands for a full minute after the call ended, then gulped down most of the bottle of beer I handed him.

'Did he forgive you?' I asked.

'I'll have to buy him a mountain bike first.' He rubbed his hand through his hair. 'What's this job doing to me? It's turned me into a shit dad.'

'Come on, you adore your kids.'

Burns's frown deepened. 'That means bugger all. They judge our deeds, not words.'

'Get yourself a calendar then.'

'This job's wiped everything that matters from my head.'

The guilt on his face made me think of Adrian Stone's reluctance to forget anything, his violence motivated by past wrongs. Unlike Burns, he was living out the dramas of his childhood, punishing anyone that interrupted his dreams.

63

Stone waits until Lily's asleep before leaving the flat, then rushes through the quiet streets of the West End. There's hardly anyone around, except a few drunks weaving home after a big night out. The journey back to where Asako Mori is hidden is so familiar, he could make it in his sleep; he follows Cromwell Road, to the area known as the Albertopolis. Queen Victoria financed the public colleges and museums in her husband's memory, the ground saturated by the monarch's grief. Stone passes the V&A, then the Science Museum, glancing over his shoulder before hurrying on. Now he scales the brick wall into the compound, then descends the ladder into the tunnel. The black air reeks of damp as rats chase away from his footsteps.

Asako is asleep on the stone floor, wrists still tightly bound. She jerks awake when the torch beam hits her face, eyes blinking furiously. He can tell she's close to breaking point, but her voice is calm, even though her teeth are chattering.

'Let me go, Adrian. My father needs me with him.'

'Play for me, that's all that matters.'

She shakes her head. 'My hands are freezing. I can hardly move them.'

Stone ignores her complaint, pulling her into a sitting position. He has brought food and drink; it's important to keep her alive, until she's served her purpose. This time she ignores the fruit, bread and biscuits he drops in her lap.

'Eat up,' he says. 'Then get to work.'

When he prods her ribcage with the toe of his boot, she gulps down mouthfuls of bread, while he watches with

213

distaste, her hands filthy from the dirt floor. He waits in silence until she finishes eating, only the guttering candlelight illuminating the cavernous space.

Now he leads her to the piano, unbinds her hands, then instructs her to play a Brahms lullaby. The music relaxes him for the first time in days. The composer's anguish echoes behind each note: Brahms never married, in love with Schumann's wife for decades. Even his gentlest melodies resonate with loneliness. Stone lets sound wash over him, trying to imagine his future. He could start a new life abroad as Seth Rivers, taking Lily with him, but not until his destiny is fulfilled. He listens to the last notes of the piece and thinks of Alice Quentin, and all the others who betrayed him. But when silence finally returns, it's his sister's face that fills his mind.

64

Friday 1st April

The remains of the previous night's takeaway still littered the kitchen table when I woke to an empty flat. It was only seven a.m. but Reg had already arrived, his squad car blocking the entrance, as if I might try to bolt. My life felt so far beyond my control I decided to make an effort with my appearance for once, clipping my hair into a chignon. I chose a French navy suit from Hobbs, a jade green silk scarf, Italian leather high-heeled shoes. My freedom might be compromised, but it wouldn't dent my confidence. I trotted down the stairs with renewed confidence, but Reg gawped at me, open-mouthed. It was hard to tell whether the old timer was appalled or impressed.

'Why are you so dolled up?' he asked.

'It's what's called looking smart, Reg.'

'All that gunk on your face doesn't suit you.'

'I'll take that as a compliment on my natural beauty.'

Reg gave me a lecture on vanity during the drive. According to him women shouldn't waste money beautifying themselves, and men who dyed their hair were a laughing stock. By the time we reached the station my teeth were so firmly gritted, my jaw ached. Luckily my bodyguard had no idea how much I spent on clothes and makeup every month; the exorbitant sum would have triggered a heart attack.

The incident room had an atmosphere of quiet industry. Everyone was working steadily, taking phone calls, poring over CCTV footage or vetting evidence reports. Tania beckoned me to her desk as soon as I arrived.

'Great outfit,' she commented. 'But we're making no headway with the film of Asako Mori.'

I dropped onto a chair beside her. 'How come?'

'The IT guys put the music through sound recognition software; there are no matches.'

'You think it's original?'

'It must be.'

'If Stone's using his own composition, we're getting closer to what matters most to him.'

'But it won't lead us to the victim.'

'Clues could be buried under the surface; we'll need expert help to find them. Is Ben Wrentham ready to see us again?'

Tania's face hardened. 'He's chatting to his expensive lawyer in the interview room.'

Wrentham looked like he had spent a sleepless night in his holding cell, his face puffy, with uneven stubble peppering his jaw. His solicitor looked far more composed; the man must have been close to retirement age, with a shrewd expression and the weather-beaten skin that comes from decades of tropical holidays. The men listened in silence while Tania explained the purpose of the interview. We had agreed that she would question Wrentham, letting me focus on his reactions and body language, for signs of lying. He stood accused of being an accessory to murder, the tension in his stance easy to read, arms folded defensively across his chest.

'Mr Wrentham, the CCTV from your apartment block shows that Matthew Briar visited you twice, the first time for just over an hour. The second meeting lasted around twenty minutes. Can you tell us what you discussed?'

The teacher glanced at his lawyer before replying. 'I was intrigued at first; Briar said he'd been a musician too. It upset me to hear that Adrian was suffering at Rampton, but the bloke was really edgy. He kept asking for money, to help buy a new piano for Rampton's music room. I ended up giving him the cash in my wallet just to get him out. It was a relief to see the back of him.'

'Yet you welcomed him back another time.'

'I had no idea he was coming. He barged his way in.'

Tania gazed down at her notes. 'That's not what your neighbour says. Mrs Abbott saw you chatting to a dark-haired young man that evening perfectly amicably; he left your flat with an envelope in his hand.'

'That's circumstantial,' the solicitor snapped. 'Any number of people may have called at my client's flat that evening.'

'Not according to the CCTV,' Tania replied calmly. 'Why did you give him more money, Mr Wrentham? You withdrew five hundred pounds from your bank that afternoon. Did Matthew Briar take it all, to fund Stone's escape?'

The solicitor leant across to Wrentham, advising him to make no comment, but the teacher ignored his advice. When he spoke again, there was an edge of desperation to his voice.

'I honestly believed the money would go towards a new piano.'

'No one could be that naïve.' Tania stared back at him. 'Tell us the real reason why you gave him all that cash.'

A muscle ticked in Wrentham's cheek. 'I had a tough time at college. Most of the other students were much more talented than me, I was out of my depth. Adrian knew I admired him, and he let me hang around. It meant a lot to me. I thought I could make his sentence more bearable.'

'That doesn't explain why you're tracking all the students in your year.'

The teacher's gaze blurred. 'We're leading parallel lives. We enrolled at college on the same day, but no one knew who'd would win all the prizes. I'll always be close to them, whether they succeed or fail, like brothers and sisters.'

'That's an interesting fantasy, Mr Wrentham, but from my viewpoint it looks like cyberstalking. It's time to drop the fantasies and tell us where Adrian Stone's hiding.'

Tania's angry tone didn't help matters. Wrentham's lips closed in a narrow line, the interview closing abruptly, before he was taken back to his cell.

'What a freak,' she murmured, when the door closed. 'I'll keep going till he cracks. We can see him again this afternoon.'

'He'll open up faster if you show some sympathy. Treat him like another of Stone's victims, he's more likely to talk.'

'How do you mean?'

'Stone groomed him too. He was a manipulator, even in his teens.'

Tania's turquoise stare fixed on me. 'There's no limit to the damage he's done, is there?'

Back in the incident room I concentrated again on the minute-long film of Asako Mori. It looked like a scene from a horror movie: a beautiful young woman, chained to a piano, forced to play for her captor, proving that Stone enjoyed Gothic punishments. It was only after I'd watched the clip a dozen times that details registered. The candles guttering on the ground cast little light on her surroundings, but I could see that the brick walls led to an arched roof. The curved ceiling made me think of Nissen huts, and railway arches, but London was full of abandoned buildings with cellars. Surely Stone would choose a hiding place inside his favourite West London territory, with a connection to music? I forced myself to watch the clip again, aware that the girl might still be trapped in that cloying darkness, struggling to breathe.

65

Stone waits until Lily leaves the flat before using her laptop. He searches for a list of London hospitals then works systematically, phoning each switchboard, using the same message each time.

'Interflora here. We've got flowers for a patient called Melissa Stone. I need the name of her ward, please, so we can deliver.'

The Royal Free, Barts, King's and the Royal London all deny knowledge of his sister. It's only when he contacts Guy's that the receptionist's voice falters.

'I'm not supposed to share patients' details.'

'Can we bring them to the front desk?' he asks.

'That would be fine.'

'No problem. Thanks for your time.'

A broad smile crosses Stone's face when he switches off his phone. Now he can pinpoint the exact building where his sister is lying in her hospital bed, breathing recycled air, tainted by bleach and sickness. Emotions wash through him as he imagines stepping through the doorway into her room, after fantasising about it for nine years.

Stone rises from the table and crosses to the piano. He practices scales at first, notes deadened by the confined walls, but the act of playing still feels liberating. Soon he will play in a venue grand enough to match his talent, its architecture loaded with history. He's still lost in his fantasy when the front door opens. Panic hits home immediately; Lily's shift won't finish for hours.

'Who's there?' he calls out.

'Just me, lad. I heard you practising, so I let myself in.'

Lily's father stands in the open doorway, scanning the room avidly. His gaze settles on the open computer, then the handwritten sheet music strewn across the table, as though he's searching for evidence.

'Lily's at work, Patrick. She won't be back till seven.'

'It's time you and I had a little talk, isn't it?'

Stone feels his muscles tighten. The old man's eyes fix on his face, but behind his thick glasses, his expression is hard to read. His scrutiny makes Stone long to lash out, but he keeps his hands locked at his sides.

66

Burns held an impromptu briefing at eleven a.m. Half of his detectives were chasing witness reports off-site, but more than twenty staff piled into the meeting room. I could read Burns's frustration in his body language. He looked isolated at the front of the room, like he was surrounded by a force field no one could penetrate. When he finally addressed the team his tone was icy.

'Stone abducted Asako Mori four days ago, in broad daylight, but we're none the wiser. The press are having a bloody field day. He can't have vanished into thin air. I want all CCTV footage inside a thousand metre radius reanalysed. Go back to the Albert Hall, talk to staff again, find the details we're missing and get results. Angie's going to recap what we've got on Stone since his escape, then the extra duties will be divvied up.'

Someone gave a quiet groan at the back of the room, making Burns head snap back.

'You think life's hard now, pal, do you? A young woman's being held by a maniac who enjoys cutting people up. Your daughter, or your wife, could be locked in his torture room. Any slacking will result in instant suspension. Do you understand?'

Burns's voice was potent as undiluted whisky when he scanned the room again, his gaze lingering on each face. He looked more like a boxer psyching himself up for a fight than a senior detective, a million miles from the quiet man who could sit for hours, completing a drawing in his flat. I'd have crossed the street to avoid him in such a foul mood, but both parts of him interested me. When I looked up again, Angie was at Burns's side, studying her case notes. Her expression was sober as she began to speak.

'Adrian Stone has been on the run since Monday, March the 21st, when he absconded from Rampton, killing two guards and wounding Matthew Briar. The next afternoon he abducted his former tutor, Gareth Keillor from the Royal College of Music. Keillor's body was found on Wednesday 23rd March, butchered and covered in stab wounds. His corpse was left in the boot of his car, outside forty-eight Dover Street, where Chopin composed the music found at the first crime scene. Then the forensics team discovered Keillor's heart buried in the grounds of his childhood home, late on Thursday the 24th. Stone killed Sacha Carlisle the following day. Her body was left on Frith Street in Soho on Saturday 26th March. A Glenn Gould sonata was playing on her headphones. The piece was first performed at the Royal Albert Hall, which is where he abducted the concert pianist Asako Mori, on Monday 28th March. Since then, he's been taunting us, uploading a film of Mori onto YouTube. He's called his sister Melissa and Alice Quentin on the phone, playing pieces of recorded music. Melissa is being treated at Guy's hospital for phobic anxiety disorder.' Angie closed her notebook and looked in my direction. 'Alice, can we have your update now?'

Most of the faces were sceptical when I rose to my feet. Police teams accept help from forensic psychologists on sufferance, believing that conventional detection trumps analysing a killer's mind set every time, despite evidence to the contrary. I touched a button on the laptop at my side, projecting the map I'd downloaded from HOLMES 2 onto the wall.

'The marked area is Stone's spiritual home. The kill sites stretch from Marylebone in the north, down to the edge of Mayfair. They're all within a two-mile radius of the Royal College of Music, the scene of his greatest disappointment. He was a star student, but when they forced him out, his violence was unleashed. His obsession with music has grown stronger since his captivity; he won't be able to resist performing in public, despite the risks. Check pubs, piano bars and clubs inside this catchment. Find out if anyone matching Stone's description has played at those venues.' I turned to study the map more closely. 'It's likely that Mori is hidden on one of these streets. You'll need to increase your foot patrol along Exhibition Road and Cromwell Road. I think he's living inside this neighbourhood. Stone's hoodwinked someone into helping him. Whoever it is, they've got a submissive personality and low self-esteem; their head's buried so deep in the sand, they won't realise their life's in danger. Put out the best CCTV shot of Stone on the next news bulletin, with a direct appeal to whoever's sheltering him. There's a chance we can panic them into talking to us.'

67

Lily's father shows no inclination to leave. Stone feels his intense stare on the back of his neck when he stands in the kitchenette, making coffee. His stomach twists with the knowledge that the old man may have guessed his identity, but Roberts's expression is calm, sunlight reflecting from his thick glasses.

'This place is too small for the pair of you, isn't it?' he comments. 'I'd help Lily to rent somewhere bigger, but she won't hear of it.'

'It suits us, for now,' Stone replies.

When he places the coffee mugs on the table, the old man's gaze doesn't shift from his face. He gives a narrow smile before sipping from his drink.

'Lily would give me hell, if she knew I was here. Can we keep it our secret?' Stone nods his head, waiting for the old man to explain his visit. 'Tell me your plans, lad. My girl's not as strong as she seems. She needs someone to stand by her long term.'

Stone's fear of exposure suddenly drops away. 'I would never hurt her, Mr Roberts.'

'Is that a promise?'

'No one understands me better.'

'Good.' The old man's face hovers close to Stone's. 'But do you love her?'

'Yes.' The word emerges from Stone's mouth without conscious thought, leaving him shocked. 'She broke down my defenses.'

Lily's father releases a laugh. 'Her mother was the same. I couldn't look away; she hit me between the eyes. What about the future? You 'll need a proper home.'

Stone shrugs. 'I want her with me, whatever happens.'

'The pair of you will work it out.'

The confidence in his tone reminds Stone of his own father, and fear courses through him. He remembers the endless criticisms and the man's sublime certainty that he was right. Suddenly a haze of fury drops over him and he has to resist his urge to reach for his knife. When he reopens his eyes, Roberts is rising to his feet.

'I'll go now, lad. You've put my mind at rest.'

The old man slips away as quietly as he came, but Stone's peace of mind is shattered. When he sits at the piano again, the melodies have fallen silent.

68

An unexpected visitor was waiting for me at the station after the briefing. It seemed fitting to find Dr Frances Pearce in an interview room that resembled a prison cell, brick walls painted stark white, a table and chairs eating up most of the space. I felt a pulse of resentment for all the messages I'd left on her answering service with no reply, but there was no point in criticising. The psychiatrist looked ready to burst into tears, her thin face white with distress.

'This is unexpected, Dr Pearce.'

'I should have contacted you sooner. Sorry, it's been a tough time.'

'Better late than never. You've spent more time one-to-one with Stone in the past nine years than anyone else.'

The psychiatrist studied my face. 'Did you read my clinical notes?'

'Cover to cover. They don't give much away.'

'It wasn't easy to describe our dialogue.'

'Why?'

'I never felt completely safe, even though he was handcuffed to his chair, with a guard outside the room. It was a constant power struggle.'

'Can you explain why?'

'He brought things to our sessions: essays and poems at first. His writing was disturbing but fascinating at the same time. Then he started collecting quotes from famous musicians, artists and writers, from books in Rampton's library. They all supported his belief that suffering produces creativity; I thought you might like to see an example.'

She pulled a dog-eared piece of paper from a folder. The page contained dozens of quotations, copied in Stone's tense script. My eyes lit on one by the artist Francis Bacon: 'The act of birth is a violent thing, and the act of death is a violent thing. And, as you surely have observed, the very act of living is violent.'

'A manifesto for brutality,' I said.

'Adrian sees it as a vital part of his talent. I couldn't make him accept that the idea was a symptom of his illness.'

'Why did you argue for his release?'

'I thought he'd made progress, but it was a trick. He needed my endorsement, for the Home Office to reassess him.'

'Have you got anything else to share, Frances?'

'Only that his violence will worsen. It feeds his music, and that matters to him more than anything.'

'He certainly seems to revel in other people's suffering.' I studied her pale features again. 'You said you never felt safe with him. What did you mean?'

'I was going through a bad divorce.'

'Stone tuned in to your distress?'

'He drew things from me, piece by piece. Private information about my marriage and kids.'

'Did you help him escape, Frances?'

She shook her head vehemently. 'I made a misjudgment, but I'm not crazy.'

'No one implied that.' I kept my voice gentle. 'Can you guess where he is now?'

'Adrian had this fantasy about an ideal life. He dreamed of living near Kensington Gardens, by his old college, so he could use the flat when he performed.' He words faded into silence.

'He may be doing just that.'

Dr Pearce seemed stricken by guilt, for allowing Stone to worm under her defenses. I couldn't help wondering if she was more involved that she claimed. She had denied assisting Matthew Briar, but might be lying, to save face. Helping a convicted murderer abscond was a far more serious offence than professional misconduct. I spent an hour in her company, trying to prise out details, but most of her answers were too general to help locate Stone. She admitted that the dialogue between them had become personal, not professional.

'Will you stay at Rampton?' I asked.

'I resigned yesterday. They're bound to take away my license; it felt better to jump, before I was pushed.'

'Is anyone supporting you at home?'

She nodded her head. 'My kids are great, and we've got a holiday planned, but I'll miss my work.'

I couldn't provide a comforting reply. With the Board of Psychiatry's inquiry hanging over her, she had made the right decision. When I met her eye again, the emotions she'd been suppressing emerged in a burst of tears. I remained in my seat, but reached out to touch her hand. My work as a psychologist had shown me that it's best to keep silent when someone breaks down. Frances Pearce's intense sobbing signaled the loss of her career. Afterwards she seemed relieved to have unburdened herself, but too shaken to leave the station immediately, so I fetched her a glass of water, wishing I could help. She had broken the professional code of practice but nine years in Stone's company could have weakened anyone. Psychopaths' stories are so seductive, I might have fallen into the same trap.

69

Stone hides between office buildings on St Pancras Way. His vantage point gives a direct view of the police station's entrance, a few journalists loitering on the steps. He's still uncomfortable about talking to Lily's father. His feelings for the girl are so unfamiliar, it seems safer to concentrate on the next stage of his plan. He's certain Alice Quentin is hiding somewhere inside the ugly concrete building. Soon he'll find a chink in her armour, or her bodyguards will make a mistake.

Hundreds of people arrive and leave. He's still there half an hour later, when he catches sight of an unexpected face. Frances Pearce is dressed in a light green coat, expression serious as she lifts her collar against the cooling breeze. The sight of her is jarring. Until now, her memory drew no anger, because she was so easy to play. But now she's let him down. She must have been blurting out secrets; he can't guess how much information she's given away.

Stone follows her at a discreet distance, face concealed by his baseball cap and aviator sunglasses. She's walking slowly, her pale clothes standing out from a sea of black-suited businessmen, marching back to their offices from long lunch breaks. When he steps onto the escalator at Kings Cross, his breathing steadies, mind blank as a clean sheet of glass. Instinct is driving him now, not intellect.

The platform is so full, he almost loses her. A crowd of Japanese tourists are waiting for the Tube to deliver them to the British Museum or the National Gallery. Frances Pearce is three metres away, checking messages on her phone. He can tell she's been crying, eyes puffy and red-rimmed, but why should he care? She could have helped him, but never took the risk. The electronic board overhead announces a train's arrival in one minute, passengers surging towards the platform's lip. It's only when headlights blaze at the end of the tunnel that he steps forward, his pulse drumming in his ears.

'Traitor,' he whispers.

There's a squeal of brakes as Frances Pearce turns round, but it's too late. With one hard push he sends her sprawling across the tracks as the engine grinds to a halt. By the time someone screams, Stone has melted into the crowd.

70

Angie found me after my meeting with Frances Pearce. Her expression had lightened since the briefing and it was clear she had good news. Someone called Nancy Morris had called from a music venue in Soho; the woman claimed that Adrian Stone had been playing piano recently in the jazz club she managed.

'It's a good lead,' I said. 'Ronnie Scott's is inside his territory.'

'How come he's got the balls to perform, when he knows we're after him?' she asked.

'Stone doesn't think like the rest of us; he believes everyone should worship his talent. I'll come with you, and see what she can tell us.'

Ronnie Scott's Jazz Club was in the basement of a dilapidated building on Frith Street, fifty metres from the spot where Sacha Carsdale's body had been dumped. It was chilling to realise that Stone might have left the girl's body then calmly crossed the road to tinkle the ivories. The last time I'd visited had been years ago, to hear Jamie Cullum. The gig had passed in a haze of cocktails, dancing and sublime jazz, but every other detail had slipped my mind. Today the venue's doors hung open, admitting us to a large hall, with tables arranged cabaret-style around the stage. The furniture was shabby, parquet floor in need of varnish, but the reason for Stone's interest were obvious. For jazz buffs the club held as much cachet as the Albert Hall. Black and white pictures of stars performing on its small stage lined the walls, from Charlie Parker and Nina Simone to Herbie Hancock and Miles Davis.

I was still studying the pictures when footsteps tapped across the wooden floor. The woman who sashayed towards us was the essence of fifties glamour, black dress cinched at the waist by a wide red belt, dark hair swept into a beehive that must have required skill as well as patience. She was close enough to touch before I realised she was middle-aged. Her skin was chalk-white, deep lines grooved round her mouth.

'You got here fast, ladies,' she said. 'Why don't we take a seat?'

She perched on a chair while we sat down. Her manner was as brittle and self-conscious as a Hollywood star from the golden age.

'Can you tell us what you know about Adrian Stone, Ms Morris?' Angie said.

'Nancy, please. I could be wrong, but the idea's been nagging at me. He says his name is Seth Rivers.' She glanced down at her glossy nails. 'A young guy walked in a few weeks ago, bold as brass, asking for a gig. Normally I tell musicians to take a hike, but his audition was mesmerising. I agreed to let him close the set that Friday, and he went down a storm.'

'But you think he's Adrian Stone?'

'He's never given his address or phone number; he takes payment in cash.' Her gaze sharpened, as she scanned our faces. 'He hassled me for a headliner gig. When I refused, it felt like he could explode. There's something scary about him.'

Angie nodded. 'Did you notice anything else?'

'His girlfriend jumps when he snaps his fingers.'

'Do you know her name?' I asked.

The manager shook her head. 'She's here whenever time he plays.'

'Are there any photos of him?'

She looked sheepish. 'Our security camera doesn't work. I've been nagging the owners for weeks, but it never gets fixed. We don't let people take pictures during gigs, but I filmed him playing on my phone. Come backstage if you want to look.'

Nancy Morris's office was a cluttered, windowless space, desk piled high with a mountain of envelopes. She gestured at them, sighing.

'Agents send me brochures every day. It's a pity the world has thousands more musicians than it needs.'

She showed us the film on her computer. It was grainy, with dull lights flickering in the background. The pianist looked years older than Stone, bald, with a thinner face and dark eyes. But when I looked again, something about his fluid movements and arrogant smile changed my mind. Angie seemed unconvinced that we'd found our man, but took a copy of the film anyway.

'When's he due to play again?' I asked.

'I booked him for the opening set tonight, before the main act, but he may come by earlier to practise.'

'That's fine,' Angie said. 'I'll arrange the security.'

When she stepped outside to make calls, it was clear that behind her glossy sophistication Nancy Morris was afraid. If her suspicions were correct, she had hired a serial killer to entertain her clients. I tried to reassure her that anyone could have been fooled; if the pianist really was Stone, his disguise was incredibly convincing.

By the time we left, two unmarked cars had parked further down Frith Street, plain clothes officers slipping inside the building via the fire escape, to protect Morris. A look of excitement crossed Angie's face as she instructed the guards to ambush Stone once he arrived, but my thoughts returned to Asako Mori, her fate still unknown. Now there was a new victim to consider; if Stone had recruited a girlfriend, her life was in jeopardy too. He would kill her without remorse, whenever he chose.

71

Stone arrives in Soho earlier than planned. He marches towards Frith Street at a rapid pace, keen to bury himself in a world of sound, but halts on the street corner. Something looks different; a dark blue sedan is parked on the yellow lines opposite Ronnie Scott's. He ducks between two buildings, and soon his suspicions are confirmed. A squad car crawls past, performing a slow recce, his hands curling into fists at his sides. Someone at the club has blown the whistle, his latest disguise failing to protect him.

He slips down an alleyway, emerging minutes later on Tottenham Court Road. The crowds of shoppers infuriate him, the seething mass of humanity forms a perfect camouflage, but they obstruct his path. Now his fake identity will offer no protection whatsoever, and Lily will know the truth. Leaving the country isn't an option, until he can buy himself a new passport. Stone shelters under an awning, watching people stroll past, a young couple laughing jubilantly. He wishes he could share the pain he's experiencing, but forces himself to walk away.

It's evening by the time he returns to Asako Mori. The girl is conscious again, gaze weakening when he shines his torch in her eyes. She's crouched beside an abandoned piano, knees hunched against her chest, still chained to the wall. Now that one of his territories has been discovered Stone's paranoia is increasing. There's a chance someone might find his empire.

'Get up,' he snaps. 'We're going further underground.'

Mori scarcely moves as he undoes the chain. Stone's hand fastens around her arm, the tunnel narrowing as he drags her further from the light.

72

I did half an hour of yoga at the safe house that evening. I would have preferred to sprint through London's streets until anxiety evaporated through the pores in my skin, but contorting my limbs into complex positions brought nearly as much satisfaction. By the time I emerged from my shower, my skin was glowing, and the world felt steady again. I was searching the half-empty fridge for something edible when my phone rang. The voice belonged to Tania, her tone unusually tense when she greeted me.

'Is something wrong?' I asked.

'Bad news, I'm afraid. Dr Frances Pearce died soon after your interview this afternoon.'

My brain scrambled to catch up. 'What happened?'

'Suicide, we think, under a Tube train at King's Cross. Someone found her wallet on the platform.'

I listened in silence to the details of Frances Pearce's last actions. Apparently she had walked down St Pancras Way straight after our conversation, then thrown herself under a train. None of it made sense. The psychiatrist had seemed upset, not broken. She knew her career was over, but had been spending time with her family, with a holiday on the horizon. My experience of suicidal patients reminded me that they could rarely imagine a positive future, convincing me she'd been killed.

'She didn't take her own life,' I said quietly.

'We're checking every detail, Alice. The boss'll come and see you when he leaves Scotland Yard.'

I huddled on the settee, unwilling to accept her version of events. It was too coincidental that Stone's former psychiatrist had suddenly met a horrible death. I pictured her in the interview room, thin hands knotted in her lap, so burdened by guilt over her malpractice that she had quit her job, before the formal investigation. I tried not to dwell on how she'd died: terror, followed by unimaginable pain.

I sat there motionless, until the bleep of the intercom brought me round. It was tempting to tell any visitors to clear off, but the guards announced that my brother had arrived, instinct making me push the button to admit him.

'How did you find me, Will?'

'Burns called.' He leant down to kiss my cheek. 'Jesus, what is this dump? Why aren't you at home?'

'It's too complicated. I won't bore you with it.'

'Suit yourself. Where's the kitchen?'

My brother pushed past me, in search of cooking facilities. Ever since his bipolar disorder was diagnosed, food had been his salvation. I sat on a stool to watch him in action. My appetite had been dulled by shock, but it was relaxing to watch him chopping shallots at breakneck speed, then filleting salmon with a professional flourish. He told me that his new job was going well; the owners at the Pont D'or teaching him new techniques with every shift. It still seemed odd that the studious, charismatic boy I'd grown up with was nowhere to be seen. This man seemed far more grounded, a smile on his face as he tore parsley into clumps, sprinkling it liberally over the fish. Within no time he put a plate in front of me which contained butter-glazed spring vegetables, beside a parcel of salmon en-croute browned to perfection.

'How did you make all that so fast?'

'I cheated,' he said, grinning. 'I brought the pastry with me. There's crème brulée, for later.'

We caught up on our personal lives while we ate: Nina's new job teaching English at an adult education college was satisfying but underpaid, mum's plans to go into sheltered housing causing long debate. Will even tested his speech for Lola's wedding on me, checking to see if his jokes raised a laugh. By the time he was ready to leave, my mood had improved considerably. He collected his jacket from the hallway then gazed down at me.

'You could say what's wrong, Al. I'm a good listener these days.'

'I know you are. You'll be the first person I call on, once I figure it out.'

He gave me a bone crushing hug then set off down the fire escape, footsteps clattering on the metal rungs. When I looked out through the window, Burns's Audi had pulled up, my brother chatting to him through the rolled down window. The sight of them conferring annoyed me; no doubt they were planning how to keep me safe, like safeguarding a valuable china doll. When Burns materialised in the doorway, I couldn't decide whether to hurl myself at him or banish him from my space. The exhaustion on his face kept my irritation in check, his skin pale beneath a three-day growth of stubble.

'There's food, if you're hungry,' I said.

'Jesus, I hate these things.' He tore off his tie, dropping it on a chair. 'I could use a drink.'

'Whisky?'

'A nice big double.'

I poured two fingers of Glenfiddich into a tumbler and watched him knock it back, like a draft of medicine, the colour returning to his face. Afterwards we sat together on the sofa, exchanging information. I explained that Frances Pearce had given no indication that she was suicidal.

'Have you got the CCTV from the platform?' I asked.

He stared at me. 'You want to watch it, before you sleep?'

'It can't be worse than the pictures in my head.'

Burns rolled his eyes, but rose to his feet to fetch his laptop. He sat beside me while the grainy black and white film clip played: on a crowded platform, people stepped forwards as the train approached. The pale fabric of Frances Pearce's coat flashed in the corner of my eye, then her body pitching onto the tracks, a split second before the train arrived. She had never stood a chance. At first sight I had to agree that it looked like suicide; maybe she had even dropped her ID on the platform to save the fire brigade from searching her mangled body. But the film looked different in slow motion. The crowd was too dense to see who had pushed her, but she twisted round as she fell, searching for a voice in the crowd.

'We can't identify Stone at the scene. Hundreds of people streamed off the platform; any number of the blokes could be him in disguise, or he might be somewhere else entirely, playing the sodding piano.'

It was the frustration in his voice that made me reach for him, to neutralise the damage Stone was inflicting. The bulk of his shoulders under my hands felt as reassuring as watching my brother cook, solid and inarguable, while everything else fell apart. I could tell he was shocked by the heat behind my kiss, desire for him mixing with determination not to let our jobs force us apart. I forgot about work while I peeled off my shirt. For once he let me take charge, climbing over him on the settee, my hands snagging in his hair, watching his eyes lose focus. Afterwards he lay against the cushions, his expression stunned.

'You never fail to amaze me, Alice.'

'Read Freud, if you want to know about the link between sex and death.'

'I'd rather just let you take advantage of me, on a regular basis.'

The muscles in Burns's jaw were tensing again. The stress of the case must have been overwhelming, if whisky, comfort and sex couldn't distract him. It made me wish I could lift the burden from his shoulders until morning, make him forget Stone's antics and the media frenzy. I reached for his hands again, leading him to the bedroom, sleep overtaking him the second he lay down.

73

At midnight, Stone is alone in the cramped flat. Lily is working a night shift while he perfects his new disguise. He stands in front of the mirror, studying his reflection. It has taken time and effort to change his appearance again. His hair is barely more than a stubble, but he has dyed it black, still wearing brown contact lenses. Reducing his food intake has given his face the sculpted look of an older man, skin darkened by fake tan. The police are hunting for a pale, bald-headed twenty-five-year-old; he could walk down any London street and escape detection.

He watches his story unfold on the news channel: badly lit photos from Ronnie Scott's show him playing the Steinway on the small stage, the newscaster's face grave as she explains that he has been using the alias Seth Rivers. He takes a deep breath and reminds himself that the most important thing is to keep his liberty, fleeing the country if need be, so he can compose in peace. The idea of dying before his music receives the acclaim it deserves terrifies him, but he's torn between settling old scores and keeping Lily at his side. She may have seen the news already; the idea making his heart beat rapidly in his chest. It's too early to test whether she loves him enough to accept his crimes.

At four a.m. Lily returns at last. He's listening to Count Basie's American jazz on his headphones, the seamless rhythm restoring some of his calm. He can tell from the girl's expression that she has no idea that his fake name will adorn every front-page tomorrow. She's rushed home from work, still dressed in her uniform, smile wide and unquestioning. He waits until she climbs into bed before pulling her into his arms, their faces close when he finally speaks.

'I need your help, Lily. I'm in trouble.'

Her smile crumbles. 'What's happened, sweetheart?'

'Promise you'll do as I ask?'

'Of course.'

'You'll get hurt if you go out alone tomorrow, you have to stay with me.'

'Who are these people looking for you, Seth?'

'Men from the cruise ship. They say I owe them money, but it's not true.'

'Let's contact the police.'

Stone's grip tightens on her wrists. 'They'd kill me, if we did. We have to leave here and start over, just you and me. Will you do it?'

'If it keeps you safe.'

The girl's eyes are terrified when he kisses her forehead, then drags her closer, her warmth soothing him to sleep at last.

74

Saturday 2nd April

Copies of the Daily Mail were circulating the incident room the following morning. PIANO KILLER STILL ON RAMPAGE the headline blared; at seven a.m. the nation was waking up to the news that Stone had struck again. The story reported the death of Frances Pearce as his latest attack. The killer's face appeared below the headline, but the image was misleading. It showed him with blond curls, wide blue eyes giving the camera an innocent stare.

'Just what we need,' Tania muttered. 'That picture's a year out of date.'

Stone might have changed his appearance half a dozen times since then, and any hope that intense media coverage could expose him was slipping away. I spent the next hour familiarising myself with the work completed by the investigation team overnight. CCTV had identified Stone following Frances Pearce into the Tube station, face partly concealed by a black baseball cap. Dressed in jeans, trainers and a dark windcheater, he had disappeared into the crowd streaming off the platform after the fatality. It was only when I read the report on Pearce that the full impact of her death hit home. Her two teenage daughters had been waiting for their mother to return from London, until a WPC and a senior detective from the Nottingham force had knocked on their door to share the bad news. Two more young lives had been devastated, but anger would only prevent me from doing my job effectively; my energy would be better channelled into finding Stone, before he struck again.

Burns's office had been taken over by visual recognition specialists from Scotland Yard. The two men were studying film footage from Ronnie Scott's, to determine whether the pianist on

Nancy Morris's film was Stone. Angie hovered in the background, fresh-faced and alert as she awaited their verdict. Her boundless enthusiasm seemed undimmed, even though nothing was going to plan. I stood beside her, watching the specialists resizing images of the performer at the jazz club.

'It's a ninety-eight percent match,' one of them announced.

'How do you know?' Angie asked.

'We take exact measurements of the facial structure, feed them through the computer and it does the maths. That's definitely Adrian Stone.'

When I peered over his shoulder, two radically different images of the killer were overlaid on top of one another, revealing identical bone structure, yet I would have walked past him on the street. Superficial changes to hair colour, eyes and skin tone would have deceived me completely.

I took a moment to digest the information. In addition to going on a killing spree since his escape, Stone was indulging his passion for performance. It brought home his ability to compartmentalise his actions. Like many psychopaths, he could commit an atrocity, then return to normality like nothing had happened. Now that his options were narrowing, his modus operandi would change again. He would react like a caged animal, lashing out wildly as the net tightened.

I found a spare computer terminal in the incident room and checked through my notes. It was more important than ever to discover whether Ben Wrentham had been Matthew Briar's accomplice, but the teacher continued to deny involvement. There would be just one more chance to question him, before he was released for lack of evidence. He would still face trial for acting as a criminal accessory, but that was a lesser offence than accomplice to murder. So far all Wrentham had revealed was an obsessive nature and a naïve ability to be deceived. It was still possible that Briar's accessory had been another of Stone's contacts from before his imprisonment, remaining loyal despite all he'd done.

When I scanned the emails in my inbox there was a reminder to attend a catch-up meeting with Christine and Mike at the FPU in an hour's time. Another message had arrived from Hari Chadha, updating me on Melissa Stone's progress. The young woman was recovering slowly; his treatment plan included one more week of in-patient care, followed by continued use of anti-depressants and counselling at home. The news filled me with relief; at least Stone had been unable to harm his sister. Another email arrived, just as I finished reading the diagnostic report on Melissa Stone. A wave of shock hit me as sound blared from the computer's speakers: piano music played at hectic speed, discordant notes tumbling over each other in their race to be heard. Everyone in the incident room turned round to identify the source of the melody.

I could only sit passively while the music rang out, but people were already crowding around my computer, to see whether the email could be tracked. The subject line was empty, no written message, the music's manic energy announcing that Stone knew my email address at the FPU, as well as my phone number. He was demonstrating that he still held the upper hand. I watched the team downloading information, checking co-ordinates from the sender's address, aware that the information would arrive too late. If he really had enlisted a girlfriend, she might be our best hope of tracking him down.

75

Stone wakes with a clear sense of purpose. Today is for righting old wrongs; one more chance to settle the score, before he concentrates on the future. Lily is already in the kitchen making breakfast, but he takes the coffee pot from her hands, placing it back on the counter.

'Text your dad, Lily. Tell him we're going on holiday, you can call him when we get back.'

'But I ring him every day, wherever I am.'

Stone puts his hands on her shoulders. 'You want him safe, don't you?'

'Of course.'

'These people are dangerous.' The girl is close to tears, so he attempts to be gentle. 'Trust me, everything'll work out, I promise.'

Her smile slowly revives, but Stone knows he can't leave her alone in the flat. She might turn on the TV and see his face emblazoned on the screen. He'll have to keep her with him, even though it will slow him down. The girl follows him downstairs without complaint, not asking why he's carrying a rucksack. She doesn't even complain when they reach St James's Park and he tells her to wait for him in a café, no matter how long it takes. Her face is as solemn as a child's when he kisses her goodbye.

It takes Stone five minutes to jog to Dacre Street. He pulls a clipboard and a small cardboard package marked with Parcel Force tape from his rucksack. Security's been reduced outside the FPU, just one uniform outside the entrance, with a bored expression on his face. Stone smiles broadly as he approaches.

'I need a signature for this. Can I go in?'

'Where's your van?'

'Parked round the corner. The wardens here are mental.'

'Show me your ID, please.'

Stone flashes a square of plastic bearing the Parcel Force logo, the guard only glancing at it, before nodding his head. But the receptionist is a tougher proposition. The middle-aged woman looks up from her work, biro hovering in mid-air, her expression irritable.

'Can I help?'

He offers a conciliatory smile. 'Alice Quentin ordered this. She wants it delivered straight to her office.'

'Leave it with me. I'll see she gets it.'

'I need her signature.'

'Dr Quentin's busy, she can't be disturbed.'

'My boss'll give me hell if she complains.'

It takes charm and perseverance before the woman finally directs him to Quentin's office. Stone senses that he's on borrowed time, walls pressing in on him as he jogs up the stairs. The place smells of dust and tradition, rooms filled with the type of people he despises; dozens of so-called experts, who love dismantling people's imaginations to kill their dreams.

On the third floor he scents Quentin's perfume; a blend of rose and jasmine, and now he hears her voice. Through an inch-wide crack in the door he sees her, seated at a table, and intent expression on her face, talking to a white-haired old man and a thin woman with her back turned. He could kill all three of them in seconds, but the noise would alert everyone in the building. He withdraws to look for her office instead. Quentin's fragrance is even stronger in the confined space, making his head spin. Stone deposits the parcel on her desk then shuts the door, before escaping back down the stairs, humming a Latin melody under his breath.

76

My meeting with Christine and Mike gave me time to review the evidence. I was grateful that both of the FPU's most senior consultants had sacrificed leisure time to help me locate Adrian Stone. My boss was planning a gym visit afterwards, dressed in a sleek black tracksuit, while Mike wore jeans and an outsize plaid shirt, designed to conceal his expanding waistline. He sat with one elbow propped on the table, watching me describe the stages of my analysis. I had begun by helping the police search for Matthew Briar's accomplice, analysing the behaviour of those closest to him for sign of complicity. The second phase had involved using HOLMES 2 to track Stone's movements, profiling software helping to map his kill sites. My focus on the musical clues had brought no direct result. Stone's calling cards had grown less specific, as if he regretted revealing too much at the start of his campaign.

'Do you still think his college friend's involved?' Christine asked.

'Wrentham's keeping his mouth shut. He gave Matthew Briar money, but could just be naïve. His obsession with the past made him an easy mark. There's no hard evidence he knew Stone would escape.'

'Who else has a strong psychological drive to want him free? It must be someone intimate to take such a big risk, after nine year's separation.'

I looked down at my notes. 'The person with the strongest connection is his uncle; David taught Stone to play the piano, often watching him perform as a child. He was his only regular visitor at Rampton, and his wife thinks he's tortured by guilt.'

'You believe he's still linked to Stone emotionally?'

'He's manifesting stress symptoms: verbal aggression, tense body language, restlessness. But that could be out of concern for Melissa. I need to speak to him again, without making him feel victimised.'

'Treat him like an expert; ask him about the musical clues,' Christine suggested. 'Did Stone have any other college contacts?'

'His ex-girlfriend's clean, and his tutors and fellow students have all been investigated. There's no one with a criminal record; they seem to be leading blameless lives.'

Donnelly gave a wry a smile. 'We've all got vices, Alice. If Briar was desperate for an accomplice, he could have used blackmail. His sidekick will be doing everything in their power to hide themselves.'

We carried on discussing the case, looking at Stone's actions from every angle. We all agreed that his obsession with performing would drive him to seek out another venue, even though his fake identity as Seth Rivers had been exposed. Burns had instructed his team to check piano bars and clubs inside his hunting ground. My sense that David Stone could yet reveal missing information about his nephew made me keen to interview him again, even though he had reacted defensively. My last option would be to seek more help from the staff at the Royal College, for insight into the latest musical clues. I still sensed that vital information could be hidden in each recording.

I carried on mulling over details when I returned to my office. Someone had delivered a pile of envelopes, which lay beside a small package in the centre of my desk. I opened the mail first, to give my brain a break from endless analysis, flicking through invitations to speak at psychology conferences and fliers promoting books on neuro-linguistic programming. I was about to open the package when something stopped me: parcels were normally left on the front desk for collection. It looked innocent enough, the printed address label held in place by Parcel Force tape. It probably contained nothing more sinister than new cartridges for my printer, but I rang downstairs, to check why it had been delivered, the receptionist sounded apologetic.

'The young man said you wanted it delivered personally. I thought it was urgent.'

'I didn't order anything, Sheila.' My heart rate quickened. 'What did he look like?'

'Youngish, black hair, nice smile.'

I put the phone down and studied the package again. Would Stone really have the guts to march into my place of work? The answer had to be yes. He'd already played in a packed jazz club and abducted Asako Mori from one of the city's largest concert halls. I hedged my bets and called Pete Hancock for advice.

'Leave your office and lock the door,' he said firmly. 'I'll send the dangerous substances team round.'

I waited by myself on the landing. If my suspicions were correct, Stone was getting closer all the time. When I peered out of the window, Dacre Street looked perfectly safe, lined with rows of respectable brownstones, taxis travelling past at a sedate pace. The environment would have suited Stone perfectly, so genteel and relaxed, no one would believe a serial killer had wandered by in broad daylight. Tania would have mobilised squad cars by now, to check the area, but Stone would have done a vanishing act long ago.

An officer from the dangerous substances team arrived soon after my phone call. I watched him pull on protective overalls before entering my office, emerging ten minutes later, with the package in a sealed box.

'I've checked the air in there,' he said. 'It's not contaminated. You're safe to go back inside; we'll check the package back at the lab.'

I sat at my desk and tried to focus, ignoring the fact that Stone had paid me a personal visit. I studied the case file again, determined not to waste the time at my disposal before Reg ferried me back to the station.

77

It's midday by the time Stone and Lily arrive at Guy's Hospital. The girl still seems tense, despite his reassurances. It would be risky to leave her in a public place, but luck is with him when he spots the chapel's wooden doors, set into the building's Georgian facade.

'Wait for me there, Lily. I won't be long.'

'I wish you'd say what's happening. This is freaking me out.'

'Trust me, sweetheart, it's best you don't know.'

Stone leads her into the chapel, inhaling candle wax and dust, picking up echoes of fables he doesn't believe. The nave is painted white, tinted light spilling through stained glass windows, a simple gold cross above the altar. He sits on a pew with his hand on the girl's arm, and when he looks into her eyes again, her calmness has returned.

'Want me to pray for you, Seth?'

'No need.' He kisses her forehead. 'Just stay here till I get back.'

Stone circles the hospital's tower block before choosing the easiest point of access. He waits outside a staff locker room, until the coast is clear. It takes little effort to jemmy the lock with a nail file and grab a white coat from a hook on the wall, a stethoscope still tucked into the top pocket. He catches a glimpse of himself in the mirror, transformed into a young medic, with a serious expression. When he reaches the tenth floor, he focuses on his breathing as he climbs the stairs. Already he can hear music playing, the knowledge that his sister is close singing in his veins.

The staff nurse gives an absent smile when he enters the ward, a phone tucked under her chin as she scribbles on a notepad. The other nurses are too busy to acknowledge him, administering drugs and taking care of patients. The place sets Stone's nerves on edge; the air wreaking of urine and stale food. An old man turns in slow circles, talking gibberish, while a middle-aged woman rocks from side to side, her face vacant. Stone's eyes scan the beds, but there's no sign of his sister.

It's only at the end of the ward that he sees a police officer sitting outside a closed door. He collects a clipboard from the bottom of a bed, pulling a biro from the pocket of his white coat, then approaches the guard.

'It's time for Melissa's evaluation. Is that okay?' he asks, smiling. 'It'll take about ten minutes.'

The middle-aged man nods. 'Go ahead.'

The music's louder now, a high insistent melody he can't ignore. His sister is asleep when he enters the room. He stands motionless, looking at her blond hair fanned across the pillow, skin dusted with freckles, just like when she was a child.

'Lissa,' he whispers.

The girl's eyes open slowly. She doesn't recognise him at first, then she's too shocked to scream. 'Please don't hurt me, Adrian.'

'You never let me explain.' Her thin shoulders flinch as he sits on the edge of the bed. He's touching her now, fingertips on her cheek, his hand settling against her throat. 'Don't make a noise, just listen.'

'Leave me now, please.'

'You were the only one who cared. Dad loved hurting us and mum criticised everything we did. By the end Jenny was worst of all. I killed them for you, as well as me. It set you free, didn't it?'

She hesitates then chokes out a reply. 'Yes.'

'Aren't you going to thank me for saving you?'

'Thank you, Adrian.' Her voice trembles, there's a quake in each word as he presses harder on her windpipe.

'Why did you lock me out? I wanted you with me; I'd have taken care of you.'

'I was too young to understand.'

'You were the only one I cared about, Lissa, so sweet and innocent. My girlfriend reminds me of you, she's studying to be a nurse.'

Melissa's eyes are losing focus, making Stone loosen his grip. He reminds himself that he came here only to explain the past, the music in his ears fading to a quiet chorus. He touches his index finger to her lips with the lightest pressure.

'Good bye, Lissa. Don't raise the alarm.'

He thanks the guard as he leaves, ignoring a nurse's voice calling him as he exits the ward, feet thundering on the concrete as he escapes.

78

The incident room was in uproar when I returned. Phones ringing endlessly, then loud conversation as detectives trooped in for a briefing. Pete Hancock grabbed my elbow and propelled me from the room.

'It's mayhem in here,' he said. 'Let's go somewhere else.'

We ended up in the canteen, with Pete tutting loudly as I downed strong black coffee.

'Caffeine's my only vice, Pete.'

'Don't blame me when your pancreas packs up.' He sipped his mineral water. 'You were right not to open that parcel, by the way. There was a membrane inside, full of sulphuric acid that would have spilled all over your hands.'

I winced, remembering Sam Wyedale's injury. 'Stone had a fake ID card from a delivery company then conned his way upstairs. He's getting bolder all the time.' My meeting with Christine and Mike could have saved my life. If Stone had found me alone, he might have thrown the acid in my face. 'Is there news on Ben Wrentham?'

'He's been released for lack of evidence. His lawyer fought tooth and nail.'

'There must be some good news, Pete.'

'Newcastle play Hull tomorrow. There's a decent chance they'll win.' Hancock's bleeper sounded as I drained my coffee. 'We're needed in the meeting room.'

The emergency briefing was just starting when we got back downstairs. Burns met my eye as I took my place; so much of our relationship was conducted in public, I had grown used to communicating with him by nods and blinks, interpreting his mood through body language. His gaze appeared steadier, as though he had a clear view of his target, his hybrid London/Edinburgh drawl sounding more upbeat.

'We've got two confirmed sightings of Stone. He delivered a package to the Forensic Psychology Unit on Dacre Street around eleven a.m., then entered his sister's hospital room at Guy's Hospital about twelve-thirty, disguised as a doctor. She was too shocked to raise the alarm for fifteen minutes. Melissa hasn't given many details yet but Stone made a kind of confession, he told her that his girlfriend's a trainee nurse. I want a media bulletin prepared, then check every CCTV and road camera within five hundred metres of Guy's. We need to know if Stone's got a female accomplice, or if it's one of his fantasies.' Burns's eyes scanned the room, with the intensity of a laser beam. 'He's in the daylight now. All we have to do is follow his lead.'

Burns's renewed confidence ignited the room. After days of uncertainty the team finally had clues to chase; I watched Tania arranging logistics with her team, Angie shepherding detectives back to the incident room. It frustrated me that the musical clues Stone had scattered so liberally at the start were being ignored. When Burns finally tracked me down his smile was several degrees warmer than mine as I buttoned my coat.

'Something wrong?' he asked.

'Only that we're missing something vital. I'm off to see David Stone again, Reg is waiting outside.'

'I'll take you. I want to hear what the uncle's got to say.'

Our journey to Richmond passed in a rush of talk about the case. Something was making Stone step closer to his targets, confidence or desperation compelling him to work faster than before. The aspect that interested me most was why Melissa had survived: after ten minutes in her hospital room, Stone had spared her life. Maybe I'd misread his motivations all along, she could be the one relative he considered blameless.

David Stone seemed subdued when we arrived. He led us into a lounge filled with books, painting and sculptures, an upright piano in the corner. A cluster of family portraits stood on the mantelpiece. One showed three children sitting together, two adults standing behind them. The portrait had a stiff formality, all of the kids wearing awkward smiles, decked out in Sunday best, their hair neatly combed. It took me a moment to realise that the group was Adrian Stone's family, before the massacre.

'The grief counsellor told us not to conceal the past,' Stone said quietly. 'We wanted Melissa to remember her family, when we adopted her.'

I nodded in reply. 'Being open makes it easier to discuss what happened.'

David Stone's craggy features looked time-worn, anxiety visible in his abrupt hand movements as he gestured for us to sit down. He gave the impression of a man who had endured enough emotional pain to last a lifetime, the burden of protecting his family heavy on his shoulders.

'We thought you'd like an update on Adrian's movements,' I said.

Stone's politeness was replaced by anger when he heard about his nephew's audacity. 'How in God's name did you people let him slip through the net again?'

'He's a brilliant escape artist,' Burns replied. 'He uses a different disguise each time.'

'Your blunders put my niece's life at risk.' Stone rubbed his hand across his face. 'It has to stop. Melissa's already in pieces.'

'Her consultant says she's got a strong will to recover, which is half the battle.' I glanced across at David Stone's piano, the wood gleaming in the late afternoon sun. 'I'd like your opinion on the music Adrian sent us.'

'Why? I'm no expert.'

'You know his style. It may hold clues that we've missed.'

Stone listened to the fragments of music on headphones, his frown deepening. 'It's definitely Adrian playing, I'd recognise his style anywhere. Both pieces start in triple time, like a waltz, then the tempo fragments. It's like being caught in a tornado.'

'Patients with schizophrenia often describe their symptoms like that,' I commented.

'It's beautiful, but there's chaos behind the melody.'

'Can you remember anything Adrian said at Rampton, that might help us find him, David?'

'Nothing specific.'

I sensed he was holding something back. 'Did he ask for help to escape?'

He stared at me before replying. 'It seemed like another of his fantasies. I refused, of course. He had all these dreams about how he'd live if he was free.'

'Such as?'

'Have a relationship, travel, play for a huge audience.'

'In London?'

'I took him to the Albert hall once as a child. It affected him deeply; he often spoke about the great pianists who'd played there.' The man's voice was mournful. 'Adrian's hurt so many people, but he's a victim too. His illness stole his future.'

I was silent as we left David Stone's home, remembering his description of his nephew's music as a type of chaos, proving that his mind was unravelling. It was a relief to return to the cool spring air, the innocent sound of blackbirds calling from the trees above. All I had gleaned from the visit was that Adrian Stone had played the piano on each of the pieces he'd sent, yet I felt sure the music held more clues, if we could only tune into their frequency.

79

Sweat trickles down Stone's back as he and Lily wander through Mayfair. He's managed to keep her in the dark, but her father will have seen the news bulletins, or heard them on the radio. He studies the girl's face, solemn in the gathering dark. It's impossible to imagine life without her now. His best music has been composed since they met, but soon he must tell her the truth, before she hears it from another source.

'We can't go home, Lily. It's too dangerous.'

She shakes her head. 'My phone's there. I need to call dad.'

'I told you, it's not safe.'

Stone scans the road quickly, checking for unmarked cars. It's a quiet side street, no sign they're being followed. He notices a small hotel up ahead. The money in the envelope is running out, but there's enough for a few nights of comfort. The manager doesn't bat an eye when he pays for the room in cash, signs in under an assumed name. The accommodation is lacklustre, with faded chintz curtains and old-fashioned furniture, but the view from the top floor is spectacular. Stone can see the sharp outline of the Royal College's towers, traffic inching down Exhibition Road, the domed roof of the Albert Hall. Lily rests her face between his shoulder blades as he stares out of the window, her breath warming his back.

'Tell me what's wrong, Seth. You'll feel better getting it off your chest.'

He turns round slowly. 'You really want to hear?'

'I'd like to know everything about you.'

'Tomorrow, I promise.'

She reaches up to kiss him. 'Between us we can fix anything.'

The evening passes quietly. Stone keeps Lily distracted, by ordering food and wine from room service, then they take a bath, go to bed, make love. It's only when she falls asleep that he rises again, removes the plug from the TV. He slips out into the night time streets alone, nodding at the porter as he leaves.

Asako Mori is hunched on the ground when he returns to the tunnel, cheek resting on her knees. He lights half a dozen candles, sets them on top of two pianos, facing one another.

'Time to rehearse, Asako.'

'My hands are freezing, I can't...' A hard slap brings her words to an abrupt halt.

'Scales first, then the duet.'

Stone busies himself setting up the recorder, making sure it will capture sound perfectly. Then he sits at the piano opposite Mori, lets his hands fly across the keys, a flurry of notes echoing down the tunnel.

80

Sunday 3rd April

The morning before Lola's wedding felt surreal. After weeks of tension, I found myself at her flat. making polite conversation with her mother and two of her aunts, while we sipped Buck's Fizz. Luckily my friend was too excited about her big day to notice my preoccupation. All of my energy since the crack of dawn had been spent on keeping her calm, but I could tell she was holding her nerve.

'Time to put your glad rags on, Al,' Lola instructed me.

A stylist from the theatre where she worked as a drama tutor was helping us prepare. Lola's hair and makeup were already finished. She looked tall and immaculate as a Pre-Raphaelite model, skin glowing, auburn hair rippling down her back.

'The booze is helping,' she said, smiling. 'I'm on my third glass.'

'Don't have another. You'll fall over halfway down the aisle.'

I spent the next twenty minutes being pampered. The stylist was called Becky, her voice low and soothing as she applied blusher and eye shadow. When I opened my eyes again, a different woman gazed back from the mirror, making me understand Adrian Stone's love of disguises. My skin looked flawless, eyes sparkling, figure sheathed in smooth green silk; a butterfly released from its chrysalis. Maybe the killer found his transformations equally exciting. They gave him the chance to slough off the past and become a new man.

'Come on, Alice,' Lola's mother said, steering me towards the door. 'The car's waiting.'

The Rolls-Royce was a thing of beauty, pristine white, with ribbons swagged across its bonnet. The sight of Lola standing on the pavement made me pull out my phone for a photo. She was pencil-slim in her floor-length dress, clutching a bouquet of wild flowers, head tipped back to examine the sky.

'It better hadn't bloody rain,' she muttered.

'It wouldn't dare,' I replied.

Burns hadn't arrived when I peered into the packed church, but there was no time to fret about his absence. The organist was playing the wedding march, and Lola's nerves had disappeared. She sashayed down the aisle like a catwalk model, Neal gazing back from the altar with a dazzled smile. I caught sight of Burns lurking in the shadows as we filed out, but was too busy handing out packets of confetti to speak to him, until after the photographer had finished taking pictures of Lola and Neal signing the bans.

'Sorry I was late,' he said, dropping a kiss on top of my head. 'You look stunning.'

'Something's happened?'

'Concentrate on the wedding. It can wait.'

I was called away for yet another picture, while Burns stayed on the other side of the churchyard, phone pressed to his ear. I waited at the kerbside when Lola and Neal were preparing to leave, avoiding the wedding bouquet she threw straight at me. Her teenage cousin caught it instead, an embarrassed blush spreading across her face. I was dragged into a waiting car, and taken to the Hospital Club in Soho, where Lola and I had spent many disreputable evenings. The place had smartened up since then, classical music drifting from the stage. Two violinists and a cellist were playing Mozart, accompanied by a pianist dressed in gorgeous electric blue dress. The function room was filling steadily, and I did my best to forget Adrian Stone. There was a chance he'd quit London already, adopted another name. When I turned away from the stage, the place was heaving, waiters circulating with trays of champagne, to whet people's appetite for the wedding lunch. My nerves must have been close to the surface because I almost jumped out of my skin as someone touched my shoulder; when I spun round my brother was standing there.

'You're edgy, Al.'

'Tell me about it. My, don't you look handsome.' I stroked my hand across his lapel, tears rising in my throat. My brother's suit fitted him perfectly, dark blond hair brushed back from his face, handsome and relaxed. I reached up to kiss his cheek. 'I always thought Lola would end up marrying you.'

'Me too, but she never appreciated my charm.' He gave a wry grin, then looked across as Nina, helping herself to a glass of wine in a figure-hugging red dress. 'Never mind, I've found someone who tolerates me.'

He drifted away to chat to Lola's actor friends, and I found myself listening to the music. My thoughts were still so focused on the case, I zoned in on the piano's melody, high and rhythmical behind the cello's sighs. I waited until the trio took a break before approaching the stage, as the pianist sorted through sheet music.

'You play beautifully,' I said. 'You must have studied for years.'

'Thanks, I can't imagine doing anything else.'

'Can I ask a technical question?'

'Fire away.'

'If you heard a piano recording, could you tell where it was made?'

She nodded. 'An experienced musician could guess the dimensions of the studio or concert hall pretty accurately. The echo and sound quality give you clues. Every room has a different acoustic, that a sensitive ear can pick up.'

'That's interesting, thanks. Let me get you a drink.'

I wandered to the bar to collect wine glasses for the musicians, then caught sight of Burns monopolising the bride. Whatever Lola was whispering in his ear had brought a smile to his face. He looked big and thuggish, beside her slender form, his battered handsomeness easier to appreciate from a distance. His stance revealed all of his contradictions: the boy from a poor family who'd loved boxing and playing rugby, alongside the young man who ran away to become a painter, then thrown himself into a police career. He must have felt me staring, because he kissed Lola's cheek with a flourish, then shouldered his way through the crowd, easily the tallest man in the room.

'Flirting with the bride will only cause trouble,' I said.

'I was giving my excuses. I've got to get back to station.'

'Why?'

'Forget it, sweetheart. You're the maid of honour.'

'Don't sweetheart me.' I grabbed his arm. 'We're co-workers, remember?'

His smile vanished. 'He's running rings round us, Alice. There's a new film of Asako Mori, trapped in another sodding basement.'

'I'll come with you.'

'You can't. Lola'll skin you alive.'

'Lunch doesn't start till three, I'll be back here easily by then.'

I dashed away before he could argue, grabbing my bag from the cloakroom. When I put on my cotton shirt, jeans and trainers in the toilets, I caught sight of myself in the full-length mirror. The butterfly had retreated back inside her chrysalis so completely, even Adrian Stone would have been impressed.

At midday, Stone is still in bed with Lily, picking over a late breakfast ordered from room service. The food is better than he expected: fresh grapefruit, croissants, good French coffee. He's already forgetting years of miserable fare at Rampton as he watches Lily, slathering jam on a slice of toast.

'I'm enjoying all this luxury,' she says.

'Me too. It's good to be waited on occasionally.'

'Can we go home today?' she asks.

'You'll have to wait a while longer.'

She gives a hesitant smile. 'It's dad I'm worried about, and my next shift starts tomorrow.'

'Forget everything outside this room.' He brushes a stray curl back from her forehead. 'You know I love you, don't you?'

'It's still hard to believe.'

'Get used to it, angel. I'm not going anywhere.' He finishes his last bite of croissant. 'I'll take a shower, then we can walk in the park.'

'That sounds perfect. I'll leave our tray outside.'

Stone hums to himself under the warm jet of water. The girl is still his ideal muse, inspiring him to compose, her innocence fresh as a clean sheet of paper. He's imagining a new melody as he emerges from the bathroom, chords bright and cool as a spring breeze. It's only when he catches sight of Lily again that his good mood shatters. Hotel staff must have left a newspaper outside the door. The girl is staring down at the front page of a tabloid, fingers covering her mouth, like she's trying not to scream.

We never made it to the station. Burns received a phone call, telling him that a Mr Roberts had called the helpline, claiming to know a pianist called Seth Rivers. Burns's face brightened with the prospect of a new lead as he drove west towards Ladbroke Grove, but seeing Lola walk down the aisle had been overshadowed by concern for Stone's new victim. The car raced down Westbourne Park Road, finally stopping outside a council block near Portobello Road. The building seemed to be the last of its kind. All the other social housing had been replaced by private apartments with glass and steel balconies, decked out with pot plants and patio furniture. Mr Roberts's block was modest by comparison, the architecture a throwback to the seventies, when yellow bricks and narrow windows were all the rage.

A grey-haired man approached the car as we parked, his face haggard. He looked around sixty-five, balding, the thick lenses of his glasses reducing his eyes to the size of pinpricks.

'Are you from the police?' he asked.

'That's right, Mr Roberts,' Burns replied. 'Can we go inside?'

Roberts led us into his ground floor flat, and I realised why he'd been waiting outside. He was unable to keep still, shifting his weight from foot to foot. When I suggested he sit down at the kitchen table, he didn't respond, so I hunted in his cupboards to make him a cup of sweetened tea, to dilute his shock.

'My daughter phones every day, regular as clockwork,' he murmured. 'I didn't hear from her yesterday, so I went to her flat, but the place was empty.'

'What makes you think something's wrong?' I asked.

'Her boyfriend's calling himself Seth Rivers.' The old man's face clouded. 'She saw him playing piano in a pub and the next thing you know, they're living together. The lad seems like an oddball to me, always changing his clothes and his hair; Lily said it was because he was a performer, but it struck me as unnatural.'

'How long have they been a couple?'

'A few weeks, stuck together like glue.'

'Do you think he mistreats her?' I asked.

The old man shook his head. 'He said he loved her. I thought he sounded sincere, but it was part of his game.' He rubbed his hand across his mouth. 'How did I miss the signs?'

'When did you guess he might be Stone?'

'I don't read the papers, and my TV's on the blink. Last night I saw his face in the newsagents when I bought some milk.'

Suddenly Mr Robert's head tipped forwards, shoulders heaving, as he pulled off his glasses, a few tears splashing on his kitchen tiles. My concern for him grew stronger when his hands jittered at his sides, small eyes still glassy with shock.

'Could I see a photo of Lily please?' I asked, once he'd regained control.

He pointed at the wall above our heads: beside a small wooden crucifix was a row of photographs of a dark-haired girl, progressing from youth to adulthood. Lily Roberts's naïve smile had changed little since her school portraits, apart from losing her thick braces. The latest picture showed a slim young woman dressed in nursing uniform, expression glowing with pride. Burns asked for the most recent photo, so it could be broadcast on the news bulletins. Robert's pulled one from the wall then stood motionless, staring down at it.

'I didn't protect her,' he muttered. 'She never sees the bad in anyone.'

We waited until a middle-aged WPC arrived, because Mr Roberts was in no state to be left alone. Burns arranged for plain clothes officers to enter Lily's flat in case Stone returned, my thoughts staying with his victims as we drove back to the station. The fate of two young women rested in Adrian Stone's hands, but Mr Roberts's reaction had differed from Mr Mori's unflinching stoicism. Both men had been cut to the quick, yet I sensed that Lily's father would crumble faster, if his daughter wasn't brought home alive.

Burns disappeared into an operational meeting with Angie and Tania, leaving me in the incident room, watching Stone's latest film. Asako Mori's appearance was deteriorating fast, her hair in rats' tails, streaks of dirt marking her face. It amazed me that she could still play the piano, hands gliding over the keyboard, while another melody kept time in the background. Stone must have been playing the second instrument, unwilling to reveal his latest disguise.

'You bastard,' I murmured under my breath.

My eyes strained to interpret details, but in the flickering candlelight, all I could see was blackened bricks and a dirt floor. Asako Mori could be in one of thousands of basements in the city's disused buildings. Stone would only have needed to walk down any residential street and work out which homes were vacant, before breaking in and claiming the place as his own. If Mori was still alive, he could keep her there indefinitely. I still felt sure she was being held inside the territory he revered. My gaze wandered over the map of his catchment area, but house-to-house searches had been carried out on every street, checking pubs and restaurants to see if he had played there. My eyes lingered on Cromwell Road. At least I had been right about one thing; Lily Roberts's flat was near the site of his greatest success and failure. He might still be strolling around Kensington, using his girlfriend as camouflage. My only hope of finding him lay in unravelling his musical clues, once and for all.

83

Stone knows he should kill the girl, but something stops him. If she would only yell or lash out, hurting her would be easy, but she looks like a frightened child, her eyes pooling with tears.

'I've been so blind,' she whispers.

'That's not true, Lily. You've helped me, right from the start.'

Her jaw clenches tight. 'Why did you do those terrible things?'

'Leave now, while you still can.'

Her gaze grows fierce. 'Do you think I'd abandon you? Something made you hurt those people. What was it?'

'I can't explain.'

'Tell me, or I'm going.'

Panics forces him to speak. 'My parents criticised me, from day one; the punishments were endless. I was scared of the dark, but they unscrewed the lightbulb in my room and left me there for hours. I got off easily, compared to Melissa. Nothing we did was ever good enough.'

'Maybe they were jealous of your gift.'

'Apart from my sister, only my uncle cared. He'd have done anything for me.' Stone feels the girl's warm hand close over his. 'But he let me down. When I asked for help, he turned away.'

'So you punished your whole family?'

'Their cruelty made me like this.'

She's still watching him. 'And the other victims?'

'It doesn't matter how much pain I cause, or how much I suffer. My music's all that matters. I've been given a unique gift.'

'I know. I bought you the piano, remember? But you can't hurt anyone else. This is where it ends.'

When Stone meets the girl's eyes again, he sees sympathy, not judgement, her hand stroking his arm. Her expression doesn't change as he explains about Asako Mori, and the duet they will perform, to prove his talent eclipses all others. She rises to her feet without question when he explains that they must leave the hotel room, but her eyes light on the glass bottle he slips into his bag.

'What's in that bottle, Seth?'

'Resin, for the piano,' he says quietly. 'We can buy food on the way.'

Stone scans the street cautiously when they get outside, before reaching for her hand.

84

Stanley Yacoub wore an ambivalent smile when he greeted me at his flat in Pimlico. He must have heard the soft rustle of fabric as I perched on his settee, his eyes hitting my face with disconcerting accuracy. The sense that he was staring at me was so unsettling that I wondered for a moment if he was only pretending to be blind.

'Is this a social call, Alice?'

'I'm afraid it's your expertise I need.'

'Pity, I was hoping you'd changed your mind. The offer of dinner still stands.'

'If you can help, the food's on me,' I replied. 'Can I play you a recording, to see if you can guess where the music's being played.'

'Go ahead, I might be able to spot a few details, if the sound quality's good.'

Yacoub listened to the music intently, frowning in concentration. When the piece ended, he asked me to replay it. His expression was perplexed when he removed his headphones.

'It's beautiful but disturbing: one piano's playing in a minor key, the other major. They're in opposing tempos too, like people arguing in different languages. I'd say the players are in a tunnel; the reverb goes on forever.'

'Nothing else struck you?'

'That's the weird thing; one of the instruments sounds like an old practice piano from college. I recognise the timbre.'

'How certain are you?'

'Ninety percent. It's the one Stone used at college; an upright Bechstein, mahogany frame, around a hundred years old. They're used so heavily we replace them every five or six years. Staff or students buy them cheaply and have them reconditioned. I'm not sure what happens to the ones no one wants. Some go into storage, but you'd need to ask our technician.'

My thoughts raced. 'You think Stone's using the piano he practised on at college?'

'If my ears aren't deceiving me.'

'Do your ex-students have any way to contact each other?'

'The alumni page. Want to see it?'

His fingers traced braille imprints on his keyboard, until rows of smiling faces appeared on screen, the graduates categorised by year.

'I'm surprised they put their contact details on there,' I said.

'They need passwords to access the site. They're all musicians, remember. If you want a cellist for a gig, it's a great place to start.'

Yacoub let me scroll through hundreds of student profiles. When I clicked on a photo, details of past performances appeared beside the musicians' employment details. Adrian Stone had been removed from the alumni page, but Ben Wrentham's profile carried a portrait of him, looking pink cheeked and awkward. It was only when I saw Bella Sanderson's picture that ideas clicked into place. Stone's ex had included her phone number and home address. Ben Wrentham had claimed not to know her whereabouts, but given his obsession with the past, he must check the site regularly. The teacher could easily have passed her details to Matthew Briar, the idea making me stumble to my feet.

'Is something wrong?' Yacoub asked.

'Someone's in danger. I have to warn her.'

There was no time to thank him before I rushed from the flat.

Stone takes Lily to the hiding place by taxi. Her skin is paler than before, but her smile is reassuring as the car edges through traffic. She's showing no sign of panic, her hand relaxed in his as the Kensington streets drift by, crowds of tourists visiting museums and parks. His knife is concealed in the inside pocket of his jacket, but he's certain she won't betray him. Her expression is calm when she gazes back at him, like nothing has changed.

'Do you still trust me, Lily?'

'More than anyone.'

'Even though you know my story?'

'It makes no difference.'

'I knew you were one in a million.' He lifts her hand to his lips, pressing a kiss to the centre of her palm.

The girl follows his instructions to the letter when they leave the taxi, following him down the narrow alleyway, watching in silence when he lifts the trap door.

'I have to go down there?' she asks in a whisper.

'If you want to help. You can go first.'

Panic registers in her eyes, a quick gleam of fear as she steps onto the first rung. Her feet clatter against the steel, then silence returns as she steps onto the dirt floor. He stands in the alleyway alone, inhaling the city's odour of brick dust, history and traffic fumes. Then he lowers himself into the opening, the trapdoor closing behind him, banishing the light.

Tania sounded incredulous when I called her on my way to Bella Sanderson's house.

'How could Yacoub identify a piano Stone played, after so many years?'

'His hearing's super-acute. If anyone can interpret Stone's music, it's him. He thinks Mori's being kept in a tunnel somewhere.'

'Great, I'll get my guys to search every underpass.' She sighed loudly. 'Where's Reg taking you now?'

'To see Stone's ex. Ben Wrentham could have given Briar her contact details; they're published on a webpage for ex-students. She may be in danger.'

'Good luck, Alice. Stone's been spotted in Mayfair, I've got real work to do.'

Tania's scepticism was irritating but understandable. She had concrete leads to chase, while I pursued a blind man's guesswork. All I knew for certain was that Ben Wrentham had access to his fellow students' details. There was a chance Stone had them too, and given his habit of attacking friends as well as enemies, his ex-girlfriend was vulnerable.

There was no guard outside Bella Sanderson's bungalow when Reg pulled up, probably because Burns was using all available officers on the streets of Kensington. Sanderson seemed aware of the threat she faced, only opening her door by a crack, peering at me and Reg through her frizz of mouse-brown hair.

'Can we come in, Bella?'

She was dressed in the same shapeless uniform as before, a grey cardigan over a long black skirt, despite the warm breeze outside. Her living room looked even messier, as though basic chores required too much effort, three cats prowling across the floor. Reg stood in the doorway as I sat down, a large black tom hissing at my unwelcome arrival.

'He's afraid of strangers,' Sanderson said.

'I'll try not to scare him. Bella, did someone called Matthew Briar ever contact you?'

Her gaze evaded mine. 'The name's not familiar.'

'Briar was close to Adrian at Rampton, but the friendship cost him his life.'

'I never met him.'

'It's best you tell us the truth now. Then you won't have to go to the police station, while we search this place. You could avoid a night in custody.'

'I can't leave here. Who'd feed my cats?' Sanderson looked horrified.

'Explain what happened then. We'll leave you in peace after that.'

'I didn't do anything wrong.'

'When did he come here?'

Her gaze finally met mine, eyes wet with tears. 'A month ago. He said Adrian needed money, I couldn't turn him down.'

'So you handed over cash?'

'All my savings. It was in a tin under my bed; I've never trusted banks.'

'How much did you give?'

'Eight hundred pounds.'

Sanderson's hands twisted tighter in her lap, as her words faded into silence. I wanted to grab her the shoulders and shake the facts out of her, to make her understand that two women's lives were at stake, but that would have halted our progress. I could only sit and wait for details, ignoring the clock ticking too loudly on the wall above her head.

87

Lily stumbles after Stone, rats scurrying past their feet. Her panicked breaths echo from the walls as they head further into the dark, with only a thread of light guiding them.

'Why did you choose this place?' she asks.

'It's near where we'll perform.'

They're getting closer now. His torchlight flickers across the instruments lining the walls, mahogany frames encrusted with mould, ivories crooked as broken teeth. It's a graveyard for abandoned pianos, the air resonant with lost harmonies. Stone pictures thousands of hands caressing the keyboards, musicians' ghosts straining to perfect each melody. Asako Mori's thin form is still chained to the wall, but she's motionless, long hair splayed across the ground. She hardly flinches when he touches her face.

'What's wrong with the stupid bitch?' Stone snaps.

'Let me see.' Lily kneels down, pressing two fingers to Mori's throat.

'She has to perform the duet. I can't leave London till it's done.'

'Undo the chain, I need to check her breathing.'

Stone unlocks the padlock then watches Lily crouching beside Mori's lifeless form, calm and competent while his panic deepens.

'I only need her alive if she can play. I have to record it tonight.'

'We can bring her fever down. She'll be ready, don't worry.'

'You think so?'

Lily's hand touches his hand in the dark. 'I promise. Then we can live somewhere peaceful, so you can compose.'

It comforts Stone that the girl understands his destiny. He stands back and watches her reviving his old rival, rinsing dirt from her face, massaging warmth back into her hands. But after a few minutes the pianist is still barely responding.

'Her temperature's too high, Seth. She needs Ibuprofen, to bring it down.'

Stone curses under his breath. 'I can't leave here till it's dark. Someone'll recognise me.'

'Let me go.'

'We can wait and see if she comes round first.'

Lily gazes up at him. 'You want her to perform tonight, don't you?'

The emotion flooding Stone's system is panic, not anger. Now there's so much at stake, the prospect of exposure terrifies him.

88

Bella Sanderson took an hour to reveal the truth. I had to use techniques gleaned from years as a psychologist, asking open-ended questions, then leaving silences until she felt obliged to speak. One of Sanderson's cats leapt onto her lap, rubbing its face against her shoulder when she finally opened up.

'Matthew Briar came here just once,' she admitted. 'He was so creepy, I was terrified.'

'But you wanted to help Adrian?'

'He said the money would buy a sound system for his room, and make sure he got time to practise.'

'Has Adrian been here since he escaped?'

She shook her head. 'I waited, but he never came.'

Bella Sanderson's face was full of longing. Once she'd heard he was on the loose, she wanted to see him, despite the lives he'd taken. It crossed my mind to explain that he had a new girlfriend, but she would find out soon enough.

'We think Asako Mori's being kept somewhere underground, near your old college, Bella. Can you guess where?'

She frowned in concentration. 'Some of the students mentioned a tunnel, connecting the college to the Albert Hall, but no one ever found it.'

'Do you know what happened to the college's old instruments, when they were worn out?'

'Sorry, I haven't clue.'

The cat jumped from Sanderson's lap with a sudden hiss, bringing our interview to a close.

Reg looked disbelieving when I recounted Sanderson's tale of a hidden tunnel, but the story chimed with Yacoub's suggestions, so I insisted on visiting the Royal College, before returning to the station.

'No one'll be there on a Sunday,' my bodyguard grumbled.

'Humour me, Reg. It's my only lead.'

I called Burns during our journey to Kensington, but he gave me an overload of information before I could speak, explaining that Stone and Lily Roberts had taken a taxi to Hyde Park, then disappeared into thin air. I couldn't tell whether he heard me explaining my return to the Royal College: tracing the practice piano Stone had used nine years before might lead me to Mori. A chaos of background noise almost drowned out his voice, so I let him get back to work. In all likelihood I was hunting for something non-existent, even Yacoub's acute hearing capable of making a mistake, but I'd pursued the idea too long to abandon it without an answer. At 5pm I checked my watch and guilt washed over me; Will would be delivering his speech at Lola's wedding. There would be hell to pay if I didn't return to the party soon.

When we reached the Royal College I asked Reg to wait outside, but he refused, chuntering to himself as he followed me from the car. A burly security guard checked our ID cards as we entered the foyer. Prince Albert's statue gazed down at us, marble face disapproving, as if he regretted his favourite district becoming a serial killer's hunting ground. The sound of a piano playing languid classical music lured me upstairs to the third floor. The corridor was quieter than on a weekday, but some of the students were still hard at work. A young man was playing the same refrain over and over in thirty second bursts, reminding me that all professional musicians make sacrifices to attain the highest level of skill, but Stone's obsession had flipped over into madness. I was still watching through the open doorway when a voice echoed at my back.

'Visitors aren't allowed up here, I'm afraid.'

The man glowering at us was an extraordinary sight. Even though he must have been in his sixties, his face was gaunt and dangerous as a pirate's; grey ringlets haloed his face in a wild cloud, a tattoo shadowing his cheek, silver hoop earrings adorning each ear. He would have looked perfectly at home on stage beside Mick Jagger, a few decades ago, playing guitar for the Stones.

'We're from the Met,' I replied, flashing my ID. 'I'm looking for an old practise piano.'

His eyebrows rose. 'I've been head technician thirty years. I might be able to help.'

'Great, thanks.'

The man told us his name was Brian Hurst, as he led us to a windowless room at the end of the corridor. It felt like walking into a giant toolbox, pliers, hammers and lengths of piano wire suspended from hooks on the wall, the air tainted by the bitter smell of varnish.

'You've got plenty of kit,' Reg commented.

'Keyboards need pampering every day,' Hurst replied. 'What are you looking for?'

'The piano Adrian Stone used nine years ago,' I said.

'My records don't go back that far, I'm afraid.'

'It's a Bechstein, a hundred years old, mahogany casing.'

'A private buyer probably bought it.'

I took a step closer. 'We need your assistance Brian, please. It could help us find Adrian Stone.'

He blinked at me. 'I can't tell you what I don't know.'

'Some of the pianos are kept here, aren't they?'

'Down in the storage vault, but the students can't be left unsupervised.'

I put my hand on his arm, the unexpected contact making him flinch. 'Two women could die, if we don't find them, Mr Hurst.'

My direct appeal finally penetrated his coolness. The technician's face relaxed by a fraction before he spoke again. 'We don't use the vault anymore. It may not even be down there.'

'If we can look, it'll put my mind at rest.'

I followed Hurst down to the ground floor, Reg behind me, muttering about time wasting. The technician unlocked a door that was set so low in the wall, even I had to stoop to peer through it. Below us a spiral staircase plummeted into impenetrable darkness.

'The lift broke years ago, I haven't been down there in months,' Hurst said. 'Health and safety would get me sacked.'

'We won't breathe a word,' I replied.

'On your head be it,' he replied. 'Watch out, the stairs are a tight squeeze.'

Only the dim light from the landing illuminated our descent, the air cooling with each step.

89

Stone remains in the shadows as he walks down the street. Lily's voice is ringing in his ears, telling him that Mori needs medication; without it she won't be able to perform. He keeps his hood raised as he follows Prince Consort Road towards Kensington. At last he finds a small pharmacy, a bell jangling as he steps inside. A thin-faced man of around thirty stands behind the counter, the Daily Mail spread out in front of him, eyes locked on his face

'Ibuprofen, maximum strength, please.'

There's a flash of recognition as the man's smile falls away. 'I'm calling the police.'

Stone turns on his heel and runs back down the street, but the man gives chase, yelling his name. He zig-zags down side streets and alleys, until his chest heaves. At last the footsteps die away, but his disguise is ruined. Now the police will know he's dressed in a denim jacket, trainers and jeans. He takes a few seconds to regain his calm then loiters at the end of the alley. When an old man approaches, leaning heavily on a cane, he drags him into the alley. Stone knocks him to ground, then swaps his own clothes for the old man's baggy stone-coloured trousers, linen jacket, and canvas hat. He's unrecognisable when he sets off down the street, his back hunched, walking stick tapping on paving stones. Pedestrians barge past like he doesn't exist, and for once Stone is glad to be invisible.

He has more luck at the next pharmacy. The young shop assistant hands him the tablets in a paper bag, the transaction complete in less than a minute.

'Thank you, love,' he says quietly.

Stone gives her a guileless smile, then takes a different route back to the hiding place, down quiet side streets. When a police car chases past, sirens blaring, his heart doesn't miss a beat.

90

Hurst collected an electric lantern from a hook at the bottom of the stairs, the small glow of light making the space seem even more cavernous. The air was sticky with damp, atmosphere creepy enough to make hairs rise on the back of my neck.

'What is this place?' I asked.

'It was planned as an emergency escape route, but never finished. I think it was an air raid shelter in the Blitz. There's another tunnel fifty metres down.'

Reg swore quietly as he stumbled in the dark. I was beginning to regret my decision to chase a false lead. I felt like climbing straight back to the surface, to escape the smothering black air, but Stanley Yacoub's statement had lodged in my brain. I couldn't leave without knowing whether his suggestion was correct.

'The pianos are up ahead,' Hurst said, leading the way.

Light flickered from the curved black walls as we walked. Our footsteps sent back a thunderous echo, as though an army was marching over cobbled ground, but when we came to a halt, silence pressed in on us. Surely we would have heard something, if Stone had hidden Mori in the tunnel? But I could only hear water dripping from the roof, rats' claws scrabbling on the dirt floor. Cellos, guitars and pianos were stacked against the wall, like an orchestra had been rehearsing underground, then got spooked and abandoned their instruments. Half a dozen pianos were wrapped in plastic sheeting, others rotting in the open air. Casings had lost their patina, mahogany filthy with mildew.

'What a bloody waste,' Reg commented. 'My grandkids would love one of those.'

Hurst was too busy checking instruments to reply. I was about to give up hope when he finally beckoned us over. 'Here's a Bechstein. I'm pretty sure it's the one Stone used.'

'It's in better condition than the rest,' I replied.

The technician ran his finger along the keyboard, releasing a string of notes. 'It's been tuned, like the one next to it. But how did someone get down here? There's only one key.'

I felt a twitch of excitement when I saw the two pianos facing each other. The stool was recognisable from Stone's films, behind it the curved black wall, half a dozen unlit candles clustered on the floor. I pulled my phone from my pocket to call in the information, but we were too deep underground to pick up a signal.

'Is there another entrance?' I asked.

Hurst's face was blank. 'God knows. I've never explored that far.'

I felt a quick stab of frustration. We had found the piano Asako Mori had been forced to play, but Stone could have moved her days ago. She might already be dead.

'Let's go back up,' Reg said. 'It's freezing down here.'

Darkness and the lingering smell of decay, combined with the knowledge that Stone had used it as his lair, made me keen to escape, until a faint noise whispered through the air. I thought it was imaginary at first, until it came again: the sound of someone weeping.

'She's here,' I whispered.

'You're imagining things,' Reg replied.

His expression was tense as he listened to the echoing silence, but I had no doubts. Two options lay before us: we could return to the surface and call for help, or rescue Mori, before Stone did her more harm. The memory or Sacha Carsdale's ruined face sealed my decision.

'We have to find her,' I said. 'Pick up something to use for a weapon.'

For once Reg didn't argue, his expression dogged. Maybe he fancied one last chance of heroism before he retired. Hurst grabbed a metal wrench from the ground, handing me a rusty claw hammer. Hysteria must have been setting in because laughter bubbled in my throat as we set off. We made an odd search party: an elderly pirate and a dour policeman armed with household tools, following a tiny blonde through the pitch dark.

'Where the hell is she?' I muttered.

The brick wall ahead signalled the end of the tunnel, and the woman's voice had fallen silent too. It was only when Hurst held up his lantern again that another tunnel appeared to our left, less than five feet wide. The sound drifted towards us again, someone calling for help, almost too weak to hear.

'Asako,' I called out, her name bouncing back from the low ceiling.

Reg must have heard her voice too, his face expectant as he grabbed the lantern and marched past. I stumbled after him, then heard him call out.

'She's here,' he yelled.

Mori was slumped on the ground, her face ashen, clothes encrusted with dirt. When I knelt beside her, she was drifting in and out of consciousness, breath rattling, her skin icy to touch.

'You're safe now, Asako. Where did Stone go?'

'The stage,' she murmured, pointing straight ahead. 'The girl went with him.'

I waited for her to speak again, but her hand went limp in mine as she lost consciousness.

91

Stone knows his followers are close behind. He drags Lily down the narrow passageway, towards a flight of stairs.

'It's not safe,' she says. 'They'll find us here.'

He shines his torch beam on her face, making her flinch. 'I have to play here before we leave. She cheated me out of it twice.'

'You can't, Seth. They know where we are.'

'It's my destiny, sweetheart.'

'I don't want to lose you.'

'Trust me, Lily, please. This is why I broke free.'

Now she follows him up the steps willingly. When the trap door opens, Stone flicks a switch, eyes blinking in the sudden light.

'Where are we?' Lily asks.

'Backstage. This way, come on.'

Stone knows the route perfectly, navigating the maze of corridors until more stairs deliver them onto the stage.

'It's beautiful,' she whispers.

He lifts his gaze to the huge dome enclosing them like a bell jar, paintwork glittering, the air loaded with a history of sound. Wagner played here, then Rachmaninov; now he will follow their legacy. Two grand pianos face each other on the wide stage, and he feels disappointed that his duet may never be performed in this magnificent place. He will play the opening of his concerto instead, imagining a huge audience watching him cross the stage.

Stone gathers his thoughts as his fingers hover over the keys. The knife is tucked inside the pocket of his stolen jacket, the bottle of acid safe in the bag under his stool: no one can hurt him, until his fate is sealed. He takes a long breath then lets both hands fall, releasing a storm of sound.

92

Asako had shown us a narrow opening in the wall, before losing consciousness. Hurst volunteered to stay behind, leaving me and Reg to follow the trail. My claustrophobia increased as we jogged over uneven ground, the lantern's narrow circle of light guiding us, but our only choice was to keep running. Relief flooded through me when a wooden staircase loomed from the darkness. There was no way of guessing what lay above, but I lifted the trap door a few centimetres, terrified that Stone might be waiting. An empty corridor lay ahead, so I beckoned for Reg to follow. I was concerned that he was heaving for breath after our five-minute jog, but there was no time to stop as I climbed out of the tunnel. My surroundings were instantly recognisable, from my backstage tour with Stanley Yacoub. It proved that the rumours were true: an underground passageway connected the Royal College of Music with the Albert Hall. Reg slumped against the wall as I phoned Angie for immediate back up, using a low whisper. I ended the call abruptly after telling her that Mori was alive, because piano music began playing above us. Reg was still panting as we made a few wrong turns before reaching the stage, concealing ourselves behind the curtains.

Stone was seated at one of the grand pianos, dressed in ill-fitting clothes, his short hair dyed black. He seemed oblivious to the fact that the city's police force was hunting for him, eyes closed as he played. On the far side of the stage a young girl was watching him too, tears rolling down her face. Lily Roberts had remained loyal, despite her boyfriend's violence. Stone's music was so compelling, I could have listened for hours under different circumstances, but something disturbed his concentration. He leapt to his feet, swinging round to stare at us, then strode to the girl's side. Now that he'd seen us, making him talk was my one chance of keeping him calm.

'That's a beautiful piece,' I called out. 'Why not carry on?'

'Leave us alone. I was meant to play here; you ruined my performance.' His voice crackled with strain.

'The hall's surrounded, Adrian. You won't get away.'

'This is my destiny, nothing else matters.'

'What do you mean?'

'Music's all we have left.'

Stone's hands kept balling into fists, his face contorting. Outside there was a scream of sirens, the sound taking his last shred of control. He pulled a knife from his jacket, pressing the blade to the girl's throat.

'Make them leave, or I'll kill her,' he yelled at me. 'I'm not going back to that cell.'

'It'll be different, Adrian. They'll let you practise as long as you need.'

The girl's eyes glittered with fear, but she didn't scream. Her arm was wrapped around Stone's waist, like she was trying to comfort him, even though her life was in his hands.

'Liar,' Stone called out. 'You wanted me locked away forever.'

'I hadn't heard you play. I made a mistake, Adrian.'

I took a step forwards, ignoring Reg's advice. Stone's body language was becoming more agitated. If no one took a risk, the girl would die in his arms.

Stone's eyes fix on the small blonde woman. The calmness on Quentin's face increases his urge to hurt her. She symbolises everything he's suffered: his parents' cruelty, frustration, broken dreams. The girl he's using as a human shield is the only one who understands. She trusts him even now, when her fate lies in his hands. The next decision is terrifying, but suddenly his fear is replaced by music playing inside his head, the sound so pure, he doesn't have to think at all.

Men in uniform race through the entry doors, but he's no longer afraid.

'Stay back or she'll die,' he yells out.

He must keep them away until the right moment. The music is building now, the melody cancelling his panic, even though a marksman's gun is aimed at his chest, a red bead of light dancing in front of his eyes.

'I'm sorry, Lily. I can't take you with me.'

Keeping the knife pressed to her throat, he pulls the bottle from his bag with his other hand. Still using her body as his shield, he removes the stopper, then concentrates on the music. The high song of a flute rises into the air as he swallows a long gulp of liquid pain. Fire sears his lips, then sets his mouth and throat aflame, the music deafening as the marksman's bullet enters his brain.

The stink of sulphuric acid filled my airways as I raced across the stage. Lily Roberts was kneeling beside Stone's body, hands on his chest, as though he could be revived. My stomach lurched when I saw white shards of bone floating on the pool of blood at my feet. The marksman had done a clean job, the bullet entering his forehead, leaving an inch-wide wound, the back of his skull blown away. The acid Stone had drunk had worked its damage too, ugly red welts marking his lips, stray splashes peeling varnish from the wooden floor. Lily was weeping inconsolably. I put my hand on her shoulder to draw her away, afraid she might touch the caustic liquid, but she refused to leave Stone's body.

The paramedics reached us first, draping a blanket round Lily's shoulders, but my first concern was for Asako Mori. Two of the officers followed me down the tunnel, so she could be stretchered out. It was only when I returned to the stage that shock set in, leaving me hollow. I rested on a stool behind the curtain while police swarmed the stage, Pete and his SOCOs already photographing the scene. The marksman stood alone by Stone's body, his grave expression filling me with pity: taking a life must leave a stain, no matter how many other lives it preserved. But in reality, the killer would have died anyway, the acid he'd swallowed making it impossible to breathe.

Burns's footsteps announced him before his arrival, heavy and rapid, pounding across the stage. When he yanked back the curtain his face was ashen as he dropped to his knees.

'You can't keep doing this, Alice.'

'What?'

'Scaring the living shit out of me.'

I touched his face. 'It wasn't deliberate.'

'You've done enough. Let's get you out of here.'

'Not yet, I want to see Reg first.'

'Paramedics are giving him oxygen; the dust in that tunnel triggered his asthma.'

'Is he okay?'

'Pretty breathless. You gave him the biggest workout he's had in years.'

When I checked my watch it was nine o'clock, my thoughts returning to Lola's wedding. She'd wanted me beside her through every stage of her big day, but I'd missed the best part.

'I should call Lola,' I said.

'Will says she's fine,' Burns replied. 'The bride's dancing on the tables.'

'That was bound to happen. Take me to the station, Don.'

'You're joking. You can hardly stand up.'

'Don't be ridiculous.'

It irritated me that my legs felt so weak when I rose from the stool that I almost fell. Burns rolled his eyes, but didn't argue. He knew I wouldn't relax until the facts were lined up neatly in my mind.

The firestorm of media attention outside the station felt overwhelming. We tried to sneak in the back way, but a clamour of voices screamed out questions. Journalists tried to block my way as I rushed inside, flashbulbs igniting in my face, but the atmosphere in the incident room was even more excitable. Detectives were swigging wine from Styrofoam cups, yet I didn't feel celebratory. Maybe it was because I'd witnessed first-hand the devastation Stone had caused: Gareth Keillor curled in the boot of his car, Sacha Carsdale's body dumped in a refuse bin, and Asako Mori struggling to breathe.

Burns called a senior team meeting once I arrived. The excitement glittering on Angie's face contrasted with Tania's hard-edged composure, while we shared details of the killer's last hours. Stone must have realised it would be unsafe to return to Lily Roberts' flat, checking in to a boutique hotel. But the thing that interested me most was his girlfriend's role in his campaign. Had she been an innocent bystander, or fully aware of his actions?

'Lily Roberts will be tried as his accessory, unless she proves coercion,' Burns said.

'Or brainwashing,' I added.

Angie looked incredulous. 'She's a nurse for god's sake. How did she fall for him?'

'Psychopaths are brilliant manipulators,' I replied. 'Stone tuned into people's weaknesses; playing with their emotions was his favourite game.'

'Thank Christ he's dead,' Tania muttered.

I kept my mouth shut, but didn't share her view. Stone's death might have saved the taxpayer the expense of keeping him locked up for decades, but it had denied the relatives a full explanation of his actions.

'At least we know what happened to Asako Mori,' I said. 'He forced her backstage then down the tunnel. But how did he keep going back, without being spotted?'

'There's an access point behind an outbuilding at the Royal College. All he had to do was climb over the wall, then lift the trapdoor. He must have known about it since his student days.'

'What was the tunnel used for originally?' asked Angie,

'My team did some research,' Tania replied. 'A tunnel runs down Exhibition Road from High Street Kensington Tube, for pedestrian access to the museums, but there's an abandoned section too. The college used the vault under their building to store old instruments.'

I listened to a flow of information, exhaustion making me too numb to contribute. Apparently Stone had attacked an old man earlier that day, using his clothes as a new disguise. The seventy-four-year-old had been lucky to escape alive: he was in hospital with concussion, but slowly recovering. Burns had placed an embargo on press coverage of the story, until all the victims' families knew of Stone's death, but it was only a matter of time before information leaked. Tania had despatched members of her team to inform Ian Carlisle and his wife, and Mr Mori was at his daughter's hospital bedside. Burns insisted that Melissa's aunt and uncle must be present when she heard, aware that another shock could damage her fragile mental health. I thought about all the collateral damage Stone had caused, by targeting so many vulnerable souls. His college contacts Ben Wrentham and Bella Sanderson would face prosecution for aiding to his escape. Both were likely to be tried for conspiring to free a serial killer, and they would face vilification by the press.

It was 11pm when I finally felt ready to wipe the case from my mind until morning, but there was a moment of discomfort as we left the station. Mr Roberts was being led inside, a thin figure, slightly stooped, dark eyes small as currants behind his thick spectacles. His expression contained relief and gratitude, and it was clear he had no idea that Lily faced a charge of assisting a murderer. A new wave of anger flooded my system as fresh air hit me: of all Stone's victims, the young nurse's fate seemed most tragic. I needed to understand her role fully before the case could close.

95

Monday 4th April

My phone buzzed loudly on the bedside table at Burns's flat next morning, jarring me out of my deepest sleep for weeks. The message was from Christine Jenkins, asking me to report to the Forensic Psychology Unit, her voice calm and authoritative. Her communication style was so enigmatic, there was no way to tell whether she intended to praise or reprimand. Burns had disappeared from the flat, not even leaving one of his hastily scribbled notes stuck to the fridge, but he was bound to be at the station. The case had closed, but dozens of issues still needed to be resolved, including making sure the press reported the facts accurately.

I looked out of the window, expecting to see Reg in his patrol car, but there was no sign of him. I was a free agent again, with no need for a bodyguard, or overnight stays at the safe house, yet my tension remained. Three weeks of looking over my shoulder had left me too edgy to relax. I ignored my sense of unease while hailing a black cab, putting through a call to Angie once it set off.

'Don't interview Lily Roberts yet, will you? She needs a psychological assessment before the case review. We can kill two birds with one stone.'

'Can you be here by twelve thirty?'

'No problem.'

I could hear a hubbub of voices, phones and doors slamming when she said good bye. Already the incident room would be winding down, photos stripped from the evidence board, final witness reports being filed, but frustration still churned in my gut. I wanted to sit opposite Stone in an interview room, piecing together his motivations, to understand the root of his psychopathy. He'd retained control until his last breath, cheating us of our chance to see him back behind bars.

Christine was at her desk when I arrived at the FPU. Her appearance made me do a double take, her monochrome clothes had been replaced by a vivid cerise dress, as if the relief of the case closing had triggered an outburst of colour. She rose to her feet quickly when she saw me arrive.

'I heard the good news, Alice, congratulations.'

'Is that why I'm here?'

'I'd like the full story, from the horse's mouth. Tell me exactly how you caught him.'

Her gaze was forensic as I explained my realisation that Stone's clues might lead us directly to him, like the pied piper. Stanley Yacoub's identification of the piano in Stone's last recording had made me return to the Royal College, to discover that the rumours about a tunnel below the Albert Hall were true. Christine listened with rapt attention, occasionally shaking her head in disbelief as I explained that two of Stone's college contacts had funded his escape.

'Amazing that he retained their loyalty,' she said. 'This gives you plenty of material for your next book.'

'I'll write some articles, in the fullness of time.'

Her gaze lingered on my face. 'Are you okay, Alice?'

'I think so, why?'

'I was so sorry to hear the news about Burns. Head office called me earlier.'

'What do you mean?'

'He hasn't told you?'

'About what?'

'He's resigned.'

I stared back at her in mute amazement.

'Human resources don't want him to go, obviously. He's keeping it quiet until the case wraps up, but he must have been considering it for a while. He wouldn't throw away his career lightly.'

'I should be at the station, Christine. Can we discuss this later?'

I left the building at a rapid jog, flagging down another taxi immediately. The buildings passed in a blur of anxiety. Burns had been monosyllabic the night before, his expression shell-shocked. We'd both tumbled straight into bed, falling asleep in moments. I hadn't asked how he'd felt about his worst case coming to an abrupt end, but the nation's media had been focused on him for weeks, the stress unimaginable. When I knocked on the door of his office, no one answered.

'Looking for the boss?' Tania had appeared behind me.

'Is he here?'

'Scotland Yard are glad-handing him. He'll get a promotion on the back of this.' She stood in front of me, blocking my way back to the incident room. 'Sorry I was rude on the phone yesterday, Alice. Stress turns me into a prize bitch; I should have kept a lid on it.'

'Let's be honest, Tania, you've always believed shrinks are pointless.'

'You're changing my mind. I may even stop snapping at you, one day.'

'And pigs may fly,' I said, smiling. 'Are you interviewing Lily Roberts with me?'

She shook her head. 'I'm observing. I can't wait to hear what goes on in that warped mind of hers.'

Angie collected me from the incident room just before twelve thirty. Burns still wasn't answering his phone, but Lily Roberts's appearance silenced my personal concerns. It looked like she'd spent the night crying, eyes raw and glistening against the pallor of her skin, tension making her thin form quiver like a violin string. Her solicitor was a well-built middle-aged woman, in a black suit, brightened by a slash of bright red lipstick. The lawyer kept a close eye on her client, as though she might fall apart at any minute. Coffee was delivered to the interview room before the interview began, but Angie's strategy for relaxing Lily Roberts wasn't working. The girl left her drink untouched, eyes boring a hole in the scratched table-top that filled the gap between us.

'Can you explain your relationship with Adrian Stone for us?' Angie said quietly. 'Begin with how you met him, please.'

The girl didn't look up. 'Seth was a private person. He wouldn't want me talking behind his back.'

'His name was Adrian, Lily.'

'The man I knew was called Seth Rivers.'

'But he lied, didn't he? You have to accept what happened, or you'll make things worse. You're facing a long jail sentence.'

A tear rolled down her face. 'Do you think I care?'

'You should, Lily. Your whole life's ahead of you.'

'That doesn't matter now.'

The solicitor whispered something to the girl, but her bleak expression didn't change. I nodded at Angie, indicating that I would take over the questioning.

'Adrian was the best pianist I've ever heard. You saw him perform at Ronnie Scott's, didn't you?'

She lifted her face, a smile animating her angular features. 'He could have had anyone, but he chose me. We loved each other. If you think he had no feelings, you're wrong.'

'I saw how much he cared for you last night; he didn't want to let you go.'

'I'd have followed him anywhere.'

'When did you find out something was wrong, Lily?'

Her eyes were glassy. 'He was different, that's all. His talent set him apart.'

'But when did you realise he'd hurt people?'

'At the hotel. He told me how his family abused him.'

'That's what he said?'

She nodded her head firmly. 'They should have believed in him, like I did.'

'Did you try to stop him?'

'I told him it had to end, if we stayed together. He promised not to kill again.'

Angie and I carried on questioning her for the next half hour but progress was slow. Lily described how Stone picked her up in a bar, then moved in immediately. Apparently he had been loving and attentive, surprising her with bunches of flowers and unexpected kindnesses, claiming that he'd written his best music during their time together. But when pressed for more details, the girl shut down, unwilling to discuss the evil acts Stone had committed. Her expression relaxed suddenly as Angie brought the interview to a close.

'At least Seth left something wonderful behind,' she whispered.

'How do you mean?' Angie asked.

'My period's a week late. I don't need a pregnancy test; I can feel his baby growing inside me.'

Lily Roberts's face glowed with pure happiness before she was led back to her holding cell, then Angie turned to me with a stunned expression.

'Stone targeted the most naïve girl he could find. She was dazzled by his bullshit, and now she's bringing that freak's kid into the world.'

I shook my head. 'Psychopaths can fall in love, if the partner echoes their narcissism. He found a girlfriend who shared his belief that he was the world's most gifted composer. I think Stone was surprised by his attachment to Lily. Remember her dad saying he seemed shocked by the depth of his feelings?'

'Much good it did her,' Angie replied. 'She'll serve years as his accomplice, and having a kid won't protect her. Lily may have helped him commit murder.'

'Her body language and speech patterns indicate she was telling the truth.'

'We'll follow up everything she says, but we can only go on hard evidence, Alice.'

Angie began filling out her interview report before I'd left the room, too preoccupied to say goodbye.

96

The gang of photographers had shrunk by the time I left the station, only a few diehards pointing lenses at me as I dashed down the steps. My thoughts were churning too fast and Burns still wasn't answering his phone. The best way to burn the excess adrenalin from my system was to exercise, so I set off at a brisk pace towards Kings Cross. I paused outside the station, remembering the psychiatrist Frances Pearce, pushed to her death under a speeding train, for reasons only a psychopath could justify. I shut my eyes and listened to a motorbike roar past, planes hovering over City Airport, a passer-by gabbling in rapid Chinese. It was a relief to forget Adrian Stone's music and concentrate on the city's soundscape. The noises changed as I entered the heart of the city. People were discussing business deals, as I walked east to Fleet Street, where London's newspaper empire once thrived. The press offices were pubs and department stores now, a woman's high heels tapping past, like the clack of a horse's hooves.

When I reached Victoria Embankment the sounds blended into a low hum of traffic. The Thames was adapting slowly from winter to spring, its shade softening to moss green, currents drifting towards the sea. Without conscious planning I was heading straight for Burns's flat. The tide led me east to Southwark Bridge, then I crossed the river to his apartment block, chasing up the stairs rather than waiting for the lift.

He was lying on his sofa, immersed in the music on his headphones. It took several minutes for him to notice my arrival, eyes opening slowly, like a cat waking from a deep sleep.

'You didn't answer your phone,' I said.

He raised himself on one elbow. 'I'm entitled to some peace and quiet.'

'You'd better deal with me, Don. I won't leave.'

'Maybe you should. I'm not great company right now.'

His skin was still as pale as candlewax under his dark growth of beard. I wanted to comfort him, but touch was the last thing he needed, when he couldn't even meet my eye.

'You wanted to talk, Don, so let's do it. I'm ready when you are.'

He shook his head, frowning. 'It's always at your convenience, Alice. You keep me at arm's length for months, then change the rules. Have you even considered it might be the wrong time for me?'

'Why did you resign?'

'I hate being a shit dad, and I've seen more than enough dead bodies. Working too hard ruined my marriage, I don't want it screwing up our relationship as well.'

'Those are good reasons.'

'I don't need your bloody permission.'

'Is this the big change you mentioned?'

'Part of it, yes.'

'What's the other bit?'

He hesitated before replying. 'I was planning to ask you to marry me, but you'd probably say no. I bet you still don't have a clue what you want.'

'I do, actually. My long walk here slotted everything into place.'

'Go on then, spit it out.'

I turned to face him. Against the odds he ticked all my boxes, from his raw-boned face and hard stare to his giant scale. 'I don't want to get married. It's nothing personal, I love you more than anyone, but the relationship's what counts, not a white dress and a hundred guests I hardly know.'

'Why are you here then?'

'I want to live with you, without getting married.'

He looked nonplussed. 'As simple as that?'

I took a deep breath, wiping Lily Roberts from my mind. 'And I'd like a baby, as soon as possible.'

The shock on his face was replaced by a slow-dawning smile. 'Lola said to give it time, sooner or later you'd realise I was your ideal man.'

'There's no such thing. But the waiting part was good advice.'

'I'll be unemployed for a while.'

'Have you got another job in mind?'

'I plan to take six months off, spend time with you and the boys, start painting again. Then I can decide what to do.'

'I'm not quitting my job any time soon.'

'You couldn't.' He put his arm round my shoulder, then kissed my cheek. 'Once a shrink, always a shrink.'

'Tell me the meaning of that Gaelic phrase you keep saying.'

'Chan eil mi 'tuigsinn thu? It means, I don't understand you.'

'You will, in time.' I pointed at his headphones. 'What are you listening to?'

'Scott Matthews.'

'At least you've got decent taste.'

I stole one of his ear plugs, the singer's pure tenor and poetic lyrics dissolving the tension of the case. I rested my head against Burns's shoulder so we could listen together, my mind emptying as the music rinsed my thoughts clean.

AUTHOR'S NOTE

London has such a rich and varied musical history, I decided to base this book on some true locations. Researching it was a great adventure, which involved many hours walking the streets of West London, becoming familiar with the Albertopolis. I was struck by the fact that Queen Victoria had most of the area's grand museums built in her husband's memory, every brick imbued with her sadness.

If you enjoy the story, why not grab a street map and explore the same streets that Mozart, Chopin and Handel trod? It's a great way to peel back a few layers of the city's history, to find the melodies hidden underneath.

ACKNOWLEDGEMENTS

Thanks are due to the staff of the Albert Hall and the Royal College of Music, for allowing me free access to their rooms and resources. Contrary to my depiction in this story, the Royal College isn't secretive at all; I was given a warm welcome by students and staff. Seeing the basement-level vaults, crammed with instruments, helped my plot to take shape. Thanks to my lovely agent, Teresa Chris, for her constant encouragement. My husband Dave accompanied me on many long walks around London, often pelted by rain and snow. My oldest stepson, talented pianist Jack Pescod, gave me lots of wonderful information about musical techniques. Cheers to the 134 Club, Killer Women and my brilliant Twitter followers, who encourage me every step of the way. My mother Wendy Rhodes, is my biggest cheerleader, and my sister Honor a great source of information on London's history. Thanks so much to you both. Penny Hancock and Miranda Doyle are both brilliant and inspiring writers, who supported me in writing this book from start to finish. Ladies, I salute you!

ABOUT THE AUTHOR

Kate Rhodes was born in London, but lives now in Cambridge with her husband, an artist and short story writer. Kate has done many jobs in her time, from being a theatre usherette and cocktail waitress, to teaching English. She is a prize-winning poet and Hawthornden Fellow, with a PhD on the work of Tennessee Williams.

Kate has written eight critically-acclaimed crime novels.

If you would like to follow Kate on Twitter, you can find her at:

@K_Rhodeswriter

Printed in Great Britain
by Amazon